THE DEAD GENIUS

A LIEUTENANT JOE SONNTAG NOVEL

THE DEAD GENIUS

AXEL BRAND

FIVE STAR
A part of Gale, Cengage Learning

GALE
CENGAGE Learning™

Detroit • New York • San Francisco • New Haven, Conn • Waterville, Maine • London

GALE
CENGAGE Learning

LIBRARY OF CONGRESS CATALOGING-IN-PUBLICATION DATA

Brand, Axel.
   The dead genius : a Lieutenant Joe Sonntag novel / Axel
Brand. — 1st ed.
      p. cm.
   ISBN-13: 978-1-4328-2514-0 (hardcover)
   ISBN-10: 1-4328-2514-3 (hardcover)
   1. Police—Wisconsin—Milwaukee—Fiction. 2. Forensic scientists—Crimes against—Fiction. 3. Murder—Investigation—Fiction. 4. Milwaukee (Wis.)—Fiction. I. Title.
PS3573.H4345D43 2011
813'.54—dc22   2011013265

First Edition. First Printing: July 2011.
Published in 2011 in conjunction with Tekno Books and Ed Gorman.

Printed in the United States of America
1 2 3 4 5 6 7 15 14 13 12 11

For Craig Johnson, with admiration

CHAPTER ONE

The death notice in the *Milwaukee Journal* announced the visiting hours. Joe Sonntag thought he could manage it during his lunch break because the mortuary was only six blocks away, and it would be a good day to walk.

Still, he thought he should check with Captain Ackerman.

"I'm going to pay my respects to Armand de Trouville," he said.

"All right, but make up the time," Ackerman said.

Old Captain Punchcard sure hated for any cop to slack, and famously raided coffee shops where he suspected beat patrolmen were sipping java.

Lieutenant Sonntag nodded. The whole force should be paying its respects to Trouville, but that would never happen. Some of the force considered Trouville a rival instead of a man with a genius for solving a certain type of crime.

Sonntag devoured Lizbeth's peanut butter and apple jelly lunch, ignored the hot coffee in the thermos bottle, and shut his black lunch bucket. The desk lunch had cost five minutes. He slid into his trench coat, plucked the gray fedora from its peg, and headed into the April wind.

Somebody had to say goodbye to the odd little legend who had transformed a whole realm of law enforcement with his pioneering research.

Most of Trouville's cases had involved civil lawsuits, but now and then the cops called on him. Trouville was a questioned document examiner, with a gift for spotting forgery and all sorts of related crimes. Sonntag had consulted with the late examiner a dozen times. If a robber pushed a hand-printed stickup note at a cashier, Trouville could sometimes trace the writing right back to the crook.

Now he was dead. A heart seizure, according to the papers. He had keeled over at his desk a few mornings ago. It occurred to Lieutenant Sonntag that he knew nothing about the feisty little document man's private life or origins. The gossip was that Trouville had abandoned his Chicago office after demonstrating in court that a mobster had bilked his divorced wife, and the mobster had applied some heat.

Sonntag hadn't known Trouville very well, but apparently nobody had. Even his assistant and young colleague, Harley Potter, had only known the little genius on a wholly professional level. But even though Trouville was something of a mystery, Joe Sonntag wanted to pay his respects, and maybe pay the respects of the police department too.

The smell of hops was in the air. That was the beer city's unique odor, unless one was around places like Allis Chalmers where they churned out tractors, or Cutler Hammer where they belched out electrical equipment. But the Madsen Mortuary was close to Schlitz, and the smell of hops would permeate the mortuary. Trouville would have smiled. He despised beer.

He found the mortuary, built of Milwaukee's cream-colored brick, and made his way into utter silence. There was a cloakroom for his coat and hat, and Sonntag debated it; he'd pay his respects and be out in five minutes. The room smelled like a sachet. But then he slipped out of his tan coat and set his hat on the shelf above it. There were no other coats hanging there. He headed for the viewing parlor, where the perfume of a fresh bouquet trumped the hops.

He adjusted his tie, and smoothed his rumpled suit. It was

worsted wool, off the plain pipe racks of Irv, The Working Man's Friend, the clothier on the south side, and not the sort of suit one would find at the Boston Store. He had two of them and wore them hard. Once in a while Lizbeth added a new tie for his birthday. She liked gaudy ties, so he kept a subdued one at work. He would wear the gaudy one on the streetcar and the subdued one in the station. He dreaded the day when she figured it out.

The coffin rested on an ebony bier, and was lit softly from the ceiling. The only other person present was Harley Potter, ill dressed in what was probably a hastily purchased black suit. He smiled wanly as Sonntag approached the bier and stared at the remains of Armand de Trouville, a genius scarcely known beyond a tiny entourage of lawyers and law enforcement people, but a genius even so.

Trouville lay serenely, and at least the morticians had not ruined him or rendered him grotesque. He had been sixty-eight. He was compact and rail-thin, and now lay in his court attire. He surely was one of the last people in the country to appear in a dove gray morning coat and striped trousers, looking professorial though he was no professor, and his realm of knowledge barely had a name.

Now he lay unmoving, framed by white satin, his lips retaining their ironic smile. It was that very smile that had been the ruin of lawyers, most of whom were eager to reduce him to a useless quack. Several times Sonntag had sat in court while the lawyers had attempted to ridicule Trouville out of the witness box. They usually began with his credentials, which didn't exist because he had pioneered a new way of examining documents, using science and technology. Then the lawyers had attempted to reduce him to a graphologist or a practitioner of palmistry, or maybe a crystal-ball reader.

But by the time it was over the chastened lawyers had

discovered that the formidable little man in the witness box could say with certitude what brand of typewriter had been used to type a document, the year the model was introduced or discontinued, and why each typewriter developed its own idiosyncrasies, as certain as fingerprints, as daily use gradually twisted its strikers and hammered the platen, the rubber roller that conveyed the paper. And from his genius had come the relentless evidence that solved crimes, the evidence that revealed fraud, the evidence that exposed faked or forged wills and testaments. A giant of intellect and insight lay there in the great hush of the mortuary.

Joe Sonntag felt an odd loss. Maybe it was because Trouville was the ultimate detective, a little man with x-ray vision, along with a passion for justice. Sonntag remembered how, on occasion, he had been invited into the man's laboratory, where rigorous test and analysis would confirm or deny the authenticity of a signature of a document. Trouville didn't say much; he just proceeded quietly toward some understanding that lay beyond Sonntag's horizon, until there it was. A date typed into a document with a font that didn't exist at the time. A case resolved.

How little he knew about that diminutive man who had left the world a few mornings ago. The death notice said that a service would be conducted in the mortuary. That fit. Trouville had spoken of his agnosticism off and on. He once told Sonntag he had no certainty at all, didn't know whether God existed or didn't exist, and hoped to examine the question if he found himself entering a second life sometime. He planned to cross-examine God.

"I hope you figure it out, Armand," Sonntag said.

He left the bier, headed for the guest registry, and added his name. There were only three entries, and Sonntag knew two: Potter, who hovered nearby, and Agnes Winsocket, the receptionist and typist Trouville had occasionally borrowed from the

10

dental office next door to his own suite in the First Mariner Building alongside the Milwaukee River.

It seemed strange that so few would remember or honor a man so amazing.

Potter was hovering about, looking bored.

"No family?" Sonntag asked.

"So far, we haven't found any," Potter said. "God knows we tried."

"There must have been a will."

"No will. We've hunted for one. He had no lock box that we know of, and nothing was in his office safe. Or his flat."

"There had to be someone," Sonntag said. "He had parents. A birth certificate. Brothers or sisters. Grandparents. Marriage?—I guess not."

Potter sighed. "We looked for all of that, Lieutenant. I had to get his lawyer, Stan Bartles, and then we had to get court permission to look in his office safe and go through his flat and look for a bank lock box. Bartles says he never drafted a will for Armand, and so far we haven't found any. We had to get a locksmith to open the safe, since the combination was nowhere but in Armand's head, and that required another court action."

"You'd think a document examiner would leave a will and make sure there were copies."

Potter nodded. "You'd think so. Bartles had to get court permission to bury him and look for heirs. His checking account's in his name, no beneficiaries. In fact, the court's made him the trustee. Someone had to handle the estate."

"Come to think of it, Trouville never mentioned his family. At least not around me," Sonntag said. "Maybe he didn't have any. Or chose to distance himself."

"I think he may have had some in Quebec. He once said something like that, but it's hard to remember. We're putting ads in Quebec papers. Chicago, too. So far, no one in Chicago's called us."

"Maybe the estate will escheat," Sonntag said.

"I'm not familiar—"

"End up going to the state. If there are no heirs, no claimants, no will."

"I had wondered about that," Potter said. "There's not much in it. His business—and mine—isn't a way to make money, to put it mildly. He did it because of a passion. A document was a riddle he wanted to solve, and that was his only religion. Rather single-minded, but wonderful too. He'd get on a case, like a forged will, and next thing you knew, he'd be shaking it like a dog shaking a dead rabbit."

That seemed an odd analogy to Lieutenant Sonntag. "I guess you and the lawyer will bury our friend, hunt for heirs, keep looking for a will, and try to settle it."

"I hope you'll come to the service. What I dread is a service with no one honoring one of the brightest persons ever to walk the earth."

"I'm not sure I can make it," Sonntag said. "But I'd like to look at his lab. I've been in there a few times, and I'd like to see what's there."

"I don't see why not. It's still a functioning office, and I'm still there, trying to finish up some of the cases."

"Thanks," Sonntag said. "Say, who found him?"

"I did. I walked in. There he was. Then I got Miss Winsocket," Potter said. "She's the dental receptionist next door, you know. She types and does our accounts. We hardly need a receptionist. No one walks through our door—maybe once a month."

"You found him?"

"Early. He was sitting at his desk. I unlocked the door, and there he was, slumped in his chair. I shook him, but it was plain he was gone. I got her, and tried to wake him up, and we called for an ambulance. Heart trouble, that's what the certificate says. Heart failure."

"Heart?"

Potter sighed. "He once told me he suffered from diabetes. That explains it."

"Not cardiovascular disease?"

Potter shook his head. "Never mentioned it. But I think that's what diabetes does. The Lord gives and the Lord taketh away," he said.

"What are your plans?" Sonntag asked.

"It's too soon to say. I'd like to continue his practice, but I don't know . . . It's all up in the air."

"What about the ongoing cases?"

"I'd like court permission to work on them. I think I can resolve one or two. I've apprenticed for three years since getting out."

"Out?"

"Of the army. Medical discharge. Vivax malaria, New Guinea, they let me go in November, forty-four, and by forty-five I had started my internship with Mr. Trouville. He liked to be called that, you know, not Armand. I learned that fast. Always Mr. Trouville, the same as appeared in his morning coat and striped trousers in court. Agnes had to learn that too."

"And so did I," Sonntag said.

"Say, Lieutenant, there's something you people can do. Help us find some heirs. Anything. His family, his distant relatives."

Sonntag nodded. It was dawning on him that Armand de Trouville might have been born under another name, and that his silence about his family and his past might be connected to his flight from Chicago—if indeed there was such a flight.

"I'll talk to the captain about it," he said. "I'm thinking maybe the man we knew as Trouville might have been someone else once."

"Why didn't that occur to me?" Potter asked.

"I'll see if I can find out anything. Identities are not high on our priority list."

"I hope you'll come to the memorial service. I'd hate for just Agnes and me to be there."

"Who's the minister?"

"There isn't any. Agnes is going to read the poems of Tennyson."

"Mr. Trouville would have liked that," Sonntag said, somehow doubting his own words.

CHAPTER TWO

Captain Ackerman was lighting a five-cent stogie when Sonntag found him. The captain sucked until the cigar glowed, exhaled yellow smoke, sucked again, and sighed.

"Cigars stink," he said. "It keeps women out of the station."

"I went over to the funeral home," Sonntag said. "Hardly anyone there. But I paid my respects. At least the police department was present."

"That's because no one in Milwaukee had the faintest idea who he was," Ackerman replied. "He was the most obscure genius on the planet."

"Well, there's more to it," Sonntag said, and outlined the lack of a will, or identification, or birth certificate, or heirs.

"They'll come up with something. If the mob was after him like we'd heard, he'd take a different name," Ackerman said.

"His colleague, Harley Potter, wants help. I said I'd ask you."

"Help? What for?"

"Finding out who Armand de Trouville was so the estate can be settled."

"We got more important things to do," Ackerman said.

"I'd like to work on it," Sonntag said. "I liked the little guy."

Ackerman exhaled an asphyxiating cloud of noxious fumes. "On your dime," he said. "Keep track of hours and make it up on weekends."

"There's not much else on the docket at the moment. Milwaukee gives up crime for Lent."

"Yeah, except for fish. Every Lent, fish robberies."

"I'm curious about this. I think Trouville was one of the most fascinating people I've ever talked to. And I'd like to help Harley Potter."

"You could start by calling my friend Manny Plevin on the Chicago PD. He's got a memory that shakes out dirt like a washboard. But it's your dime. The department won't pay for long distance."

Sonntag nodded. This was going to be on his hook. "I'll call your buddy," he said.

He returned to his grimy carrel and had the operator put the call through, and somehow got the right man.

"Plevin," a gravelly voice said.

"This is Lieutenant Sonntag, Milwaukee police, sir. Captain Ackerman said—"

"Oh, Ackerman. I remember that fart."

"We're trying to identify a deceased. He's a—they call it a questioned document examiner. He used to practice in Chicago, or that's what we've heard. But the word is he got chased out by the mob. Can you come up with anything? Like a name? Relatives? Or the case—a lawsuit, I think?"

"Who'd you say you are?"

"Sonntag. Milwaukee PD detective."

"I don't remember nothing like that."

"Captain Ackerman said you might come up with something."

"He's full of beans."

Sonntag left the information and a contact number after extracting a promise from Plevin to look into it.

"What do you want to know for?" Plevin asked.

"Trouville, or whoever he once was, is the foremost document examiner in the world. That's what we hear. But he didn't leave a will, and there's not a scrap of paper connecting him to anyone or anything. We're trying to help the estate."

16

"Huh. You've been eating too much cheddar up there in Wisconsin, Sonntag. But I'll check it out."

The phone clicked dead. Sonntag rang the operator and asked for charges. He learned that he owed the PD a dollar ninety-two.

Lizbeth wouldn't be thrilled. She scrimped and saved pennies so they could have some chop suey on weekends or go for a little Saturday drive in the old coupe. This weekend, he'd be putting in hours at the station, and she'd be spending another weekend dusting the furniture.

Sonntag decided to put in an afternoon on the deal, certainly no more than that. The bullpen was quiet, and there were no fresh bodies in Milwaukee, and no one was eating meat. He'd work backward, not forward. He wouldn't look for heirs, he'd look for ancestors.

He'd have Potter take him through the office and lab. Maybe he'd find something that got overlooked. And he'd talk to that dental receptionist, Agnes Winsocket, who typed stuff for Trouville. Secretaries knew more than most people imagined.

A brisk walk along Wells Street and Water Street brought him to the north entrance of the gloomy old bank building that housed Trouville's operation. The lower floor was a gray-marble bank lobby that stretched from Wisconsin Avenue northward. Up the hard, mean stairs, or by a grinding elevator, were professional suites. Agnes was the dental receptionist next door who handled Trouville's secretarial needs. It had been a good arrangement for many years. Maybe she could pull something out of her memory.

The dental office belonged to Karl Kessler, a product of Marquette University's famed dental school. But Kessler had evolved a fame of his own for being the most intimidating tooth puller in his profession, and for pressing a forearm across women's bosoms while he whittled their molars. Sonntag knew of cases where little boys ran away from home rather than having to face the maestro of maul. Kessler was never happy unless he had humiliated his patients as well as tormented them.

"You going to be a sissy and ask for the pain killer?" was one of his favorite ploys. It was the way he said it that evoked shame and terror. It was always in a voice dripping with scorn, a voice that promised worse torment for anyone who chose the Novocain.

But this time Sonntag simply wanted to talk to Agnes. He headed down the gloomy corridor, metered by pebbled glass doors with pebbled glass transom windows above, most doors displaying the name of the firm in prim, black block letters. This was the lair of accountants and wholesalers and insurers and people who did mysterious things behind desks. The building was grim enough to increase the local suicide rate.

He found her at the Underwood upright, typing prim bills. She wore her usual navy blue suit and white blouse. Her graying hair was tight in a bun.

"Why, Lieutenant," she said after she had reached a stopping place.

"You have time to talk?"

"I think so."

"I mean, over in Trouville's?"

She consulted her appointment book. "I have twenty minutes. Doctor's at lunch."

"I'd like to do a search for anything that would connect him to anyone."

"Harley called and said to assist you," she said.

"I hope I can. I gather that there's no will, no birth certificate, no letters, no nothing."

"We looked, and looked again," she said. "But you're the detective."

They headed out of the dental suite, and she unlocked the

door to the left, which was labeled *Trouville and Potter, Document Examiners.*

There was a cramped reception area with a couple of gray horsehair chairs, Trouville's office, and a lab that also had a desk for Potter. The cluttered lab had a giant enlarger, a copying camera, and trays of developer and fixer. Trouville sure didn't rent much space.

"I don't like the smell," she said. "But now it's not bad."

"What I want to do is work backwards in time," he said. "Think back to your first months with Armand Trouville. Did he dictate any letters to family? Mention any friends?"

"My first impression was that he was terribly alone. And that was why he worked so hard, so feverishly, if I might say it. That was the only life he had."

"Did he say where he was from?"

"No, but for some reason I thought he talked about Cicero once. He talked of being a boy, delivering the *Tribune,* a penny for each delivery, and I think that must have been in Cicero."

"South of Chicago?"

"Yes. That seemed so strange, you know. A man like Armand wouldn't come from Cicero."

"Why not?"

"It's—well, just a place. Armand had to come from a, oh what's the word? A genteel place. He was a gentleman. He knew more law than lawyers. More medicine than doctors. He could have been a professor, or a duke."

"Did he ever talk about a college degree, or a certificate from some professional institute?"

"No, sir, he always took pride in the opposite. He said he was self-taught."

"No degree, then. How long have you worked for him?"

"Oh, many years. Let's see. I started with Dr. Kessler in thirty-eight. Sometime after that, he approached the doctor and me and asked if my part-time services might be available. We made an arrangement."

"He had someone before?"

"I believe he had no one, Lieutenant. If there were letters to type, he would type them, and if there were bookkeeping, he would do it."

"He never talked of his past, his family, his childhood?"

"Oh, no, sir. He lived in a private world, and no one could intrude."

"Not his colleague?"

"Harley knows no more than I do. We simply can't find any family or heirs. We really tried."

Sonntag wasn't able to elicit anything more, and marveled that the two people closest to Armand de Trouville had absorbed so little about him.

"I need to go back. Lock the door and bring me the key when you leave," she said.

"Back to the dungeon, eh?" he said.

She eyed him coldly, and stepped out.

Sonntag's sense of helplessness increased. If Armand de Trouville wanted to cover his past and blank out his future, he was skilled enough to do it. The files consisted of two black three-drawer metal cabinets. He slid the drawers open and found the contents labeled by cases and also organized by dates. He found a financial folder for each year, dating back to 1936. *Follow the money*, he thought, and pulled it.

The first entry was for rent, paid for February nineteen thirty-six. There was nothing prior. And no file in the cabinets extended back to nineteen thirty-five. That suggested that something, maybe cataclysmic, had happened to Trouville in nineteen thirty-five. He had come to Milwaukee from somewhere, left a vocation he was pursuing—somewhere. Maybe Chicago. Maybe some clippings locked in the morgue of the

Tribune would reveal a past. He'd put someone on it if he could. People did not just come from nowhere. A life had been lived before Trouville's time here.

But the business files didn't offer a clue. Sonntag was unfamiliar with some of the early cases, but the more recent ones were alive in his memory. *Madsen vs. Madsen,* for example. A case that involved fraud. A brother and sister, Wilbur and Sally, jointly owned an electroplating company. They had a falling out and he agreed to leave the company. She was the treasurer, and her signature was required on checks. There was to be a final payment to him of two thousand dollars, covering some of his expenses, so he drafted the check for her to sign. She signed it. But the two-thousand-dollar check had become a twenty-two-thousand-dollar check and was legitimately signed by the sister—who'd hired Trouville to prove that the check was a fraud. Sally was in a rage and feared the check would bankrupt her and the company.

It wasn't easy to do. Her signature was genuine. She had signed it. Trouville set to work. First he noted that Wilbur hadn't left quite enough space to write "twenty" in front of the two thousand, and his addition was cramped. Trouville photographed the cramped handwritten twenty and made a huge enlargement for the court. Then he subjected the check to more intense examination: it had originally been written while in a checkbook, which meant that the pen left a slight furrow as it wrote, and raising a faint ridge on the bottom side.

After Sally had signed the check, Wilbur wrote the additional "twenty" and the additional number two, but he'd altered it on a desk because the check was no longer in the checkbook. What was written on the hard surface did not furrow the check or raise a ridge on the reverse side. So Trouville went to work in his photography lab. He photographed the back of the check using a light source that was parallel to the surface, thus illuminating the faint ridges, the way a setting sun illumines one side of hills and throws the other into shadow. Then he made enlargements. With these huge photographs resting on an easel, he was able to show the court what had happened. Part of the check had been drafted in a checkbook. But the part that increased its face value by twenty thousand dollars had been written later on a hard surface. With his pointer in hand, he'd made the case. He won, and had rescued Sally and the company.

Sonntag remembered that one well, because the civil case had resulted in a criminal fraud case against Wilbur Madsen and the district attorney had employed Trouville as an expert witness. Over the years the police department and the district attorney had made more and more use of Trouville. There were stickup notes, there were fake wills, fake incorporation papers, faked licenses, faked diplomas, forged signatures, questionable holographs, faked suicide notes, and anonymous threats. And the little genius who'd invented a whole field of expert sleuthing had become the most celebrated forensic examiner in the country, a man regularly appearing as an expert witness in the courts of California, Texas, Delaware, New York, and elsewhere.

Trouville's practice soon spread far beyond Milwaukee, and he was taking cases that originated everywhere. He became an occasional consultant for the FBI, especially in bank robbery cases. He eventually obtained his apprentice, Harley Potter, and the firm flourished, even as Trouville trained the younger man in all the arcana of his unique vocation.

But Sonntag was no closer to knowing who he was. And these files weren't telling him anything.

CHAPTER THREE

The longer Joe Sonntag poked and probed in that gloomy office, the more he realized he wasn't doing any better than Trouville's colleague and lawyer. The dead man's past was artfully concealed. The office was orderly; Trouville and Potter had been disciplined. The case files were orderly, with no stray papers. The correspondence was perfunctory. The accounts were inclusive and current. The invoices for such items as photographic paper, developer, typewriter repair, or utilities were paid and filed.

Sonntag dialed Captain Ackerman.

"Whatcha got?" Ackerman asked.

"Nothing. It looks like Trouville's estate will end up in escheat."

"Don't use them big words on me. You calling it quits?"

"No, I'll get Trouville's key and have a look at his flat, and if that doesn't yield something, I'll quit."

"Well, it's your call. Just make sure you make up the hours," the captain said. "We got nothing going here."

Ackerman hung up abruptly, as was his wont, leaving Sonntag with a dead phone in his hand.

Sonntag flipped off the lights, locked up, and returned the key to Agnes in the dental abattoir next door. He swore he heard a patient whining, but perhaps it was just Kessler's mean little drill burrowing holes through enamel. Agnes, making an appointment on the phone, nodded and smiled at him.

It was a good afternoon for another walk, so he set off for the law offices of Crumley and Bartles, where he hoped to get a key and permission to probe Trouville's flat. It was all walkable, and that suited Sonntag fine. He did a lot of his thinking while hoofing it.

He was starting to feel his old stubborn streak boiling up in him. He'd get the skinny on Trouville one way or another, and wouldn't quit. Everyone had a past. Trouville had a past. He'd find it. It was odd: A man died of heart failure and left a mystery behind him. That's all there was to it.

He loved his detective work because it was a challenge. He had to think his way through Gordian knots. He tried to bring evil people to justice, but the thing he liked best was to demonstrate that a suspect was innocent. In his day, he'd seen people in desperate corners, the accusing fingers of all the world pointing at them, only they weren't guilty. He'd watched as miserable people were exonerated, and somehow, that reached deepest in him. There was good in his work that inspired him. But now he was on a mission that would do little but satisfy his curiosity about a dead genius. That was okay, too.

A breeze off Lake Michigan cooled the city's east side. Sonntag passed Chapman's and the Pfister hotel, turned right, and climbed the broad steps of a noble old office building where the firm occupied two floors above the street-level shops. He found the door, featuring the same ubiquitous pebbled glass that guarded most of the professional offices of Milwaukee, and soon found himself being welcomed by Stan Bartles, who was about three feet higher than Trouville, and sporting a woven gold watch fob with a Phi Beta Kappa key dangling from it.

"Ah, Lieutenant. Good to see you. I happen to have a few moments so we can chat."

"I just want the key to the flat," Sonntag said. "And permission."

"I'm glad you're doing this. Harley and I have hunted everywhere, and asked for help from banks with lock boxes, and we've come up with beans. With your excellent training, maybe you'll do better."

"I'm taking the afternoon to try," Sonntag said. "Not much else doing at the moment."

"No axe murders?"

Sonntag smiled. "You want to talk a little bit? What you know about Trouville? What you guess? Why he apparently left no will? Stuff like that?"

Bartles suddenly studied his Bulova. "I really couldn't say, and have no inclination to guess, Lieutenant."

"Much in his bank account?"

"I'll tell you this, Armand wasn't getting rich at his game. No, no one's going to inherit much. The state's not going to collect much. He may have been the foremost document man on the planet, but that didn't translate into big fees."

"You have a notion or two where he came from?"

"Some place like Virginia, where lawyers and witnesses might get suited up for court. Any man who wears a morning coat to court ought to be someone you can trace somewhere."

"I was thinking the same thing," Sonntag said. "And an outfit like that would cost me two weeks' wages. Why would he wear one? It's out of fashion."

"There's men who are stuck in the past like a fly in amber. He was one of them."

"But he was the future. He was finding more and more ways to authenticate a document."

Bartles smiled. "You're right. A paradox. Look, I've got a client coming in, and . . ."

"Sure," Sonntag said.

The attorney dug in his desk and pulled out a key with a tag on it. "Here. Bring it back, please. And let us know."

The tag read Trouville, 1114-1/2 Downer, upper.

"I'll let you know," Sonntag said.

Sonntag headed north. It would be a long hike. He checked his watch. Maybe he should phone Lizbeth and tell her he'd be late again. But he was late so often she usually didn't start dinner until he walked into their bungalow on the west side.

Downer was a pleasant enough, mostly commercial avenue, mixed with apartments, well shaded in summer but now the arching elms were just budding. He passed a young mother wheeling a child in a gray pram, and two retired duffers sitting on a bench soaking up the sun, and a mournful basset hound tied to a bicycle rack.

A little to the east rose the solid old brick mansions along Lake Shore Drive, most with a grand view of the inland sea. But Downer was more modest, an engaging street that seemed to blend rich men and poor men together amid a cosmopolitan world of shops and cafés and apartments.

The upstairs flat on Downer was accessed from an entry hall. Sonntag climbed the green-carpeted stairs and slid the Yale key in the lock, which opened easily. His first impression was casual chaos. Whatever discipline Trouville had imposed on his workplace, his hearth was apparently more undisciplined. And yet not really messy. A lair, a den, a library, a place of the mind. What Sonntag registered at once was heaps of books with bookmarks in them, stacks of papers and documents, an oversized magnifying glass, an easy chair with a Tiffany lamp nearby with a table bearing heaps of reports and papers. Trouville had obviously done much of his detective work here, rather than his office. Here is where he examined handwriting under a two-hundred-watt lamp, kept up with academic reports, and took copious notes, judging from the heap of papers covered with the cramped cursive writing that Sonntag knew to be Trouville's.

This seemed a more likely place than the office to find heirs, discover a will, trace the origin and previous whereabouts of the man who had changed the whole world of crime detection. Sonntag hesitated to plunge into all those papers and notes; not yet. Not until he had some sense of the man whose life had vanished behind seven veils. The kitchen was tidy. Trouville apparently ate out, but there were a few dishes in the drying rack in the sink.

On the dining table, where they had been left by Bartles, were Trouville's insurance papers. The name Armand de Trouville had been typed into the car insurance contract as well as a liability insurance contract. Date of birth March 10, 1881. He had turned sixty-eight only a few days earlier. He had lived a normal life span. There was no birth certificate among these items. Three pairs of glasses rested on the table, two of them bifocals and one a magnifier. Trouville had grown farsighted, a common enough event in old age.

Sonntag found himself reluctant to probe Trouville's flat, or invade his privacy. He was a detective, used to digging deeply into people's lives. He was used to digging through closets, emptying pockets, poking through desk drawers, hunting for clues to crimes. But here was only a man's wish to hide something of his past, and remain anonymous at death. So it was different. He felt he was violating Armand de Trouville's space and life. And violating his deliberate design for life's end. The dapper genius wanted to leave the world his own way, and not the way his colleague Potter and his lawyer Bartles wanted. But of course the colleague and lawyer were simply doing what was necessary. A search had to be done. An effort made. The weight of law and court required it. A man had died. It was necessary to dispose of his possessions. And they had called in Sonntag to employ his skills toward that end.

Even so, Joe Sonntag felt a certain embarrassment, and

silently voiced his apology to Trouville's spirit as he looked around the place. Sonntag missed little. He discovered Wheaties and Quaker one-minute oatmeal. He discovered a bottle of homogenized milk, now sour. He discovered a can of Folger's and a stovetop coffeemaker with a perforated basket. He discovered Lennox cups and saucers, but no mugs. Under the sink were bottles of bleach and ammonia, and Fels Naptha.

In Trouville's bedroom he found a neatly made bed. There were no family photos on the dresser or bedside table. A closet held a variety of suits and shirts on hangers. Trouville had a lot of suits and shirts and ties. Other clothing remained in packages wrapped in butcher paper from the Chinese laundry down the street.

Sonntag felt even worse poking around the bedroom. He wondered how it would be if a stranger were to poke around in his and Lizbeth's bedroom after they had died. It wasn't indecent; it was just a brutal spotlight, like a photographer's light, piercing every corner. The dresser revealed several pairs of navy blue flannel pajamas with white piping on them. There was a stack of pressed, fresh handkerchiefs, some of which were monogrammed with a large T and an A and R on either side. Come to think of it, Sonntag didn't know what the R stood for. Armand R. de Trouville.

There was a drawer of black silk hose, the sort that required ankle garters, and there were spare pairs of those as well. There were four pairs of shoes in the closet, three of them oxfords and one of them patent leather. All but one pair was black, the other brown. Made-in-Milwaukee shoes.

The bathroom offered up a shaving mug; straight-edge razor; shaving brush; a tube of Pepsodent, wintergreen flavor; two toothbrushes; talcum powder; bath towels, hand towels, and washcloths, none of them monogrammed; and some spare rolls of Scott toilet paper. There was a fingernail kit with scissors, clippers, file, and cuticle smoother, all of stainless steel. Made in Germany, it said. Probably prewar. A bottle of Bayer aspirin and another of Phillips Milk of Magnesia occupied the medicine cabinet, along with a box of Band-Aids. There was some digitalis in a bottle. Trouville apparently was getting along until his heart seizure.

Most of the suits had been purchased at MacNeil and Moore, an elegant men's clothier on East Wisconsin Avenue, but another came from Chapman's. Some had handkerchiefs artfully tucked into their breast pockets. All had knife-edged creases in their pants. Trouville had taken care with his grooming.

A cutaway and pinstriped trousers hung in a paper sheath from Jessen's, the dry cleaners. Sonntag spread them out on the bed and pulled the lapel so he could read the label. These bore a Marshall Field label, sewn into the inner breast pocket. Chicago. The formal attire probably antedated Trouville's exodus to Milwaukee in nineteen thirty-six. Of course, even this was no proof that Trouville had once lived in the great Illinois city. He may have ordered it. But it was a clue—a dubious, miserable clue that stretched back to Trouville's past.

Sonntag returned the formal attire to its sheath and hung it in the closet. He'd take his quest to Chicago next—a trip to the morgues of the dailies, a talk with any of the old cops who'd spare him a half hour.

He spent a while probing magazines, books, business papers, and closets, to no avail. It was after four. If he hurried, he could return the key before Bartles left his offices for the evening.

He hiked swiftly down Downer, past Kilbourn and the Women's Club of Wisconsin, and on to the lawyer's lair, reaching the offices just as the afternoon exodus was filling up the elevators, which paused endlessly at every floor. Sonntag opted to dash up the stairs, and oddly, that is how he ran into Bartles, who was dashing down the stairs, wearing a homburg and trench coat and clutching a briefcase and umbrella.

"Well, this is luck," Sonntag said. He handed the key to Bartles.

"What did you discover?" the lawyer asked.

"Not much. Whoever Armand was before nineteen thirty-six, he had erased it all."

Bartles sighed. "We were thorough. Potter and I made a systematic search. We literally left no page unturned. We even poked around in the wastebaskets. The man will go down as a genius, a mystery, and perhaps a legal tangle."

"I found one small thing, sir. One of the cutaways he used in court was from Marshall Field."

"It was?"

"Are cutaways available in Milwaukee?"

"Not that I know of. Of course, a tailor—"

"Trouville's cutaway had a label. I'll see what can be found out in Chicago. Not easy without a name. But he did have a profession, and he did wear cutaways or morning coats in court. So I'll see what I can find out."

"I hope we haven't blotted up too much of your time, Lieutenant."

"I'm as curious as you, and now I won't quit. But it may take a few months."

"Do we owe you anything?"

"Send Captain Ackerman a valentine. He could always use one," Sonntag said.

"He'd like a box of nickel cigars," Bartles said.

They hiked down the stairs together, the lawyer to wherever he lived and Sonntag for the orange Number Ten Wells Street streetcar that would rattle him home if it made it over the trestle high above the Menomonee River.

CHAPTER FOUR

After a hard day, Joe Sonntag usually felt so tired he would sit in a stupor and stare at the walls after work, at least until Lizbeth put supper on the table. This afternoon he didn't feel so tired, and he mused on it as he waited to board the orange Wells streetcar.

Maybe it was because his effort all afternoon hadn't involved crime. The question was simply about a man's identity, and the purpose would be to settle an estate. Maybe it was crime that wearied him by the end of each day, he thought. Maybe it was because most of his days as a police detective were a struggle against the sinister, the cruel, the vicious, the rapacious, the stupid, and the self-destructive. Maybe what tired him was his understanding that but for the police, terrible forces would tear apart families and homes, children and grandchildren, spouses, good businesses, and the peace.

He hadn't figured out whether Armand de Trouville had once lived another life, and his curiosity was piqued now by how well the little document examiner had buried his past—and future. But he would figure it out. He would do it on his own time, not municipal time. Which reminded him, he owed the city half a day. He would make it up on Saturday. Lizbeth wanted to go for a country drive on Saturday, with stops at some of the cheese factories north of the city. He loved those drives too. The roads were empty, and the cheese factories open and offering delightful varieties. He had especially come to enjoy the green cheeses, those barely aged, with delicate flavors. She would be disappointed. But maybe they could go out for chop suey instead.

The streetcar squealed to a halt and Sonntag boarded, let the motorman punch his monthly pass, and found his way down the aisle, past yellow wicker seats. The familiar ozone smell filled his nostrils, unsettling him a bit. He'd left his black lunch bucket at the station, and would brown-bag it tomorrow. Lizbeth was used to his delinquencies, especially that one. It would mean there would be no hot coffee from the thermos bottle.

The orange streetcar cranked west along Wells Street, past seedy shops, and eventually reached an area of seedy apartments and a few old homes with steep stairs. A flood of working-class humanity boarded, filled the wicker seats, clung to the hand straps above as the car screeched its way west. Milwaukee was an industrial city, and this car was filled with tired men in bib overalls and brogans, with worn women wearing brown babushkas, with young clerks, and a few trim girls in pastels. The hemlines in Milwaukee always stayed low, no matter what was fashionable nationally. One could sometimes see pictures in *Look* or *Life* of young women with tight skirts and a lot of calf, cleaved by the seam of silk or nylon stockings. But Milwaukee was different. There were Lutheran or Catholic or Orthodox churches in every neighborhood. There were Slovenian or Rumanian or Greek or Polish or Czech or Danish churches, their architecture faithfully imported from the Old World.

At 35th Street, Sonntag gripped the seat back ahead of him, facing once again the ordeal of crossing the Menomonee River valley on a towering wooden trestle bridge built especially for the streetcars. He had taken that journey over the viaduct thousands of times, but the terror never ceased. He had no idea what he was afraid of; he simply knew that sometime, someday, the streetcar would careen over the edge and crash far below, and that would be the end of him.

It was an ancient enemy, and it defeated him, and suddenly he was tired. The conductor slowed the car to ten miles an hour and suddenly it seemed to be floating on air, past the Miller Brewery, past the tangle of factories and warehouses, and the brown river far below, while Sonntag clung to the seat back, felt his hands turn wet, and felt the car rock as winds battered it, and then they were on the other side, and Sonntag wiped his hands on his pants, and his pulse slowed down again, and he wasn't tired anymore.

He got off at 56th Street and walked home, dodging a coaster wagon owned by that brat Horace down the street.

"You had a good day," Lizbeth said as he pecked at her cheek.

"I guess I did. But I didn't solve anything."

She was armored by her white apron. The house smelled of meatloaf. At least he hoped it was meatloaf.

"You were doing something you enjoyed," she said.

"I'll pour some bourbon and water," he said.

"I'll join you."

That was rare. She usually was so busy in the kitchen that she didn't share a cocktail with him. He wondered when he had started pouring a drink after work. Usually Old Crow or Jim Beam. One a night. That was all he allowed himself.

He returned with his drink, amber in a perspiring glass, and her own, about half the size. Sometimes she wanted a Manhattan. That's when she was frisky. Or bored.

"Tell me," she said. She had settled into her corner of the sofa. She loved to listen to him. For her, it was better than reading the comics in the Green Sheet of the *Journal.*

She always loved his cases, his stories, his guesses. Crime committed and solved. Mysteries clarified. Cold cases. A sudden break in an old case. A sharp deduction. A lucky pinch. A jailbird who squealed. An informant with a hot tip. The witness who suddenly had a stroke. The anonymous letter. The axe-

33

killer who turned himself in, walked right up to his desk. For her, his life was a marvel, filled with tragedy and sometimes joy, with crazy stories and moments of triumph. With some danger and a lot of foolishness. With maddening colleagues and sometimes brilliant ones. Once in a while she got to brag over the bridge table about some case or other he'd cracked.

"I've got to work half of Saturday," he said.

That stopped her short. "But why?"

"Because the captain decreed it. I owe the city some time. I spent this afternoon doing a favor for the estate of someone."

She sipped, waiting. He sipped, enjoying the splash of cold bourbon in his throat.

"The document examiner who died a few days ago. Armand de Trouville. It seems he left no will, no lock box, and no one can find any heirs, and his past prior to nineteen thirty-five is a blank. They asked for help, so I volunteered. It turned out I didn't do any better than they did, trying to find a living heir."

"Have I heard of him?" she asked.

"Probably not. Hardly anyone has. Hardly anyone at the station has. I think maybe a few lawyers have, and the DA's office. He wasn't like a movie star. But he was the best in his field—in fact, he invented the field."

"Like a handwriting expert?"

"That's one of many things he did. He could examine a document and tell whether it was forged, and when it was written or typed, and whether the type of paper matched the date on the document, and whether it was written on an Underwood or Remington or Smith Corona or Woodstock or Royal, and what year, because the fonts varied from model to model. Sometimes he could tell things from the ink that had been used. He could spot a forgery because even the best forgers make mistakes, one of them being too perfect. A person's signature varies constantly, it grows and shrinks, it flattens, it changes with the mood of the writer. But a forger has mastered just one signature, and repeats that one, and it's a giveaway."

"And he's gone?"

"Yes, gone. Heart attack. Cardiac arrest, I guess it was. And the world's lost an unknown genius. He was worth the whole FBI. He's changed the whole face of crime detection. He was a Shakespeare of the justice system. He was a Thomas Edison."

Her eyes shone. "Wow! And you knew him?"

"Professionally. Some of those cases. The note the stickup man shoved into the cashier's cage a few years ago—Trouville's insights led us straight to the robber. He wrote his stickup note in perfect Spencerian script, which is taught at the vocational college."

"I wish I could have met him," she said. "You meet such interesting people. My friends are sort of vanilla. I don't mean—they're sweet, but vanilla. I mean, we're vanilla and our world is sort of vanilla. Oh, you know what I mean."

She was laughing. She had some great friends, and their world was quilts and making dresses and bridge and raising children. But now she was alone, one boy dead of polio, the other off at Fort Bragg. Her world was vanilla, and sometimes he added some chocolate to it.

"Anyway, I spent the day helping out Trouville's colleague and the lawyer. They asked me to look for a will or anything that would help. So I did."

"Nothing?"

"A Marshall Field label in a cutaway."

She laughed. "The great detective Sonntag," she said.

He smiled. "It might lead somewhere. When did he buy it? Where was it shipped, if he didn't pick it up?"

"I think this man didn't want to be revealed," she said. "Did he have a driver's license and Social Security?"

"Both. In his name, Trouville. I think the Social Security

card's legit. That deal was enacted in nineteen thirty-five, and they signed people up in thirty-six. So all he had to do was sign up."

"Well, the forgery expert might have forged his own documents," she said.

"Could have, but didn't."

"Didn't you find anything at all?"

"I didn't look in the Wheaties boxes," he said. "I didn't read the coupons for Dick Tracy watches."

"No lock box? No wall safe?"

"Not even some bucks stashed in the mattress."

"Maybe it was a puzzle that Trouville deliberately left behind him. Figure this out, you dummies. Keep ya guessing!"

That hadn't occurred to him. That's what he loved about Lizbeth. She was all angles and often threw him curves.

"What's the colleague's name?" she asked.

"Harley Potter. Young. In his thirties. An apprentice, more or less. You work with a master and learn the deal."

"Figure this one out, Harley Potter, and you can inherit my practice!"

"He'd like to. He'd like to buy the equipment from the estate. There's a lot of it. Photographic stuff, big enlargers, a copying camera—but most of all, a reputation. If he's the colleague who survives, he has an unbeatable career."

"How so?"

"If you learned art by apprenticing with Rembrandt or Michelangelo, and learned it well . . ."

"Gotcha," she said. "Is he good?"

"I have no idea. But his mentor was a legend, at least for those in the know."

The meatloaf was great. She had a way of mixing in a certain blend of spices, and using ground beef and pork together with diced onions and peppers.

"You have to work on Saturday? Did Ackerman really say that? He couldn't just let go of you for a while? Like for a little public service?"

"The aldermen love him, Lizbeth. He keeps costs down."

"I can see why," she said, toting some plates and saucers to the kitchen. "But I wish I could trade him in. Maybe I'd get to see you now and then."

He felt the usual guilt. A city detective put in long and ir-regular hours, and got little for it, and was all too often the cause of an empty place setting at the table. He couldn't blame it all on the department, either. Often he'd get so absorbed he'd forget to come home, and then he'd face a hurt wife, who knew she sometimes lost out to his vocation. Worse, he'd often forget to phone her when he was going to be late.

She drew water and added some Ivory soap flakes and plunged the dishes in, and began scrubbing them hard. Then she rinsed them and set them in the drying rack.

He eyed her guiltily, having just cut her weekend into rib-bons. He grabbed a dishtowel and started wiping.

"Don't," she said.

But he continued, wiping tumblers and plates and knives and forks.

"I'll take you out for a big dinner Saturday night, babe," he said. "We'll go to Mader's for some sausage and sauerkraut."

"Don't," she said. "It's not your fault. They want sixty hours a week from you and give back nothing."

"Well, let's go anyway. You're my date."

She had always been his date on Saturday nights, when they were courting, when they had little boys, and after the nest was empty. And she still was.

"You sure are a handsome guy," she said.

He laughed. Joe Sonntag knew what he saw in the mirror when he shaved. Lumpy and middle-aged and a brow furrowed forever. A balding worrywart.

"You pick it, and we'll do it," he said.

"Greek?"

He laughed. That was her way of saying she would enjoy a little romancing next Saturday. He slipped a hand over her shoulder and kissed her.

"Don't you know that was a Greek meatloaf?" she said.

"It had never occurred to me," he said.

"Well, a gal who gets stood up on a Saturday morning has to do something about it," she said.

CHAPTER FIVE

It felt peculiar, going to work on a Saturday. He hadn't done it for years. He was the senior detective, head of investigations, and got regular weekends off.

But now he faced the Wells Street viaduct once again. This time there were only three passengers on the streetcar, which meant the car was light and any gust of wind might blow the car off the track and into the valley. When the car was jammed, and people in the aisle hanging onto the straps, that's when the viaduct might collapse. But the thing he feared most was bad maintenance. Some day, some worker would fail to put in a bolt and screw down the nut, and that would be the end, and there would be a front-page story in the *Journal.*

He closed his eyes and gripped the seat as the car sailed into space. He knew exactly when to open his eyes on the other side, because it sounded different when the car was running on solid earth.

The bullpen in the downtown station looked forlorn this Saturday. He wished crime would take a holiday over weekends so everyone could go home. But Saturdays were the worst of all. A lot of people decided Saturday was the right day to kill a spouse or rob a saloon or push a sister's head underwater on a Lake Michigan beach. Bank robberies declined on Saturdays, but nothing else did. He tossed his fedora on a peg and added his trench coat and settled at his battered oak desk, scalloped with cigarette burns. There were no messages awaiting him. He paused, wondering how to make himself useful to his employer, the City of Milwaukee, on a Saturday morning in April.

His young colleague Frank Silva resolved that for him.

"Hey, what're you doing here?" he asked.

"Making up time."

"Ah, Captain Ackerman's been on your case. What did you do? Take time out for a toothache?"

"Tried to help an estate find heirs," he said.

"Oh, Trouville. I heard about that. Find anything?"

"A Marshall Field label in his cutaway."

Silva was grinning. "The word was, he fled up here when a mobster down there threatened to exterminate him."

"Well, that's the word, but it's all air. I've got a Chicago detective on it. And I want to spend a day in the morgue of the *Tribune*, nineteen thirty-five."

"Why then?"

"Trouville's earliest Milwaukee records date from February, thirty-six."

"Where'd that rumor come from?" Silva asked.

"Beats me."

"Maybe Trouville spread it himself. Where else would it come from? You might ask why. I've heard that Trouville liked to tell stories that were pretty much doggie doo."

That's Frank Silva at work, Sonntag thought. The boy—a man in his thirties, actually—had a way of cutting to the heart of things. He was an alderman's son, an active socialist, purveyor of anti-capitalist tracts, street fighter, picketer, labor union organizer, anti-fascist, and the best detective Milwaukee possessed. *Better than me,* Sonntag thought. That's because Silva mixed with people better, and knew human nature better.

"I get it," Silva said. "You took some time to help the estate, so Ackerman's got your nose jammed into his grindstone."

"You need help with anything?"

"Well, not really. All the killers have taken a spring break in Florida. The robbers are all at a convention in Tucson. The rapists are all on saltpeter. The panhandlers have sworn off for Lent. The strippers at the Empress are keeping their pants on. A beat cop found a revolver in Ace Pawn, the serial number ground off. He confiscated it and we're going to do some ballistics."

"Cold cases?"

Silva sighed. "Always those. Look, there's a Wild West exhibit opening at the museum. Go look for pickpockets. See if Wyatt Earp's wandering around with six-guns."

Silva knew how much Sonntag laughed at the West. There was nothing Sonntag despised more than westerns, with guys in cowboy hats marching down the main street of some little berg intent on killing each other, all according to a code. Hollywood swagger, he called it. And don't get him started on John Wayne.

Sonntag settled in his carrel and began reviewing some of the cold cases in weary old folders stuffed into a drawer. They were mostly his notes, plus an occasional photo. The ones that seemed to endure the longest were not crimes of passion, but mob stuff. The numbers runner who got offed. The south-side gal who got her throat slit. The body with the missing head. The case of the disappearing satchel of hundred-dollar bills.

That's when Harley Potter walked in.

"I hoped I'd find you here," Potter said.

"I don't work Saturdays," Sonntag said. "How'd you find me?"

"Called the lady of your house."

"You got some news for me?"

"No, I was hoping you had news for me. What did you find?"

"Searching? Nothing more than you and Bartles found, I'm afraid."

"Mind if I sit and visit?"

Sonntag nodded. The young man, skinny and blond, settled in the wooden chair across from the detective. This all seemed peculiar. A Saturday morning visit to the Milwaukee PD.

"You want a report?"

"Well, yes. This is all so worrisome to me. Here I am, a partner in a firm that seems to be falling apart. My future—"

"I see. You're a partner?"

"Not formally or legally. A colleague would be a better word. I sort of, well, apprenticed myself to Mr. Trouville. There's no other way to be a document examiner. On my part, I wanted the best training. On his part, he wanted a successor, and someone who was familiar with every aspect of his work. He said so, once. He said if anything ever happened to him, I should carry on. I've never forgotten that."

"So your relationship was teacher and student?"

"Oh, I wouldn't say that. It was at first, but not now. We're partners, colleagues. I've been with him since early forty-five, you know, and I wouldn't say I'm a junior partner. I joined him after my army service ended."

"What were you in the service?"

"A tech sergeant, sir. Medical corps, Pacific theater. Field hospitals need a safe environment. They're more than just big tents in the jungle. I directed spraying crews. Insecticides, water purification, sanitation, hang mosquito netting, that sort of thing. Only I caught malaria trying to eradicate it."

"So you like tech stuff?"

"You bet, sir, and that's how I ended up with Mr. Trouville. He was the ultimate scientist. I was lucky he was interested. He's not young, you know. And he must have been thinking about a successor. And I was thinking about being that person. And advancing the science. And taking it further someday."

"And now you don't know what tomorrow will bring."

"Yes, sir. I'd like to work on his cases. He has several pending. I'd like to purchase his equipment and practice from the estate. I'd like to continue but Mr. Bartles, the trustee, won't let me. Without heirs, and without a will, and without known relatives, everything—"

"Is a mess." Sonntag pondered it. No wonder the young man was anxious. "Well, I wish I could help. It's going to be a drawn-out process."

"I don't even have a paycheck anymore. I used to receive a monthly check from him, drawn by him. What am I going to do now?"

"I'd be anxious too. I wish I had better luck. I didn't take the time to open every book and magazine hoping a will and testament would tumble out, but I covered anything else that intrigued me."

"And?"

"He opened shop in Milwaukee in nineteen thirty-six. Back from there, it's a blank."

"He supposedly practiced in Chicago before then," Potter said.

"Where did you hear that? I'm interested in that. Where did it come from?"

"Himself, sir. One time, when we had just cracked a forgery and the court bought our testimony, we were at dinner—Houston, Texas. He got to reminiscing and mentioned Chicago, starting there, on his own, not much help, courts skeptical, no credentials, lawyers laughed at him. And then he changed the subject."

"Like he had slipped up?"

"Yes, sir. He swiftly steered away from that. He'd seen Chicago, loved State Street, loved the Chicago Opera, loved the Art Institute . . ."

"The only thing I found in his flat was a Marshall Field label sewn into that cutaway of his. But that doesn't mean much. You can live here and order from Marshall Field. Or go there. Ninety miles to Union Station, six or seven blocks to Marshall Field's."

"That's it? The office and his flat?"

"That's it. Trouville had a few friends around town, and I'll talk to them. Who knows what he told his pals? But the odds are getting pretty slim. You and the attorney did a thorough job yourself, and if there's no deposit box you've about covered it. The courts have appointed Bartles the trustee. He'll advertise for heirs. And in a few months the court will authorize him to dispose of the property."

"And I'll be out in the cold."

"Maybe not."

"Look, detective, I'm out. There's nothing I can do."

"Start your own firm?"

"I'd like to. But I can't claim success. I have no record. Every case was his case. Every client was his client. I was mostly his errand boy, digging up stuff."

"Like what?"

"He'd tell me to call Remington Arms and find out when a certain model was discontinued. Or call Parker and ask me to find out what year they changed the dye in the blue ink to blue-black."

"So? He started with no credentials. In your business you win them pretty gradually. In time, you'll have them. You got the best training anyone could have. Armand de Trouville is a name known from coast to coast, at least in certain circles."

"But everyone knows he took all the cases. He told the lawyers he'd done the work, even when I'd done some." Potter smiled suddenly. "But I learned a lot, anyway."

Sonntag stared out the grimy window into an April morn. "It must have been hard on you to find him gone."

"Yes! I walked in and there he was, slumped in that swivel chair, his mouth open, his arms dangling. He didn't fall out of it, but only because the wooden arm held him.”

“You called an ambulance?”

“I don’t remember very well. I shook him. I took hold of his hand. It was cold. I shouted at him. I put my hand under his nose to see if he was breathing. I was getting very, very upset.”

“I would too,” Sonntag said.

“I didn’t call right away. I went next door, to the dentist, and got Agnes, who works for him and us. She came right over.”

“Why her?”

“Dentists have drugs. Smelling salts. They know something about that.”

“She tried to awaken him?”

“She took one look and called for help. After that, all we could do was wait.”

“That must have been a long wait,” Sonntag said.

“I’ve seen a lot of dead,” Potter said. “They turn gray in the face.”

Sonntag could see the young man revisiting the moment. “He was a great man. I knew him professionally,” he said.

“Well, he was great, but he wasn’t easy to work for.”

“What did Agnes say?”

“She knelt beside him in his swivel chair, and tried to will life into him. She tried to blow into his lungs, and thump on his chest. I’d seen too much death during the war to try that stuff.”

“Seizure, heart failure,” Sonntag said.

“Is that what the death certificate says?”

“Don’t you have a copy?”

“I haven’t seen one. Mr. Bartles has it.”

“Had he been ill, sir?”

Potter spent a long time peering into himself. “Not so the public would know,” he said. “Diabetes. He had to be careful what he ate. He had a list of forbidden foods a mile long. He didn’t say much about it in public.”

"What's a heart arrest?" Sonntag asked. "I'm not familiar with that on a death certificate. Was this something to do with diabetes?"

"It could be," Potter said. "Doesn't that cause cardiovascular disease?"

The conversation petered out. Potter seemed to draw into himself.

"Thanks for keeping me posted," he said, and left the station. Sonntag sensed he had been looking for something, and hadn't found it.

"Something wrong with that guy?" Frank Silva asked.

"He looked into the crystal ball and saw snow," the lieutenant replied.

CHAPTER SIX

Lizbeth's response was resigned. "I knew you would," she said.

Sonntag had called her to voice a decision: "I think I'd better go to that service this afternoon," he said. "I'll be home around four, and we'll go to dinner."

"Okay," she said.

He did not miss the sadness in her voice. His life as a cop had intruded so much on her own hopes to do things together that he felt bad. And this was one time. He wasn't required to attend. He had already paid his respects. But here he was, going to Armand de Trouville's service, and he couldn't say why. He'd make it up to Lizbeth. He'd take some time off. He'd take her on a trip, maybe to Chicago. Or maybe not. He knew how he'd spend time in Chicago. He'd be digging through nineteen thirty-five clippings at the *Tribune* while she wandered around the Loop all alone.

He bought a Twinkie for lunch and hiked over to the funeral home north of downtown Milwaukee, all the while wondering why.

The funeral chapel seemed oddly hollow. There was no casket in sight, which meant that this would simply be a memorial service. Sonntag shed his wraps and settled himself in a pew. Captain Ackerman, in dress blues, occupied the pew ahead. That was good. The Police Department was present, as it should be. The attorney, Stan Bartles, and apparently his wife beside him, sat near the front. Agnes Winsocket sat nervously in the

47

first row, dressed in black silk, along with her employer, the dentist Karl Kessler, looking stern. The young colleague, Harley Potter, sat importantly near a lectern. Sonntag waited for more, but as the minute hand on his Bulova slid past two, it was plain this would be it.

Potter glanced at a pocket watch and rose, settling himself behind the lectern.

"Good afternoon. We've come to celebrate the life of Armand de Trouville this day. We will begin with a stanza from the poem 'In Memoriam, A. H. H.,' written by Alfred, Lord Tennyson, upon the death of his friend."

Agnes Winsocket arose, carrying with her a collection of Tennyson's poems. It took her a moment to adjust herself at the lectern and open to the selected verses.

She began tremulously:

> *"Oh yet we trust that somehow good*
> *Will be the final goal of ill,*
> *To pangs of nature, sins of will.*
> *Defects of doubt, taints of blood;*
>
> *"That nothing walks with aimless feet;*
> *That not one life shall be destroy'd*
> *Or cast as rubbish to the void,*
> *When God hath made the pile complete."*

Sonntag was reminded that funerals are for the living. If Trouville's spirit was present, he would probably be enjoying the absence of an audience most of all. There never had been a person so indifferent to the affections of others, or their opinions, Sonntag thought. The man lived in a professional bubble: every document was a challenge and a mystery that must be resolved and understood. If Trouville had ever pondered the large questions of life and death, or even purpose, or good and evil, Sonntag had never heard any of it escape the examiner's lips.

> *"Behold we know not anything;*
> *I can but trust that good shall fall*
> *At least—far off—at last, to all,*
> *And every winter change to spring.*
>
> *"So runs my dream: but what am I?*
> *An infant crying in the night:*
> *An infant crying for the light:*
> *And with no language but a cry."*

Miss Winsocket, visibly relieved to have discharged her duties, swiftly returned to her pew and the dubious safety of Dr. Kessler.

Potter announced that Stanley Bartles would share some remembrances of Armand de Trouville.

The attorney rose amiably. He was accustomed to public speaking, and settled behind the lectern as if born to enjoy life there. He wore three-piece black gabardine this day, which only accentuated the woven gold watch fob and the Phi Beta Kappa key.

"I've been pondering how I might honor an amazing life at this moment," he began. "It wouldn't be easy. If I focused on one thing in these brief remarks, I would miss a dozen others. If I spent these moments on his innovations in the field he virtually invented, and listed the techniques he developed to authenticate documents of all sorts, I would neglect the other things that made this man's life remarkable.

"If I said that he was a genius in the courtroom, who astounded lawyers and made believers of judges, I could fill my entire time here with anecdotes and telling moments. Or if I turned to his impact on the commonwealth, and explained that

Armand de Trouville's forensic techniques gave the nation unprecedented defenses against fraud and deceit; who gave families a sure and authoritative means to settle their estates; who occasionally altered our understanding of the past by examining the authenticity of historic documents; who was the terror of kidnappers who conveyed their demands with notes; the terror of crooks and forgers, fakers and swindlers, all of whom used wills and contracts and licenses and endorsements to perpetrate their pillaging—these too could occupy my brief time here."

He paused. "So I will talk about the man I knew, without referring to the ways he changed the world."

Sonntag listened, rapt. He had known all sorts of crooks, some of them bright. He had known politicians and public servants, swine and saints, yet none of them had quite caught his admiration the way Trouville had. Surely that was what had drawn him to this ill-attended memorial on a Saturday afternoon.

He saw that Captain Ackerman was impatient. The man would want stories, about the way a *T* was crossed or a lowercase *A* was left open, or how a European *7* with a crossbar convicted this scoundrel or that. But Sonntag sensed this was going in the right direction, and that the attorney was reaching for something important, something of value for this tiny assemblage.

"The man I knew as Armand de Trouville may have been born with a different name. Once he came close to telling me what it was. In vino veritas, goes the aphorism. And in this case, our late friend was enjoying some rum and Coca Cola with me, which in itself surprised me, since he was abstemious. But we were in Miami, where he had given expert testimony in a forged-will case, and in our celebration, he began to talk of his past. He had started out to become an artist, he said, studying as a young man at the École Supérieure des Beaux-Arts in Paris. For reasons unclear, but perhaps scandalous, he enlisted in the Foreign Legion under the name of Bolivar Newman. He told of eating sheep's eyes with Bedouins near Marakesh and riding camels and fighting fierce bandits. During the first war, he fought in the Legion, but afterward won his discharge. He was no longer interested in painting, but in etching, and began to produce handsome etchings, all of them under this new name. There were splendid etchings of Notre Dame, Westminster Abbey, the cathedral at Chartres, and other great edifices. But this etcher known as Bolivar Newman soon discovered there was no living in it, and that was when he turned to the as-yet little-known world of what was then called questioned document examining. And there he flourished, employing the tools and techniques he had mastered in other fields. When and how he became, or returned to, the name we know him by remains a mystery. He died the foremost questioned document examiner in the world, and the inventor of the discipline.

"That's all I know. I've chosen this brief confession he made years ago as the way we might remember him. A genius with a romantic past. Either that, or a genius with a gift for spinning amazing fables about his prior life. It doesn't matter whether the stories he told me while he grew increasingly dizzy are true or not. They are the way we all should remember our friend, our treasured Armand."

Sonntag sat, astonished. Nearby, Captain Ackerman sat squinting, running this new material through his crap-detector mind.

Agnes Winsocket followed with some predictable verses from Tennyson's "Crossing the Bar":

> *"Twilight and evening bell,*
> *And after that the dark!*

And may there be no sadness of farewell,
When I embark."

It ended in quietness. Half a dozen people stirred, reached for hats and coats.

Sonntag waited at the door for Bartles.

"You surprised me," he said.

"Oh, it was just some of Trouville's malarkey. Heaven knows what his real past may have been. I thought it would make our goodbye party here a little more entertaining."

"It might help me find out who he was," Sonntag said.

"He invented that stuff. He was plainly having fun, concocting a past. So that seemed fitting for a farewell."

"Do you have any of those etchings?"

"Sure do. The Notre Dame one. It's hand-signed, Bolivar Newman, in the margin. He gave it to me."

"Then there's some truth to the story," Sonntag said relentlessly.

"Well, I suppose. But consider the name he used. Newman. New. Man. Obviously, our friend Trouville was entertaining himself with an invention like that."

"Were there other etchings in his flat? I'm afraid I didn't study the art on the walls."

"If there are, I don't know what good it would do."

"Everything leads somewhere. Including etchings. He must have learned the art somewhere. There would be dealers who know the etchings, if they're good. Maybe we can find out who he was, track down some relatives."

"Lieutenant, your instincts are wonderful and much appreciated. But I'm hoping to complete the advertising and petition the court to close the estate if no one responds. These things can drag on forever. I'd just as soon close the estate as swiftly as we can manage it."

Sonntag had the odd sense that his offer to pursue this new

material was being rejected. Even though the etchings by Bolivar Newman were real, apparently the story was only a story. It set off faint alarms in him. He noticed Captain Ackerman shamelessly eavesdropping.

The assemblage drifted out. Kessler, the dentist, departed with his receptionist and bookkeeper. Potter donned a black London Fog and vanished into the April day. Bartles, brandishing a folded umbrella, departed wearing a brand new homburg. Ackerman, in stiff blue uniform, watched them go.

"Something's not right about all this," Ackerman said.

"Just a gifted man with a mysterious past," Sonntag said.

"There's a crime around here somewhere," Ackerman said. "I'm putting you on it."

"Such as?"

"I don't know. But something's haywire. I can smell it."

"Let me get this straight. This is now a formal PD investigation? You want me to find out what?"

"Just my gut feeling," Ackerman said.

Sonntag grinned until the captain started looking huffy.

The funeral director hovered at the door, waiting for the last visitors to depart.

"Was Mr. Trouville buried?" Captain Ackerman asked him.

"No sir, he was cremated yesterday. We've given the urn to Mr. Bartles."

"And the dental gold?"

The director looked pained. "Of course, sir."

They stepped into the overcast day and the door closed behind them.

"They got rid of the body in a hurry," Ackerman said.

"Not in a hurry, Captain. That's a pretty standard arrangement."

"Now we can't have a look at the body."

Sonntag was truly baffled. "Captain, it's not a criminal case.

It's a man with no will or heirs. And a hidden past."

"Find his dental charts," Ackerman said.

"Probably Kessler," Sonntag said. "He was next door."

"Teeth. That's the secret. Teeth solve half the homicides and three-quarters of identities."

"I'll look for teeth, Captain. And once I get Trouville's dental record, what would you advise?"

"Look for the dental records of Bolivar Newman."

"I'll do that, Captain."

Ackerman eyed Sonntag. "You might be chief of detectives, Lieutenant, but you're missing a crime here. So get to the bottom of it, or I will."

"What crime, Captain?"

"Oh, it's lurking in there. I know one when I see one," Ackerman said.

He wheeled away. Joe Sonntag stared after him, wondering how much cop time would be wasted on Ackerman's folly.

Chapter Seven

Sunday morning played out the usual way. Joe Sonntag didn't want to go to church, and Lizbeth did.

"You could at least go for Lent," she said.

"I just want to read the comics."

He knew that would irritate her, and it did. "You of all people, a cop, need to go to church and not read L'il Abner."

He knew how badly she wanted him at her side. She was all dolled up in a spring frock, gray cloth coat, and a blue straw hat with a mess of artificial roses perched on it. She wanted him there, thanking God for all good things on a fine spring day, surrounded by good people, solid and kind, the sort who filled the pews of Our Redeemer Lutheran Church each and every Sunday, rain or shine.

But Joe Sonntag was weary of God, and all the crooks and thugs supposedly made in God's image that he ended up dealing with. He felt very bad, not going with Lizbeth, but he wasn't going to change his mind. That was the high point of her week, the five-block walk to the sturdy church, erected of white limestone. He didn't know why he treated her that way, denying her the one thing she wanted most out of each week. He just knew he couldn't walk into that building and listen to a sermon every week, not when he knew what men did to their fellow men and women every day.

She stared sadly at him, her face filled with pain and forgiveness, and then she headed into the sunlight. He watched her walk up 57th Street, determined and alone.

He was lucky she'd stuck with him. A lot of women ditched cops. They didn't like the danger, the irregular hours, and especially the cynicism that afflicted cops who had seen too much of the rotten side of life. But she'd raised two sons with him, one dead of polio now and the other learning to become a paratrooper. She hadn't gotten much from life; not on a cop's income. She vacuumed too much now, running the Electrolux over everything twice a day, like she wanted to sweep up all the sin in the world.

He didn't give a damn about the comics. Especially Prince Valiant, the long-haired fop.

The afternoon would be good.

He was shaved and dressed when she returned. Whatever else church did, it lifted her spirits, and as soon as she had doffed her cloth coat, she flashed him her sweetest smile and set to work in her kitchen. Frank Silva was coming over with his girlfriend, Molly Pistek, better known as Red Molly. Lizbeth liked the young detective, but wasn't very sure about Red Molly, secretary of United Auto Workers Local 248, the most radical and turbulent union in the nation.

Red Molly wasn't a Communist; she was a Socialist, like Frank Silva. But nothing triggered her fury more than the attacks on her Communist bosses that pelted the union from all quarters, including the CIO's big boss Phillip Murray. Joe thought it would be an interesting afternoon, if Lizbeth didn't go lock herself in the bedroom if the talk got too heated.

But now Lizbeth was busy with the bratwurst, the buns, the onions and relish, the charcoal for the little burner on the back deck, and all that stuff. There would be plenty of beer, too. And some harder stuff for Joe. There he was, in Beer City, home of Schlitz, Pabst, Blatz, Miller, and a few lesser brands, and he didn't really care for beer. In fact, he hated some brands, which tasted like dishwater when they didn't taste like piss. It was heresy in Milwaukee. Anathema. A defect of character. Sonntag was German, wasn't he? Or part, anyway. His mother was Bohemian, his father a quarter Danish. Well, then he should act like one. Older men shook their heads, advised him to switch to ale or lager or pilsner or some other species of malted liquid, but it didn't do any good. Sucking beer was like swallowing varnish, and that was that.

Frank and Molly arrived at around three. They'd taken the streetcars from the south side, which involved a transfer. On Sundays the cars didn't show up very often. Molly was toting some daffodils she'd grown on her porch. Lizbeth clucked and cooed and slid them into a vase and set them on the kitchen table, where bright sun made them glow.

"How are you, Molly?" Joe asked.

"Unfine. Totally unfine. I won't be fine until there are no Republicans left standing."

"I think you said that about cops last time," Silva said.

"You two are the exceptions," she replied. "I could tell you a few hundred things about police brutality. Have you ever been pounded with a billy club? I have."

Joe thought it would be a good afternoon, even if Lizbeth was looking pale.

Molly was talking about the new Taft-Hartley Act, enacted by the Republican congress, which required unions to certify there were no Communists in the leadership if the union wished to engage in collective bargaining. Local 248 was a holdout, and the upheavals made it into the *Journal* and the *Sentinel* every few days.

Lizbeth was starting in on the sink, with a generous dose of Bon-Ami, even though the sink looked just fine to Joe. Scrubbing the sink was her way of escaping whatever was happening in the parlor or out on the deck.

"Come on in; everyone's been served," he said. "They've got beers and I'll have a Coke."

"No, I'm busy. You go entertain them," she said.

Joe thought Red Molly didn't mix very well with Pastor Gruber's Lenten sermon.

"Hey," said Frank, "you ever find a last will?"

"No, Trouville didn't leave one, it seems. Unless a lock box shows up that no one knew about. Not until box rental's due . . ."

"A loner, then. There's lots like that. They're cut off. Either don't have a family, don't want one, or they're hiding something."

"That's what Ackerman thinks. He showed up at the memorial service."

"Did he know Trouville?"

"A little. Ackerman's got a way of showing up sometimes, and I don't know what's going through his mind."

"You went, though?"

"I did, and that was the darndest thing. Trouville's lawyer—this was between some poetry—he got to telling about the time Trouville had a little too much rum and began telling a story about being an artist in Paris, joining the Foreign Legion, fighting in the first war, dining with Bedouins in the desert, and turning to making etchings, which earned him nothing."

"What the hell are etchings?" Red Molly asked.

"I've got to look it up," Sonntag said.

"I know what it is," Silva said, sipping away the suds in his glass. He was in no hurry to explain it. "It's like an engraving. The artist works with a copper plate covered over with something or other. Some gum, I think. He scratches his picture, lots of fine lines, through the stuff on the surface, and when he's ready, he dips the plate into acid, and that eats away the copper wherever it's exposed to the acid, and after a while the artist has sort of an engraving. He cleans the plate and rolls ink into all those fine lines, and presses soft paper to it in a press, and has an etching for sale."

"I'm glad someone knew," she said. "All I know is how to make bombs."

"How'd you learn that, Frank?" Sonntag asked the younger detective.

"An artist showed me once."

"That must have been useful knowledge for Trouville," Sonntag said. "I wonder if he could spot counterfeit money."

"Hell, he could probably make it," Silva said. "He might have a few million stashed somewhere."

Sonntag thought he'd take a closer look at Trouville's darkroom. As far as he could tell, there was nothing but Kodak stuff in there. Enlargers, chemicals, trays, a copying camera, and a heap of photographic paper, some of it very large. He caught himself up short. What was he thinking? Trouville was a man impassioned, a man determined to expose fraud and forgery and fakery.

"That's not the man I knew," Sonntag said. "But you know something, Frank? Ackerman smells a rat. You know what he told me after the service? He thinks some law or other got broken, and he put me on duty to find out what."

"Ackerman did? What's his reason?"

"He has none. And he told me if I didn't see it myself, I'm a lousy detective."

Silva grinned. "He's crazy."

"Like a fox is crazy," Sonntag said.

"What did he say?"

"He said he could smell a crime in there even if his chief of detectives couldn't."

"You just leave Local 248 alone," Molly said. "We'll solve our own crimes."

"I can't believe it. Ackerman wants you to take on the Trou-ville case as an official investigation?"

"Yep."

"I think I'll join the Foreign Legion," Silva said. "When cops get hunches, run for cover."

Sonntag saw Lizbeth out on the deck, firing up the tripod grill with a mess of charcoal in it. "Guess I better help her," he said.

They nodded and sipped their Blatz. There were odd loyalties in Milwaukee. If you drank Blatz, that meant you were proletarian. If you drank Pabst, you were respectable. Sonntag could never quite figure it out, but he kept getting into trouble by offering people the wrong beer.

"I'll help," he said to Lizbeth. "It's cold out here."

"No you won't. You always cook the brats half to death."

She waved the tongs at him and had that steely squint he had learned to respect. That was another thing. He was the only male in Milwaukee who regularly got chased away from a charcoal cooker.

Defeated, he returned to the party, where Red Molly was berating Phillip Murray, head of the CIO, for betraying the proletariat and trying to kick Local 248 out of organized labor.

Frank listened patiently, but that wasn't what he wanted to talk about.

"What else did Ackerman say?" he asked.

"Go for the dental charts. Trouville's already been cremated. If we get to the right chart, we might find out what the crime was. He said dental charts are the key to solving crime."

Silva didn't shake his head, even though Sonntag wished he would.

"Could be," Silva said. "Dental charts are like fingerprints."

"We're gonna strike Allis-Chalmers," Red Molly said. "Whip their ass."

"According to the lawyer, Trouville turned himself into an artist named Bolivar Newman. So I get to look for the dentistry," Sonntag said.

"Bolivar the new man. That's pretty obvious," Silva said. "Trouville's probably just plain Trouville."

"If they hire scabs, we'll pound the crap out of them," Molly said.

"It'll blow over in a few days. Ackerman's just itchy because all the crooks in Milwaukee took a spring break, and his detectives aren't up to their eyeballs in doodoo."

"Keep me posted," Silva said. "I love toothy mysteries."

"Come eat," said Lizbeth.

"Anyone want some beer?" Sonntag asked.

"No, I won't be able to drive the streetcar," Silva said.

Lizbeth herded them into the dining room, where there were paper plates, cloth napkins, brats on a platter, Milwaukee-style vinegary potato salad, sliced onion, relish, dill pickles, and iced tea.

"It sure beats brown bagging," Silva said, loading two brats and all the trim onto his wobbly paper plate.

"I like to think of all the people in the world who are hungry, crushed to death by capitalism," Molly said. "But there's a new world coming, a new world coming."

They had a fine repast. Lizbeth vanished into the kitchen and refused help. Silva and Sonntag discussed Captain Ackerman and the Trouville case, if there was one. Molly discussed Mao Tse-tung and the forthcoming social utopia of China, now that Chiang Kai-shek and all his crooked generals and corrupt warlords had been nearly whipped. Lizbeth discussed the making of potato salad.

Silva saw the night descending. "We've got to catch a car," he said. "Or wait for a night owl car."

"I'll drive you," Sonntag said. "It's a coupe, but three can get in."

"No you won't. We'll just catch a car."

They compromised. Sonntag warmed up the prewar Hudson coupe and drove them downtown along State Street, where he could look upward and see the Wells streetcars crawling along the viaduct far above. From Wisconsin Avenue, downtown, Frank and Molly could catch a car south.

As he drove back along Wisconsin Avenue, his mind turned toward what the morrow might bring. He wished Ackerman would just let Trouville go in peace. It didn't matter who he was, or what he was, or whether there were heirs. All that mattered was that Trouville's pioneering science applied to questioned documents not be lost. He thought he'd talk to that assistant, Harley Potter, about writing down everything that Trouville had taught him. If the forensic science of document examination would survive, it would be Potter who would carry the ball.

CHAPTER EIGHT

Joe Sonntag found himself waiting in a small cavity tucked beyond two dental examination rooms. Agnes Winsocket had put him there, not wanting him in the waiting room where he might terrify the patients. There was no getting around it. Sonntag dressed in plain clothes, but people always spotted him for a cop. He wondered what there was about him.

The detective eyed the diplomas on the wall and listened to the mosquito whine of a dental drill as it chopped canyons in enamel. But in time the whine ceased, the muffled sound of voices stopped, and Karl Kessler, in his white smock, settled himself behind a small desk.

"Yes, Lieutenant? I have only a few minutes."

"We were wondering whether you have dental records for Armand de Trouville."

"He was my patient, yes. But I fail to see why you should have them. Is this a criminal case?"

"No, but they might help us find out who he was, and might lead us to his family."

"I'll have Agnes get them for you. You'll return them, of course."

"Certainly."

Kessler stirred as if to conclude the meeting. He was a be-jowled man in his sixties, with wire-rimmed glasses and gray hair slicked straight back.

"Could you tell me anything about Trouville? He seems to be a mystery."

"Some sort of young bohemian long ago. French dentistry. I had to redo it. Several molars. Rotten job. The French don't know a molar from an elephant tusk, and wouldn't know how to save a decaying tooth if their life depended on it. I had to start over."

"Did Trouville say what he was doing in France?"

"He was full of stories, mostly hot air. I'm looking forward to having a new tenant next door."

"Was he a problem?"

"Certainly a most difficult man. Our arrangement was that he would pay a third of Agnes Winsocket's salary and use a third of her time, but he gradually consumed most of her time, and without increasing his payments. I would have patients enter my offices, and Agnes would be tied up next door. A mess."

"Ah, I see. And Agnes took dictation, typed his letters, that sort of thing?"

"If she'd let him, he would have had her making his lunch and cleaning his chambers. And cleaning up after Potter, too."

"She didn't complain?"

"She should have. The trouble with Agnes is that she's too mild. Trouville was a burden on everyone around him. Poor Potter. The young man would do most of the work on a case, and Trouville would take the credit—and the pay. If you ask me, Trouville was a parasite."

"How so?"

"He was an unorganized crack-brain who persuaded the world that he was some sort of genius. If it weren't for Potter, busy in the darkroom, Trouville would be considered a quack. I'll tell you something I don't want repeated: Potter was the master, and Trouville the dithering apprentice. Trouville leeched off Potter. You want to know something interesting? None of

Trouville's correspondence even mentions Potter. I got that from Agnes. Say, I have patients waiting. I'd better get on with my business."

"You're a Marquette Dental School graduate?"

"Unfortunately, yes. And now I teach there. If it weren't for me, those dimwits wouldn't amount to anything, and the school wouldn't be so . . . esteemed. There isn't an instructor over there who knows what he's doing. I teach one day a week, and they keep asking me for more. They've even got a woman on the staff. Just more academic nonsense. But I won't spend time there. Half those students shouldn't be dentists, and the other half should practice in a place like Alabama where they don't have much of a board of examiners. Half of Alabama wears bad dentures."

"Did Trouville talk about his past?"

"You would never take seriously anything he said, Lieutenant. He always wanted Novocain, and didn't have the character to let me drill without it. So I would just shrug off anything he said. A sissy."

"Did he have serious dental problems?"

"Rotten teeth and rotten care until I started to repair his ruined mouth. Look, Lieutenant, I don't know why I'm forced to spend time with you. You're drilling into my day."

"Okay. One last question. Didn't Trouville talk to Potter about himself? Colleagues share lives. Didn't Potter ever say anything to you?"

"Why should anyone talk to Potter? He's a whiner. When I filled a cavity he whined for weeks. I finally told him if he didn't like my services, he should hire some kid out of Marquette and get his tooth filled on the cheap. The filling would fall out in a year, but so what?"

"Was Potter unhappy as an apprentice?"

"Potter would be unhappy if he had more wives than King

Farouk." The dentist arose abruptly. "Agnes will get the records for you."

"That'd be helpful, sir. And thanks for sparing me the time."

She found them in moments. A simple chart marking what teeth had been worked on, and when, plus a few notes.

"I'll have them photocopied and get them back," he said. "Maybe we can match them to someone. Somewhere, someone worked on those choppers."

Sonntag borrowed the key to Trouville's suite from Agnes, and let himself in. The place was quiet and gloomy. Harley Potter wasn't around, but why should he be? Everything had come to an abrupt halt with Trouville's death, including the cases. Sonntag didn't know what he was looking for, only that Trouville remained a mystery. The suite had a hollowness to it. Once it had been staffed by people at the forefront of a new discipline; now it waited for the trustee to pack everything up and the court to dissolve an estate.

Karl Kessler didn't exactly think the world of his neighbors. Or the Marquette Dental School for that matter. And Sonntag suspected there were others on his list of unsatisfactory people, many of them his patients. Trouville didn't get a passing grade. Neither did Potter. Neither did Agnes. He thought maybe any detective from the police department might not make the cut either.

Harley Potter's desk occupied a corner of the laboratory. Sonntag studied Potter's desk, which was barren except for a Remington typewriter and an in-and-out basket. There were no mementos, and no awards or citations or family photos hanging on the wall. Potter had family; he'd spent months with his parents after he was discharged recovering from the malarial wasting of his body. But apparently no one merited a photo on his desk. Perhaps he was a loner of some sort. Or maybe he'd already moved his stuff out.

Sonntag slid a desk drawer open, and felt like a snoop. It was one thing to pursue a crime, and quite another to poke around in private lives where there was nothing more sinister than a man who had buried his past and had no heirs. The file drawer in Potter's desk was empty. So were all the other drawers. There wasn't even a pencil. Well, that made sense. Potter's duties here had come to an end, and he had cleaned everything out. He had hovered a day or two, waiting to see what the estate would do, or whether he might continue to operate the office, but then he was directed to stop. There would be no pay, no pending case could be pursued, no client could be contacted.

Sonntag felt a little sorry for Potter. An apprenticeship had come to nothing, and there was nowhere else to go, although the FBI did make occasional use of questioned document examiners. There wasn't much demand for such services. A door had closed in Potter's face, and all he could do would be to wait. If he hoped to buy the photographic and lab gear and go into business himself, he'd probably be out of luck. It would probably take a year to wind this estate down.

But there still were files in Trouville's cabinets. And correspondence. And accounts.

Sonntag debated whether to get into that. What he really wanted to do was tell Ackerman to quit pursuing chimeras. The man had hunches and ran with them, and they almost always came to nothing. Sonntag has wasted countless hours tracking down one or another of the captain's hunches. There was no felon hiding in the bulrushes here.

He poked into various files, but his heart wasn't in it. He took a look at the books. Trouville's income was uneven. He paid Potter a hundred a week, which was good money. A lot more than any factory worker was taking home in a manila envelope. It seemed plain that a questioned document examiner wasn't going to get rich. Most of those who employed him were lawyers, and most cases had to do with contested wills and probate. He had consulted on criminal cases for police departments across the country. He had taught his field at police academies and occasionally had lectured at universities, mostly in law schools. He was not carrying a load of bad debt. He had been an expert witness in countless courtrooms and had been paid for his services.

There were a few competitors or rivals, all of them in big cities. His files were stuffed with commendations. The public might never have heard of him, but most every law enforcement official in the country had known where to go with a questioned document.

Was there anything missing in all this? Not that Sonntag could see.

He settled in the oak swivel chair in which Trouville had died and stared at the man's orderly desk. There was a desk calendar and a few books. The top one was *Making Money: A History of Counterfeiting* by Gilbert Merchant. Underneath were two blue-bound technical manuals on industrial papermaking. He thought about the man who had perished right there in that chair. From that chair, the little genius had been carried away to Milwaukee Hospital, dead on arrival.

"Are you going to tell me anything?" Sonntag asked.

There was only silence. He didn't believe in ghosts, spirits, necromancy, or any of that bunk. Lizbeth did, though. Sonntag had never seen a ghost and knew he never would. He waited patiently. If Trouville's spirit was hovering around, now was the chance. He could whisper in Sonntag's ear: "Lieutenant, it was a spasm, and a feeling of suffocation, and that's the last I remembered." But nothing happened. The room didn't get cold. Sonntag didn't feel some bleak eminence hovering. No stirring of the air.

"I'm supposed to find a crime," he said. "But Ackerman has

neglected to tell me whether you did something illegal, or someone did something to you. Now's your chance," he said. "What got you into trouble? Who's messing with you or the estate?"

But there was only sunlight filtering through the Venetian blinds, making the room pleasant. Slats of sun slid across the orderly desk, illuminating the tempered glass desktop that rested on the waxed oaken surface. The sun caught the circles of residue where a coffee mug had rested. The mug was nowhere in sight, long since washed and stored somewhere.

The hell with ghosts.

The hell with the whole thing. To hell with Ackerman and his hunches. To hell with the PD. Maybe he could retire early. How could anyone operate the city's detective bureau when Ackerman was squandering valuable resources on lousy hunches? The man was getting crazy. Sonntag quit for the afternoon, left the key with Agnes, and hiked back to his station, feeling he had wasted most of a day on nothing.

He enjoyed the messiness and grime of his bullpen, somehow more satisfying to him than the polished perfection of Trouville's suite. Travis, a beat cop, was questioning a witness to a stickup. Morgan, the desk sergeant, was furtively picking his nose. Popov, an informant recently sprung from Waupun, was watching the second hand of the clock.

Sonntag's carrel was his home, his dining room, and sometimes his hospital. He had rehearsed what he would say to Captain Ackerman, and after checking his inbox he headed that way, past the men's room, and into Ackerman's antechamber.

"It's early. What did you find?" the captain said.

"I want to talk to you about this. There's simply no evidence. I checked with Trouville's ghost and he remained silent. Either that or he pleaded the Fifth Amendment. I will go to the cathedral and get down on my knees and ask for divine guidance if you wish. With a little luck, a blinding light will fill the cathedral and a voice will rumble down and tell me who did what."

Ackerman gazed sulphurously at the lieutenant. "What did the dentist say?"

"He said that everyone else is unsatisfactory."

Ackerman simply glared.

"He said that Trouville paid a third of the receptionist's salary but used much more of her time; and that he treated his protégé, Potter, badly by taking credit for Potter's work."

"There, you see? A criminal case. Keep at it."

"Captain, you'd better explain."

"It's obvious. Trouville joined the Foreign Legion. No one joins the Foreign Legion unless he's on the lam or in trouble. Would you join the Foreign Legion?"

"Is that it? Is that why you're pushing for a criminal investigation?"

"What better reason? No will. No relatives. Assumed name. A genius who's cracked some major forgery cases, put some crooks away, and made enemies. A healthy man dies suddenly. There's a few felonies lurking in there, Sonntag."

"I think you should assign someone else, sir."

The captain sighed cheerfully. "I feared it would come to that. I trust my hunches. But I can't expect anyone else to. Maybe I'm wrong. Maybe I'm imposing on the whole detective bureau." He pondered, a massive blue presence at his desk. "I tell you what, Joe. You do a few more things, and if it comes to nothing, I'll set it aside for the time being. You go talk to the doctor who signed the death certificate. I happen to know he's an intern at Milwaukee Hospital. And find out who Trouville's doctor was. I want a medical record."

"You really think he was killed? He fell over dead early one morning, alone in his office. He was sixty-eight."

"There's a homicide in there somewhere, Sonntag. Just one more day. You find out what you can tomorrow, and if it comes to nothing, okay. It'll be okay. You can spend your valuable time finding out who's stealing hubcaps."

Sonntag laughed. Captain Ackerman laughed too. Sonntag gave up any plans he had for an early retirement.

CHAPTER NINE

Lizbeth wasn't around. Sonntag eyed the living room and kitchen and dining alcove, and glanced at the backyard, and listened at the stairwell. He set his black lunch bucket on the kitchen counter, opened it, drained a little coffee from the thermos, and rinsed it. She'd made an egg salad sandwich for him this day, and added two Oreo cookies and a small orange. He rinsed the inside and set it on the counter. Early in the morning she would make another sandwich, wrap it in wax paper, brew some Maxwell House, pour it hot into the thermos bottle, add an apple or an orange, and maybe some cookies. Oreos sometimes, or her own chocolate chips. No matter how early he started his day, the lunch bucket would be ready for him.

It was thirty-five after five, which meant he had gotten home on time; theoretically he left work at five, caught the Wells car, braved the life-or-death trip over the Wells Street Viaduct, and arrived at his house on 57th Street right about now. But it rarely happened that way. She was used to seeing him show up after six, and often closer to seven.

But there were some red potatoes slowly boiling on the range. He headed for the pantry, where a few bottles of booze were primly stored, far from prying eyes. They sometimes shared a drink before dinner. He liked his Old Crow with a splash, over ice. She would, on occasion, go for a Manhattan, but sometimes she would pour a little schnapps and sip it lightly.

"Lizbeth?" he called, but she was elsewhere.

So he dug some ice from a metal tray in the old Kelvinator, and poured one. He wanted a double tonight, but resisted. If he had to put up with Ackerman's nutty hunches every night, he'd pour a double every night. Tonight he would pour a single, and maybe another single, and nurse his grievances for an hour or two. He was good at nursing grievances. Ackerman had mauled Sonntag's day, and was likely to maul tomorrow. In fact, Captain Ackerman was getting crazier by the week, making Sonntag think he should request a transfer. He was too young to retire. But he could spend his last years on the force as a beat cop at some outlying precinct station. Not downtown. Not in sight of crazy old Ackerman.

He heard a thumping and realized she was upstairs after all.

He headed for the stairwell. "Lizbeth, you want a drink?"

"Just a minute," she said.

He heard the sound of the pull-down attic ladder retreating to its place in the hall ceiling, and realized she had been up there, God knows why.

She trudged down the steps, seeming more thin than usual, but somehow energized. She was carrying something.

"You were up there?" he asked.

She nodded, kissed him lightly, and headed for the sofa.

"You want a drink?"

"Not yet," she said.

He settled beside her, curious about the thing in her hand, and knew with a jolt what it was.

It was the old brown photo album. The thing she had banished to the attic almost two years earlier because she couldn't bear having it in sight and mind.

He stared at it, and her, but she lifted her jaw and returned the stare, defying him to say something.

"You're home early," she said. "Caught me by surprise."

The album was simply a collection of the snapshots of their boys, Joe Junior and Will, simple black and white photos, most taken with her Brownie, caught on the dark gray pages of the album with pasted-down corners. She had not looked at it since the fall of 1947, and at that time she had carried it up there to fade away, along with boxes of boys clothing, baseball bats and gloves, and a beautifully crafted model airplane of balsa wood and tissue paper, lacquered until it shone.

"I want to look at it," she said.

Sonntag wanted her to. He had intended to talk to her about Ackerman, and requesting a transfer, and leaving the detective bureau, but this was more important. She smiled bravely and plunged in, looking at photos of the boys, little boys, then older ones roughhousing, playing baseball, Will on roller skates, the skate key in hand. There were other things too, report cards, certificates of merit, school memos printed in purple mimeograph ink. But most of all, pictures of the boys, growing up year by year, page by page.

The album ended abruptly, the remaining gray pages empty.

It was complete into 1947, the year Will had played American Legion baseball in the summer, his team competing on diamonds all over the city and suburbs. He was a shortstop. That is, until he took sick one day in July, fevered, had trouble breathing. They had rushed him to the hospital. Polio, the doctors said. There was a long, agonized week of helplessness, and the horror of that monstrous iron lung that imprisoned Will, and the unabated pain, and the terror in his eyes, and his inability to form words, and then his sudden swift decline and death. They had buried their boy Will, and had worried that Junior might have caught infantile paralysis too, but Junior didn't, and a year later he joined the army just hours after he had finished high school.

One day soon after Will had died, Lizbeth had picked up the

brown album, along with some portraits in cardboard frames, and carried them up to the attic of the bungalow, and she had not ventured up there since. Until now.

"I just wanted to see him," she said.

That was all. Sonntag didn't push it. Didn't ask questions, such as why now?

"He was a fine boy," she said. "I miss them both. The house still is so empty."

Their other boy, Junior, was a private first class at Fort Bragg, and not much good at staying in touch with his mother and father. There were long stretches with no news.

"I miss them too," he said.

She nodded, and she held the album in her lap, her hand restlessly rediscovering it.

"I thought it was time," she said. Her hands caressed the brown album.

He nodded. She had buried Will in the attic of the house, and the attic of her mind, for nearly two years.

"Oh, the potatoes!"

She plunged toward the kitchen. He heard her clatter around in there, and then she returned.

"They're okay. But two minutes more . . . and you would have taken me out for chop suey."

"We can still go if you want."

"You're blue," she said.

"Just annoyed at Ackerman. He's playing one of his hunches again, and you know where that always ends up."

"One of these times he'll be right," she said, and smiled.

Ackerman had yet to see any of his hunches lead to an arrest and conviction. Street cops sometimes had good hunches. Detectives often got good hunches. But administrators resting their fat bottoms in office chairs got bad hunches.

She served dinner, her special meatloaf and boiled red

potatoes and green beans. She cooked meatloaf often because it lasted if he was late, which was routine. It'd still taste just fine if he got home two hours into the evening.

They skipped dessert. She said it was for Lent. He thought some ice cream would improve Lent, but he'd never quite figured Lent out anyway.

"Okay, what's Ackerman's hunch?" she said as soon as she'd dropped the dishes into a pan of hot water to soak. They seemed to wash themselves when she did that.

Sonntag told her. The death of the questioned document examiner, the lack of will, the lack of heirs, a concealed past, the young assistant, the lawyer, the fact that Trouville was a legend in some circles. And Ackerman's obsession with crime.

"I asked him what crime, and he said anyone in the Foreign Legion was running from something. I said Trouville invented that romantic story, and Ackerman said there was a felon in the woodpile."

"But who? Was he talking about Trouville or those around him?"

"Beats me," Sonntag said. "Tomorrow I'll talk to some doctors because the captain wants me to, and then we put the hunch on the shelf—unless Ackerman gets another brainstorm. If he gets his brainstorms any more regularly, I'm going to ask for a transfer."

"Really?"

"I'm an investigator. I try to solve crimes. I want to make the world safer. I think I have a knack for it. I've even solved a few that no one can prosecute because we don't have the evidence to make it stick. But we know what happened and who did it. But now my superior thinks he has some pipeline to God, and all we have to do is find the evidence for a crime no one knows about. A crime that never was."

"I've never heard you talk like this."

"I've always talked like this."

"I mean, about transferring."

"It's been on my mind for a while. Ackerman's too good a cop."

"I don't—"

"The perfect cop wants to solve every crime, put every crook in jail, and ferret out every crime we never even hear about. When your boss has a pipeline to God, things are going to hell."

"Just wait it out. Just ignore him. You're the head of the detective bureau. Just ignore him and keep on going."

"It's called a chain of command, Lizbeth."

"Just get past him. Do what he wants tomorrow, and that'll be the end of it."

"Until his next hunch."

"I wish you wouldn't talk like that."

"I'm going to keep on talking like that."

"Do you hate him that much?"

"I don't hate him at all. I just think he's gotten crazy."

"You could talk to someone higher up."

He laughed shortly.

She looked worn. In the very evening she had reached the time when she could accept Will's death, her husband was saying he hated his job. He did hate it, at least now. That was because he loved it so much. He was born to find out what happened. It was in his blood. As long as he had the rest of the force with him, he felt fine.

"Maybe it's the way you see your job," she said.

"I'll do what I have to do," he said, dismissing her concern.

But she persisted. "Maybe your job is simply to get the facts. Maybe getting the facts is all anyone wants from you. Maybe justice, or putting crooks behind bars, maybe that's for someone else to worry about."

"Lizbeth, that would be like cutting off my hand. I get facts, but I also decide what facts count, and what are meaningless. What facts score a hit, get some killer convicted. That's part of my work. Sorting out facts. Using facts to discover motivation. Using motivation to eliminate suspects and point to others. It's deduction. It's looking at the evidence and figuring out what happened. If I were just a fact-collector, I'd . . ."

"You'd what?"

"I don't know," he said. "But right now, Captain Ackerman's wasting me, wasting my life."

"Your life is not wasted, Joe, not at all. You've supported me, given me love, raised two boys. We live a good life. Not wasted."

It was an affirmation and a plea.

"Not wasted, then," he said. "But I've hit a wall."

That night they lay sleepless, both aware of the other, in the soft dark. The Big Ben ticked through the minutes. A window had been cracked, letting an occasional April breeze stir the air. Sonntag tried to sleep, but couldn't. Was she mad at him? Disappointed? Was his life as a good detective grinding down?

"Hug me," she said.

She turned to him, and he drew her close, until he felt her softness through the white cotton flannel of her nightgown, and felt her arms burrow around him and her hands caress his shoulders and neck, and felt her peace. His own hands encased her and he felt the knobs of her backbone under his fingers.

They hugged for a long time, until it became uncomfortable, and muscles needed release, and she pulled free and simply lay beside him.

"Would you promise me something?" she asked.

For one wild moment he thought to say he never made promises, especially ones he could not keep. "If I can," he said.

"Just for one day, tomorrow, would you treat Captain Ackerman's hunch seriously? Would you, just for one day, suppose he's on to something that needs a close look, and would you give the mysterious Mr. Trouville's life and death a close look?"

"Okay," he said. "But just for one day. After that, he'll be a crazy bastard again."

She laughed.

He knew he'd fall asleep in moments.

CHAPTER TEN

Sonntag caught Dr. Ray Schwartzkopf in the middle of rounds on the second floor at Milwaukee Hospital, which annoyed the purse-lipped physician.

"Yes? I only have a minute."

"I'm Lieutenant Sonntag, Milwaukee police."

"Police? Is there something wrong?"

"Mostly a mystery we're looking into, sir."

All this was occurring in a hospital corridor. Nurses sailed by. People pushing equipment carts rolled past. A gurney carrying a comatose pale old man rolled by, steered by an orderly. A bell was dinging. Sonntag felt himself being coolly assessed by the muscular physician in the white examination smock, and maybe found wanting.

"You were Armand de Trouville's physician, were you not?"

"Yes. What about it?"

"We're simply trying to tie up a few ends, sir. You didn't do the death certificate, I gather. It was signed by David Mauss, M.D."

"A resident, sir. University of Wisconsin College of Medicine. I happened to be on hand when Trouville was brought in. DOA, of course. I had Dr. Mauss do the examination, but I supervised. That was fairly early that morning, after eight."

"And Mauss concluded it was heart failure?"

"Heart failure, the previous evening, around nine."

"Previous evening? How do you know?"

"Several ways. Temperature. Rectal thermometer. A body cools two degrees Celsius the first hour, and one degree Celsius an hour after that until it reaches ambient room temperature. That put it at about nine. Also, his blue pallor and rigor mortis were consistent. Is there something I should know about this inquiry?"

"He died intestate, no heirs—and no known history prior to nineteen thirty-six. We're looking into it. Given his reputation, and what he did for us, we thought we could help. Now, was an autopsy considered, sir?"

"No. Mauss did the usual external body exam, looking for wounds, trauma, but it was clear straight off that Trouville had suffered cardiac arrest. He was a type two diabetic, that's the late-onset type, and vulnerable to heart disease, especially at his age."

"He saw you about diabetes?"

"I hardly saw him at all until he came to me with some complaints a few years ago. He was terrified of going blind. His whole career depended on sight, and diabetes could be ruinous."

"The death certificate was routine, then?"

"Certainly. What else was there? Quite ordinary in a diabetic Trouville's age. So Mauss signed it."

"Did Mr. Trouville ever talk to you about his youth? His family? His past? We're trying to locate heirs."

"Only to joke about living life unwisely. I think maybe he had a few scrapes as a boy, but I'm just guessing."

"Nothing about where he was from, where he spent time?"

Schwartzkopf sighed. "Sir, I practice medicine; I don't operate a confessional. And if that's it, I really need to continue—"

"One last question, doctor. Did you preserve any fingernails or hair or skin or whatever?"

"Again, we didn't do an autopsy, detective. One wasn't called for. There was no anomaly evident. No, nothing was preserved."

"All right, sir, thank you."

The doctor nodded curtly and sailed down the corridor, his stethoscope flapping.

Sonntag watched him go. What was it about Milwaukee Hospital? Gloom. It had been decorated to be as somber as the eye could absorb. Sickness was a serious business in Milwaukee, so the hospital walls would be painted battleship gray. That would encourage patients to take their illness somberly and not engage in the folly of hope. They had entered a dark world and ought to be reminded of it.

So Trouville had died the previous night, and not after coming to his office early on the morning of April 17.

Sonntag walked down to Wells and caught the mostly empty orange streetcar east. He stayed on board until the car had clattered over the Milwaukee River, and then got off. His destination was the First Mariner Building, where he chose the stairs rather than the elevators that made him itchy.

He found Agnes Winsocket at her receptionist post in Dr. Kessler's waiting room.

She smiled brightly.

"Mrs. Winsocket, did Mr. Trouville routinely work evenings?" he asked straight off.

"Why yes, detective, sometimes he did, when he was keen on a case."

"Did you work late to help him?"

"Oh, no, sir, I knew when he was in because he would leave Dictaphone belts for me to transcribe. And sometimes when I left letters for him to sign, or accounting, before going home, it would all be taken care of when I first entered his suite in the morning."

"Did he drink coffee when he worked at night?"

"I wouldn't know, sir."

"Do you remember offhand whether Mr. Trouville was sipping juice or something when you first saw him that morning?"

She sighed. "I didn't notice. I wasn't thinking about that. I was just thinking about the poor man, and how quiet he was, and how he was gone, and how we needed to get help. His assistant seemed almost helpless. He just stood there and stared." She paused. "I guess I'm curious about all this."

"We're trying to find heirs. Piece together his last days."

"I'm afraid I don't quite understand."

Sonntag smiled. "I don't either. I've been asked to look into Mr. Trouville's life."

"Well, it wasn't very complicated. Every Monday he caught the train to Chicago. He practiced one day a week there, and usually caught the afternoon Hiawatha home, so he didn't stay over. A lot of his business came from there. He had an office on Wacker Drive."

"He did? Trouville?"

"Certainly."

"And you typed letters from there?"

"Just like the ones from here."

"Same name and all?"

"You mean the firm? Yes, but the letterhead had a Chicago address. I use it for his Chicago correspondence."

"May I have a sheet?"

She pulled open a drawer and withdrew a sheet of letterhead. The best quality paper, an engraved letterhead, Armand de Trouville, Questioned Document Examiner, and a Wacker Drive address. It did not list Potter's name as an associate.

"Harley Potter's not listed on this letterhead."

"It's the same firm, Lieutenant. Mr. Trouville took his assistant down there once or twice to acquaint him with the office. But he usually went down there alone, and let Harley man the office here."

"This is helpful," he said and tucked it into his breast pocket.

"Well, I'm glad I helped someone. It really bothered me that none of his Chicago clients showed up for the memorial service. None even showed up for the visitation. That's what Harley Potter told me. It's an easy trip, just one and a half hours on the train. Not one!"

"Who were his Chicago clients?"

"Law firms down there, sir. They hired him as an expert witness. I'm sure you'd find their names on his books."

"Did he have that office on Wacker Drive a long time?"

"Goodness, I wouldn't know. Certainly longer than I've been working for him."

"Prior to nineteen thirty-six?"

"Oh, I wouldn't know that. I started part time about nineteen thirty-seven, and full time in forty-two after my husband was drafted."

"Say, do you have some of his Milwaukee letterhead?"

She nodded, and drew a sheet from a drawer.

One glance revealed what was puzzling him. "Is there any reason it doesn't include both offices? This lists just the Milwaukee address. I don't quite understand."

"I wouldn't either," she said. "But I'm sure Mr. Potter could explain."

Harley Potter, it turned out, lived in a near west side walkup not far from Marquette. Sonntag hoofed it, which is probably what Potter did when he was working. On a hundred a week, he could afford better, but was probably husbanding his cash. Like most people in the turmoil after wartime rent and price controls were lifted, Potter was no doubt worried about the future. The end of price controls and rationing had torn the lid off, and now unions were striking, people were seeing big leaps in rent, food prices were dizzy, and nothing seemed secure.

Sonntag knocked and got no response. Maybe the young man was out job-hunting.

But just as Sonntag turned to leave, a muffled voice from within stayed him.

"Who?"

"Lieutenant Sonntag."

The door creaked open. Potter looked sleepy. "Taking a nap. Nothing much to do," he said.

"Could we talk?"

Potter stood at the chipped four-panel door, debating. Then he swung it open. A rank smell smacked the detective. The room was close, fetid and dark. Sonntag wanted to yank the ancient window sashes open, but they probably were painted shut. There were sinister cooking smells as well, like thousand-day-old cabbage. The kitchen off to the left looked worn and grubby, with battered linoleum countertops. Maybe this had once been a student warren for the university.

Potter rubbed a hand across his unkempt jaws. "Sorry. There's not much to do. I'm out of work." He eyed the detective. "You find out anything about Armand?"

They stood there in the middle of the room. Potter had not gestured Sonntag toward either of the ancient horsehair chairs or lime green couch.

"A little. He has a Chicago office."

"Of course. I've been there. He has clients there. The main work was done here, though. The lab's here."

"He had different letterheads, Agnes Winsocket says."

"I don't know much about that end of it. He's had that office a long time, and that's his original letterhead. I came later. I've always been sort of like a dental assistant, the guy back in the lab, soldering braces together, while he's out front with the clients." He shrugged. "That's how it was. Why pitch out old letterhead? Use it up; that's how he was. You get anywhere finding heirs? I sure want to know. I'm sitting around waiting to see if I have a future in Milwaukee."

There was something bitter in Potter's tone. He wanted to be a partner, not Trouville's obscure lab technician.

"We're still looking—mostly as a favor to the estate, you know. Armand de Trouville helped the PD several times. If it wasn't for him, analyzing the lipstick messages a killer named Krank left on bathroom mirrors, we wouldn't have nailed him a few years ago."

"Yeah, I remember. Well, I wish you'd get this settled. I'm in limbo now. If I could buy the lab stuff from the estate, I'd pick up where he left off. I've done my apprenticeship, and I don't like just waiting for this whole legal business to unwind."

"We're looking hard, sir. It takes time to connect someone to a past somewhere. Did he ever say anything to you about his family? Where he's from?"

Potter stared at a grimy mug on a side table. "Yeah, once, after we had dinner somewhere. He said he was from Huguenot stock. His family barely escaped the St. Bartholemew Day slaughter." He smiled. "I had to pull out the Britannica. That was in the fifteen-forties. In sixteen eight-five, the tolerance of Huguenots in France came to an end, and they fled to England and America."

"Did he say where?"

"I wish I could remember."

"If you think of it, let me know. He might still have relatives there."

"I don't think so. In all the years I've known him, worked for him, he never talked about relatives."

They still stood in the middle of that gloomy room. Apparently Potter was not going to invite him to sit down.

"Was it Canada? Did he have roots in Quebec or up there?"

Potter shook his head. "Lieutenant, I've got a headache.

Would you mind?"

"Okay. Here's what I want you to do, Mr. Potter. Come on down to the station and ask for me. We'll just sit and reminisce. You tell me stories about your boss, and I'll tell you stories about the way he solved some mysteries for us. Maybe if we just share some coffee some afternoon, you'll remember more."

"Yeah, like all the times he forgot I existed."

"Stuck in the lab, I guess."

Potter smiled. "Oh, I was treated very well and paid pretty well. And he was always complimenting me, too. I don't want you to think there was any trouble."

"Sure. You pop an aspirin and stay in touch, okay?"

Potter seemed relieved and steered Sonntag straight to the door. It wasn't until Sonntag got out into the sun, and got some air in his lungs, and some breezes cleaned out his suit and shirt, that he began to feel clean again.

He headed for the station, rehearsing what he would tell Captain Ackerman. There wasn't much to tell the captain. The rumors of Trouville being chased out of Chicago after a court case were nonsense; he still had an office and clients there. Trouville apparently was a French Protestant, or his family was. And Trouville's doctor said the man's death was natural, consistent with diabetes, and that he had died ten or eleven hours before he had been found.

But that's where the medical record didn't jibe with anyone's story. They all said Trouville had come to work early that day.

CHAPTER ELEVEN

Joe Sonntag always knew when Captain Ackerman was around. The stink of five-cent Tampa cigars the color of dog turds spread mercilessly from his office and the adjacent corridor. On this April morning, the aroma was especially fierce, which meant that the captain would not listen to anyone, but would talk a lot between exhalations of brown haze.

The captain glanced up from his paperwork, fixed Sonntag with his sulphurous eyes, and exhaled through both nostrils like a Disney dragon, which was very bad.

"No crimes in sight," Sonntag said.

"Tell me."

"Talked to the doctor; entirely routine cardiovascular episode for a diabetic. Talked to Agnes Winsocket, Trouville's steno, and discovered Trouville had a Chicago office, so the rumors about being driven out of there are probably so much gossip. He went there one day a week. Talked to Harley Potter, the assistant, about Trouville's colorful past. Not much to learn from that, but I did hear a couple of new stories. One was that Trouville came from Huguenot stock, that's persecuted French Protestants, and another was that his family is from Quebec. Potter was annoyed because he thought he should get more credit for the lab work he did from his boss. Routine."

Ackerman sucked until the end of the cigar crackled.

"Keep on it. There's a crime down in there."

"But you said—"

"I'm revoking that. Keep on it. Maybe there's a religious murder. Maybe he's wanted by Canadian law. Teletype the Mounties."

"What else do you want me to look for?"

"Felonies, Lieutenant. Any and all felonies."

"Done by who?"

"By anyone. By Trouville. By his guardian angel. By his landlord. By Chicago crooks."

"What sort of felonies?"

"Murder, fraud, armed robbery, cooking bank books, that's for you to find out."

"Who murdered what?"

"That's for you to find out. I want this solved by tomorrow, Sonntag."

"What's to be solved? Who used the fly swatter on the fly?"

"You'll know it when you see it," Ackerman said, and flicked ash off his soggy-ended stogie.

The captain began studying a paper, dismissing the lieutenant.

Sonntag laughed. He swore Ackerman was laughing too, but the captain's demure smirk was hidden from view. Sonntag left, but as he wheeled out the door he caught the cat-grin on the captain's mug.

Well, one more day then. The captain wanted him to waste another day. God knows why.

He wandered back to his carrel, wondering what sort of high crimes and misdemeanors to hunt for. He decided to forget about Canada for the time being. He'd go pick on someone, maybe Trouville's lawyer, Stan Bartles. Picking on lawyers was always good for an hour or two, and for some reason he liked Bartles, Phi Beta Kappa key and all.

"Hey, I can smell the stogie," Frank Silva said.

"So can I," said Sonntag. "I am on a wild goose case."

89

Silva smiled warily, so Sonntag filled him in. Hunch on hunch on hunch, and little more.

"He sure goes on a tear now and then. Have any of his hunches ever come to anything?"

"Not since I've been here," Sonntag said.

"Where do they come from?"

"Some volcano in his head. They erupt and there's no stopping it."

"Has he ever come close?"

"Actually, he sniffs up stuff sometimes. He gets an itch to look into something, and it does lead somewhere but often not to a crime at all; just to something odd about somebody. What Ackerman loves is quirks. Anything weird about anyone."

"Do you believe in hunches?"

"Supernatural ones, no. But intuition, sure. Sometimes we get a sudden idea out of nowhere, and it pans out. It's just our brains at work. It's never happened to me. I've never had any sort of hunch. My brain's about the size of a golf ball. For me it's all legwork, collecting facts, checking what you know against testimony or things that seem contradictory. But no. Ackerman's hunches are wasting time for all of us."

"I'll spring you," Silva said.

"Huh? Spring me?"

"I need help. There's an auto theft ring, bunch a smart-ass apprentice crooks in it, and what they do is get ahold of titles of wrecked cars, valid titles, and then steal an identical car to the one that's on the title and alter the serial number of the stolen car and resell it, often out of state just to be safe. I've got a lot of things to look at, including every body shop in town. Who's selling junk car titles. Who's buying the good titles. Who's altering serial numbers. Who's delivering stolen cars. Who's buying them. Who can hotwire a car. You want to join me?"

"Sure."

"I'll tell him I need you," Silva said.

Sonntag watched the younger man plow into haze and vanish in Ackerman's lair.

It didn't take long. A minute later, Frank Silva retreated, coughing, with tears leaking from his brown eyes.

Silva was laughing. "I got assigned to you," he said.

"What?"

"He said the hell with titles and cars and scrap metal; go help Sonntag catch a real piece of work."

Sonntag found himself laughing. They both hung there at his carrel, laughing like hell.

"Okay, where are we and what do you want me to do?" Silva said.

"Come with me. We'll talk to a lawyer," Sonntag said.

At least the day ought to be entertaining.

He slid into his trench coat and popped the fedora onto his golf ball–sized brain and they headed out, and into an iffy day, with a few black-bellied clouds throwing chill at them now and then. Stan Bartles's office was across the river on Jackson and down a block. That part of the downtown area was old, sedate, and definitely classier than the western side, where sailors from Great Lakes Naval Base hit all the bars, and there were plenty of pawn shops to hand out a few bucks.

"Fill me in, real close," Silva asked.

Sonntag did while Silva absorbed it all without a word.

"So all we're trying to do is find some heirs?"

"Ackerman would like to find a few crooks in the crankcase."

Silva chuckled. "This'll be good. What better way to spend a spring day?"

They got lucky. The receptionist vanished into Bartles's office, and swiftly returned.

"He's delighted to see you," she said.

She was pretty. Lawyers knew who to hire and why.

Bartles awaited them. He was wearing navy pinstripe and his Phi Beta Kappa key this time. He circled his shiny desk and shook hands.

"Gentlemen, I certainly want to thank the Milwaukee PD. We never expected this sort of support," he said.

"Captain Ackerman is determined to find the answers," Sonntag said.

"Have you anything new?"

"A little. Not much. Did Armand Trouville ever talk about his past? His family?"

Bartles smiled broadly. "I couldn't slow him down, and every story headed in a new direction."

"French Huguenot, according to his associate. Did he ever tell you anything like that, or where his family settled?"

"I never heard that one. No, I still know nothing about his family or heirs. But there must be a dozen stories. Have you heard the Devil's Island one?"

"Devil's Island?"

Bartles was amused. "The same. Off French Guiana. It's still going. Still the worst hellhole on earth."

Silva was grinning. "Do I live in a big cold city on Lake Michigan?"

Bartles was enjoying himself. Sunlight poured through the tall windows, momentarily turning a gray city into a bright one.

"Devil's Island was one of three small isles well off shore. France sent tens of thousands of criminals there—and also political prisoners. There were actually several camps, one on each island and one on the mainland. Most everyone sent there perished. The handful who escaped had to reach the mainland, braving thirst and heat and sharks; but the mainland was malarial jungle that couldn't be penetrated. If one tried to cross a river, piranha fish swiftly devoured him to the bone."

"So you're going to tell us that Trouville escaped Devil's

Island," Sonntag said.

Bartles smiled again. "Oh, no, it's much worse. Trouville loved to say his father was administrator of the worst camp down there in the eighteen eighties and nineties and into this century, and oversaw the death of tens of thousands of wretched Frenchmen banished there. Trouville said he grew up there until his father sent him to France to be schooled."

Sonntag smiled too. That was a good story, which would please Ackerman.

"Did you check it out?" Frank Silva asked.

"I did. I talked to the French consul in Chicago. He wired their ministry. No one named Trouville was an administrator or held a lesser position on the islands."

"If that was even his name," Sonntag said.

"Exactly," Bartles said.

"You said it's still operating?" Silva asked.

"Yes, but there's pressure on France to shut it down."

"People are still being destroyed there?"

"I think prisoners have more rights now. And the worst camp's been closed. The war has changed the way we all think. Even the Frogs."

"It is hard to call myself a human being," Silva said. "Is there no mercy in this world?"

Bartles eyed him solemnly. "I had the same sense sometimes when Trouville was spinning stories about his past. Alleged past, I should say. He was a mystery. I have no idea why he toyed with his history, and who he really was. Part of why I'm glad you're on this is simply my hope that you'll find out something. Anything real."

"Did Trouville have any other stories that might steer us toward a family? Or heirs?"

"Oh, I don't know. You've already heard about the art student in Paris who got into some sort of jam, the Foreign Legion, the etcher. He does seem to have been an artist. I don't know why he had a story for every occasion. We'll advertise for heirs, and we'll close the estate."

"What's in it? Much of value?" Sonntag asked.

"Not much. Office and lab, household things, a few thousand dollars."

"And a reputation," Frank Silva said. "Armand de Trouville was the most successful and sought-after questioned document examiner on earth."

"An ephemeral value," said Bartles. "Gone now, except in memory, and a few papers and techniques he shared."

"Maybe his legacy is knowledge, not bucks," Sonntag said.

"The state of Wisconsin gets it all," Bartles said. "And you'll no doubt be looking for a document examiner as good as he was."

"His assistant Potter would like to start up his own practice," Sonntag said. "I talked to him yesterday. He's hoping to bid on the equipment. Hoping to inherit the two or three cases that Trouville was working on."

"I had to stop him from pursuing that for the time being," Bartles said. "Nothing can be continued until the estate is settled. He's a good chap, and maybe when it's over, he can step into Trouville's shoes."

"Do you know what cases?" Sonntag asked.

"They're still in separate file folders on Trouville's desk. I took a look. None involve law enforcement, and all involve civil suits. If any had involved law enforcement, I'd have notified you."

"Do you remember the investigations?" Sonntag asked.

"No, not just now. But if you wish to look at them, for whatever reason, just tell Agnes Winsocket next door that it's fine with me, and you'll get the key."

"What's the time frame for settling the estate, sir?" Silva asked.

"We'll be advertising for ninety days, and closing the estate in six months, assuming there are no responses and we've exhausted all avenues."

Bartles's secretary steered them out.

"Want to go over to the First Mariner Building?" Sonntag asked.

"Yeah, let's see what Trouville was trying to figure out."

They hastened through threatening weather to reach the bank building, and made their way up the gloomy gray marble stairwell and corridor, past grim pebbled glass doors with names on them painted in flat black paint.

Agnes Winsocket supplied a key, and they opened up the bleak office next door. Sonntag thought he smelled something, but couldn't say what. Armand de Trouville's office was silent and bleak, just as before.

"This is where he died?" Silva asked.

"About nine in the evening, apparently working late."

"Here in his office chair?"

"That's what both Harley Potter and Mrs. Winsocket said."

"And he was slumped over his desk?"

"That's what they said. They called for an ambulance, but they knew he was gone."

"If he was working late on something, were there files on the desk when he fell into it?"

"Why are you asking that?" Sonntag said.

"I just have a feeling," Silva said. "You ever have those? You sort of intuit something? Something you can't put your fingers on, but it's there? Well, that's what I'm thinking. There's something here that needs explaining."

"You, too? I guess I'm alone. All I want is facts, just facts."

"Do you believe in ghosts, Joe?"

"Nope."

"Well, maybe one's yakking at me."

CHAPTER TWELVE

Trouville's current work rested in three files in folders on his desk. He and Silva would look at them, but first some underbrush had to be cleared away.

"I suppose we should look at these," Sonntag said. "Frankly, I don't know what we're doing, but it might keep Ackerman happy."

"Yeah, this is an Easter egg hunt," Silva said.

"Maybe we should think a bit about what we're trying to do," Sonntag said.

"We're looking for a crime that has not yet shown up," Silva said. "How do you beat that for a new game?"

"Well, let's come up with some sort of approach. Otherwise we're just spinning wheels. What I'm thinking is to eliminate things. Eventually, we'll eliminate most everything. Are we looking for something criminal in Trouville's deep past? The reason he hid behind a lot of wild stories? The reason his past, before nineteen thirty-six, is a mystery?"

"It doesn't fit him. He was a serious man and dedicated to his science. He may have been embarrassed about something. But not something criminal."

"So we're looking at a recent crime? Maybe one that was done to him? In short, was this death natural?"

"Yeah, like who killed him and why," Silva said.

"The doctor said no. Ordinary heart failure, common in a diabetic. Or at least the senior doctor thought so. The resident who signed the death certificate I haven't talked to."

"Who would kill Trouville? How, and why?" Silva asked.

"Someone who didn't want a document looked at very closely. Maybe someone with high stakes in the outcome. Would you kill the document examiner if he said the million-dollar will was a fake?"

"We're back to how did he die?" Silva said. "Can you kill someone and make it look like a heart attack?"

"He may have eaten something rotten or poisonous that evening."

"That's as good as anything," Silva said. "Are we still looking for heirs? Or a will? Or Trouville's past?"

"We'll leave no tern unstoned," Sonntag said. Somehow, Ackerman's obsession was turning into something funny.

"Is this a crime scene?"

"The perfect crime is one that never shows up," Sonntag said. "So let's call it a crime scene. Someone did in Trouville here. Knocked him off around nine that eve."

This was too much for Frank Silva. "All right, name the perpetrator, and the motive, and what it was. Homicide?"

"That's as good as any, and that's what's got Ackerman breathing fire, I'd guess. If we tell Ackerman it's probably homicide, he'll put the whole force at our disposal."

Silva should have laughed, but instead he grimaced.

Silva, sitting in Trouville's chair, opened the top folder and rifled swiftly through a few papers, finally reading a letter. "This is a fraudulent will case. The will might be a forgery."

Silva handed Sonntag a letter from the law firm Gruen and Dolby. The firm represented six heirs of Joshua Prague, who owned a well-known tannery in West Milwaukee. Immediately upon Prague's death, an estranged wife, Stella, produced a long and complex will giving her about ninety percent of the estate. The will was signed by Prague, dated, notarized and witnessed, and apparently of more recent origin than the will possessed by the heirs. Counsel for the wife objected to any forensic examination, but were overruled by the probate judge, who permitted the examination with representatives of both sides present, and with the privilege given the wife to have another questioned document examiner look at the will. Apparently Trouville was in the process of setting up the examination and opening the process to the witnesses and had yet to see the questioned will.

"If it's the Prague Tannery, there'll be a bundle of money in this," Silva said.

The second folder contained a request to authenticate a holographic will in which an elderly widow, Martha Mondragon, had donated her entire estate to the Society for the Prevention of Cruelty to Animals, leaving nothing to her five nieces and nephews, who, apparently, had been orally promised the estate while the woman lived. An issue was the competence of the old woman, and what the obvious tremor in the writing might signify. The questioned document examination was actually being undertaken by lawyers for the SPCA. Trouville was in the process of collecting and authenticating samples of the woman's handwriting over many years.

"Can a questioned document examiner point to diseases?" Silva asked.

"Trouville once told me that in a limited way, yes. A tremor points to some diseases. An inconsistent slant to the letters can point to some medical problems, especially if the slants are chaotic. A signature where it shouldn't be or slanting on the paper points to blindness. And of course constant crossing-out or rewriting can point to stress or duress. But he went out of his way to warn me that such conclusions are speculative. And there's no hoodoo in it. He's not a graphologist reading character from someone's hand creases or wobbly lines."

"I think I would have liked Trouville," Silva said. "No

nonsense, and no speculation beyond what's there in front of him."

"No one else with his abilities, I'm told," Sonntag said.

The third folder contained a questioned contract. One of the signatories to the prewar typewritten contract was dead, but the contract was binding on assignees and heirs. One party was the operator of a small millpond and dam in central Wisconsin near Portage. The dam had been converted to electrical generation and the power was to be sold for a fixed amount for the following twenty years, at which point the rates could be renegotiated. The recipient of the power was a village cooperative, which fed the electricity into about fifty homes and stores and shops. Hauser Brothers, owner of the millpond, dam, and generator, was claiming no such contract existed and it intended to raise rates. One brother, Amos, was dead. The remaining brother's counsel, Babcock and Judge, had sought help from Trouville. The cooperative possessed the sole known copy of the nineteen thirty-seven contract.

"Money again," Silva said.

"Trouville always said that money is at the root of all forgery," Sonntag said.

"If any of these people did in Trouville, who would you pick?" Silva asked.

"Stella Prague has the most to lose and has the least plausible story, showing up with a will no one knew about."

"Well, this is getting to be a fine Easter egg hunt," Silva said. "We don't have a homicide yet, but we have a suspect."

"You game to talk to David Mauss, the resident out at Milwaukee Hospital? Who signed the death certificate?"

"Sure. Maybe we'll find some baby blue eggs mixed in with some pink ones, hidden in a basket in the bushes."

"I think you're enjoying this more than I am."

Silva smiled. "I've never had any recreational cop work before."

They caught a streetcar west, clanking through some spring showers, and hopped off at the somber portico of Milwaukee Hospital.

"Why is it that this place reminds me of sin?" Silva said. "Do they think sickness is caused by being bad?"

"There's some biblical stuff along those lines. Lizbeth likes to jujitsu me with it."

"I guess I'm going to be sick," Silva said.

They found Mauss in the puritanical cafeteria sucking a cup of hot chocolate. He looked haggard.

"Gentlemen?" Mauss asked.

"We're Milwaukee PD," Sonntag said. "This is Detective Silva, and I'm Lieutenant Sonntag. Could we ask you a few questions?"

Mauss stared. "Is something wrong?"

"Could be. We don't know. Maybe you could help us."

"I'll try. I'm pretty tired—residents work eighteen-hour shifts—everything blurs together."

"You remember the DOA that came in a few days ago? Armand de Trouville?"

"Sure I do. That was the first death certificate I've signed."

"You know anything about the man?"

"I never met him. He was brought in and I started to examine him, and Trouville's own physician, Dr. Schwartzkopf, sailed in and supervised. I was glad he was there because I was on new ground."

"Trouville was considered the foremost authority in the field of questioned documents. That's like forgeries, things like that. Suddenly he's gone. Our captain wants us to look into it real hard. There's no evidence of trouble, but he's pushing us to check things out."

"Are you sure you're talking to the right person?" Mauss asked.

"No, not sure at all," Sonntag said. "But we're doing what we've been asked to do. Did you see anything at all on the body that raised any doubts in your mind?"

Mauss pondered that a moment, and smiled. "You know, in med school, you have to get the facts, the symptoms, the history, and then sort them out; keep what's valid, toss what's not, and come to some sort of diagnosis. Same with a body. I'd hardly started when Mr. Trouville's own physician arrived. He was in a hurry, and asked me what I'd found."

"Which was?" Silva asked.

"Very little. No visible injury or puncture. Death around nine the previous evening. Temperature, you know. A blue pallor and rigor mortis consistent with that. I was going to draw blood and some gastric contents. I thought maybe the man had overdosed, maybe imbibed too much. Then Dr. Schwartzkopf said Trouville was diabetic, and I thought to look at blood sugar."

"So you drew blood?"

"No. Dr. Schwartzkopf said cardiac arrest. He knew the man, knew his entire history, no need to go further. It'd just waste time. Eleven hours since his death. That makes it much tougher."

"Well, I said, 'I'd like to do this right, look at tissue.' Schwartzkopf pulled Trouville's jaw open and shone a light in there. Nothing unusual. 'Satisfied?' he asked. I nodded. 'You'll pick up speed with some experience,' he said. It wasn't much of a cause-of-death exam, at least what we were taught, but if that's how the world works, that's how it is."

"So you filled it out, like Trouville's doc said?"

"I did. He'd supervised. I'm a resident. Everything was up and up."

"Did you see anything at all out of the ordinary?" Silva asked.

"I thought I'd answered that, sir. I would have looked for a few things, mostly what can be found in gastric juices or blood."

"Did you suspect anything?"

"Most likely diabetic coma and death. A man can even put too much sugar in his coffee and pay for it."

"Anything else unusual?"

"Unusual?"

"I mean like Dr. Schwartzkopf signing off after a quick exam."

Mauss grinned. "They tell me it's a long way from medical school to being an experienced doctor. No. Dr. Schwartzkopf left it to me to fill in the blanks, and he was off on his rounds. Do the police think something's wrong?"

"Maybe. Trouville's expert testimony in some big-dollar cases didn't win him friends," Silva said.

"That makes me wish I'd done more."

"Too late now. He's been cremated."

They sat uncomfortably around the Formica cafeteria table.

"I've got six more hours in receiving," Mauss said. "I hope I'm awake enough to do a proper job."

"Thanks," Sonntag said, rising. "You've helped. I'll tell the captain things looked pretty routine to Dr. Schwartzkopf, and you had hoped to do some further examining."

They fled down bleak corridors and into a blustery day.

"Nice young man," Silva said.

"He's only a few years younger than you."

"Yeah, but who wants a doctor that looks like he just got out of high school?"

"You ready to look for more Easter eggs, Frank?"

"Yeah, but I wish we'd find the chocolate rabbit."

Sonntag laughed. "You still got a hunch about this?"

"I'm getting worse than Ackerman. Trouville's nothing but ash, and there are crooks and forgers and confidence men out there who got themselves in a jackpot because of him. What's the perfect crime? One that is not perceived as a crime. Like a heart attack."

"Show me some evidence," Sonntag said.

"Well, the doctor was in a hurry," Silva said.

Sonntag laughed. "He's not the chocolate rabbit, Frank."

They hopped into a car heading downtown and chose to stand, hanging onto the overhead straps.

"You mind if I talk to Trouville's assistant? What's his name, Potter?"

"About what?"

"About cases. Who was mad at Trouville?"

"That's either a green Easter egg or a red herring," Sonntag said.

But when they reached twelfth, they dropped off the car in a haze of ozone and hiked toward Potter's boardinghouse. In fact, Sonntag had a few more things he wanted to ask the young man.

"Hold your nose," he said.

"What stinks?" Silva asked.

"Rotten eggs," said Sonntag.

"You think Potter's guilty of something?"

"Yeah. He hasn't cleaned his flat since his boss died."

CHAPTER THIRTEEN

Potter opened, and startled Sonntag. The young man had cleaned up. He wore tennis stuff, white slacks, deck shoes, white polo shirt, and a blue cardigan.

"Why, it's the Lieutenant," Potter said.

"Yep, and we're hoping to visit with you a minute. This is Detective Silva. Can you spare some time?"

"Oh sure. I'm not employed and I have all the time on earth. Come in."

If the young man was now looking good, so was the old flat. A window was open, and breezes were toying with the curtains. The floor shone. Some demon had dusted and vacuumed and scrubbed and scraped and wiped the whole place. What had once been rancid air now was sweet.

"You've been busy," Sonntag said.

"You bet. I'm past the funk I've been in ever since Armand died. I'm feeling like myself again."

He motioned the detectives to the couch. The glass-topped coffee table gleamed. Potter settled in an armchair across from it.

"We're still probing Trouville's death," Sonntag said.

"Well, that's good."

"Why is it good?"

The question obviously startled Potter. "Because it'll help settle the estate," he said. "And that may open my future. I've been talking to people at First Wisconsin Bank, and it looks like

I might be eligible for a loan to buy the equipment and also the library. Trouville had quite a technical library."

"And open up shop yourself?"

"I'm ready. I worked with him over three years. I know every technique he used. I know his methods. How he analyzed handwriting. How he could practically fingerprint a typewriter. I wouldn't hesitate to say so, either. I'd like the business and that's what I want to do."

"I guess the bankers think it's not a bad bet."

"It's a good bet! I'll show them what I learned, and what I can do."

Sonntag processed that for a moment. "We'd like to know something about his new cases. The ones he was just starting on when he died."

"I'm not familiar with two, but one of them I know well. The one with the phony contract."

"Tell us," Sonntag said.

"That's the one with the millpond, dam, and generator, operated by two Hauser brothers, one deceased, and the village cooperative that bought the juice. I worked on that for a few days after Armand died, until the estate told me to stop; do no work on anything."

"Who said that?"

"Stan Bartles. The court named him trustee of the estate. I actually did much of the work on that document, and have come to conclusions, but that has to wait for the estate to settle."

"What's the story?" Silva asked.

"Well, first, the questioned contract is the only copy in existence. The copy owned by the two Hauser brothers had vanished. Or maybe it was swiped. Whatever the case, the cooperative introduced the surviving copy of the contract into the price dispute. The surviving brother, Sylvester, wanted to jack up the price, you know. The co-op said you can't; you're committed to selling us electricity at the same rate. It's all here in black and white. Sylvester simply couldn't remember any such long-term arrangement, and finally brought in Armand."

"And he turned it over to you?"

"No, but he did ask Sylvester for some samples of Amos Hauser's signature, and received three, which were in the file when Armand died. I took it from there on my own, filling time after his death, when everything was uncertain and I was whiling away the hours in there."

"Okay, what did you come up with?" Silva asked.

"Whoever drafted that faked contract was sure an amateur," Potter said. "I nailed him three ways. Boy, it was crude. Whoever did it's lucky he's not in the forgery business."

Potter's expanding self-regard amused Sonntag, who listened closely.

"First, the typewriter! That was supposedly a nineteen thirty-seven contract. That was the date. But it was written on a postwar Underwood. It had a nineteen forty-six font on it. Typewriter makers are constantly fiddling with fonts. A big problem was the parts of lower-case letters that formed complete circles, or hollows. Like the little hollow in a lower-case A. Or the two little hollows in a lower-case G. These kept gumming up with residue from the typewriter ribbons, until the hollows would print black. So the designers gradually improved the fonts, making those little areas larger or wider. It's easy to compare a typed page with the date the font was introduced. The typewriter that produced that contract was manufactured in February, forty-six, or later.

"Here's the second thing. The paper. It was all fresh, and only slightly wrinkled. Documents don't sleep in files. They accumulate dust, they get withdrawn and read and returned. The paper itself was whiter than was customary in thirty-seven. The document had a paper clip in the corner, and the pages had been turned while the clip was in place, leaving some creases. But there was little else showing age. A document in a file that long will have dented corners, flattened edges, and often marks, slight pencil or pen marks made by readers.

"And here's the third thing. The signature. It was signed by Amos. The one on this contract was an exact duplicate of another on a different contract. Signatures actually vary constantly. They are always larger or smaller, scrawled or tight. There's a whole science. But when you see an exact duplicate of a signature, same size, so you could lay one signature on top of another and they would be identical, then you likely have a forgery. Someone practiced that one signature until he got it perfect, and then used that to forge the document. If we were in the office I'd show you. We'd line up a few of Amos Hauser's signatures and you'd see at once that they varied sharply. A good document examiner tries to collect scores of authenticated signatures but a forger is intent only on duplicating one perfectly. And the one on that contract was a perfect reproduction."

"Wow!" said Silva. "I've gotten a lesson today."

"So where is the case now?" Sonntag asked.

"It's nowhere. My report didn't get written up. I've been instructed to leave all that alone until the estate is dissolved or settled."

"That must be frustrating," Silva said.

"Well, when I get launched, I'll contact these people."

"You haven't done any work on the other new cases?"

"Read the material. I'd like to take those with me too, and half a dozen old cases that were inconclusive. Armand couldn't come up with anything that would hold up in court."

"That would give you quite a start, Mr. Potter," Silva said.

"You bet it would! I think I can resolve some of those cases. You're detectives. I'm a detective of a different sort."

"Yeah, well, our boss, the captain, he thinks something's not right," Silva said. "A man of great intelligence and worldliness died without leaving a will. At least one that can be found. And he's got a mysterious past. And he spins romantic yarns about it. And along the way he shifted some of his business here from the big city of Chicago. So our captain, he's got an itch that needs scratching, and he says go out and hunt. And Sonntag here, he says Captain, we haven't got a crime, and the captain says, go look anyway because I'm itchy. So, Mr. Potter, where would you steer us? I mean, not to look for anything amiss, but to prove to the captain that everything's hunky-dory?"

Sonntag marveled. Frank Silva was the most intuitive and disarming detective on the force.

Potter gazed out the window, which overlooked a sunny alley, and offered a novel idea: "I'd look at Mr. Trouville's own documents. But not for fraud. He was the most honest and reputable man I've ever met. I'd have a psychologist look for signs of depression or, you know, turmoil. I'd record all of Trouville's stories, the stuff he told people, and give all that to a shrink, and see what he comes up with. I'd guess offhand that Mr. Trouville—that's how we always addressed him—was wrestling with a dozen demons, and sometimes despaired. In fact, I think he was driven by despair. What made him so brilliant was just that. He was always walking along the edge of abyss. I think once a psychologist supplies a pattern, and your captain can see what really drove the man, that would scratch his itch."

It sure made some sense. Captain Ackerman's malaise rose from Trouville's disorderly and mysterious life.

"Did he have enemies?" Silva asked.

"Rivals. Questioned document examination is a hot new field. There's two or three firms, like Wall and Wall, in New York, or Bates and Gloucester in Philadelphia. Enemies, no."

"I mean, like crooks that got the short end of it because of Trouville?"

Potter shook his head. "I guess there were a few. But in my years there, I never witnessed anything that was a threat or pressure. I mean, he never worried about his security, or whether his apartment door was locked, or things like that."

"Hey, you mind if I use your bathroom?" Silva asked.

"Go ahead. Down there," Potter said.

"You going out for some tennis?" Sonntag asked.

"Some practice on the Marquette courts. I don't have anyone to play with, but I can work on my swing."

"What's in your future if the estate gets tied up in knots, or the bank won't lend?"

"Oh, boy, I don't even want to think about it. Try to join another firm, I guess. My years with Trouville ought to be as good a recommendation as it gets."

"You're in a field with no formal training," Sonntag said.

"Apprenticeship. That's all there is. Everything's too new."

"It's six months before the Trouville estate can close. What's on your agenda while you wait?"

"School. Right here. I'm eligible for the GI Bill. Some science, chemistry in particular, would strengthen my work."

"You're still going to be a questioned document examiner?"

"I never wanted anything more."

Silva returned. "You set?" he asked Sonntag.

Sonntag stood. "Thanks for the tips, Mr. Potter," he said.

They abandoned the old boardinghouse and headed east along Wisconsin Ave.

"He's got a sleep problem," Silva said. "I took a gander at his medicine cabinet."

Silva never leaves a stone unturned, Sonntag thought.

"A bottle of Phenobarbital. Aspirin, an empty eye dropper bottle. The sleep drug was prescribed, and the prescription was filled at that pharmacy in the Wisconsin Tower."

"I can see it," Sonntag said. "This time he was so awake I can hardly imagine him getting to sleep. When I came by here before, he was so inert he couldn't keep himself or his flat clean."

"Ups and downs. Lotta people like that," Silva said.

They hiked toward the station along the avenue. Cars moved quietly on the asphalt. Milwaukee was a quiet town, where quiet people lived, and they usually spent their evenings quietly in the local taverns that dotted the corners. This morning, the familiar odor of hops blanketed the heart of the city.

"Well, what do you think?" Sonntag asked.

"He could be the chocolate rabbit in the Easter basket," Silva said.

"How so?"

"I dunno. Hunches again. You got any more Easter eggs?"

"The Chicago office. We can probably get a key from Bartles and let ourselves in. That'll take a day. One good thing. Chicago Union Station's only a couple blocks from Trouville's address. It's on South Wacker and Monroe."

"Yeah, let's go down there. Maybe we can go to Minsky's."

"Yeah? What's there that's not here? What's wrong with Red Molly?"

"I'm for socialist sex. Equal opportunity for all," Silva said. "From each according to his ability, to each according to his need."

"You go try that out," Sonntag said. "Only you've got to get Red Molly's okay first."

They reached the police station, with its old-world quaintness, just as a shower splattered their trench coats.

"You want to talk to Ackerman about the Easter egg hunt?" Silva asked.

"Yeah, sure. And I'll tell him we're off to Chicago on the nine-fifteen, and we'll catch the three-forty-five back. That'll give us four hours on South Wacker Drive. I'll get the key in the morning."

But Captain Ackerman wasn't in. Sonntag opted to type a brief report. He hated two-finger typing but sometimes there was no recourse. He added that they'd head for Chicago and be gone all day. He suspected that he and Silva would end up paying for the tickets unless they found something pretty hot down there, and he doubted it would come to that.

CHAPTER FOURTEEN

Lizbeth was waiting for them at the Milwaukee Road depot. Joe Sonntag had tried to reason with her, but she was going and nothing would keep her. A trip to Chicago was a prize worth fighting for. And Marshall Fields would turn over some merchandise.

"She coming? That makes it better," Frank Silva said.

"You bet I'm coming," she said. She was all dolled up in a green spring frock, high heels, and nylons.

"Frank, you go with her, and I'll look over Trouville's shop."

He knew all the bad stuff that could happen in the Windy City and he wanted someone with her.

"I can find my way just fine," she said. "It's no big deal from State Street to Adams to Union Station."

"We'll talk about it on the train," he said.

This whole thing was bizarre. Captain Ackerman was being bizarre. He not only approved the trip, but approved sending both detectives. It was unheard of. Ackerman anted up the tickets and told them to keep an expense sheet.

All because of a hunch. Ackerman thought they'd find the golden egg in Chicago, or something or other that would light up the sky. Never in the history of the Milwaukee PD had Captain Ackerman smiled so broadly, nor had anyone ever heard him say, "sure sure sure," before, like it was a new word for him. He even okayed Lizbeth, so long as the PD didn't pay her fare. Sonntag wondered that morning whether Ackerman had been drinking sloe gin fizzes, or had a new twenty-year-old wife, or won an illegal lottery somewhere.

But there they were. They boarded at nine, and settled in the maroon horsehair seats, while the cars filled up. Promptly at quarter after the hour, the conductor and trainmen pulled up the step stools, and the steam train slowly huffed out of the station.

"I'm going to get something for Easter," she said. That was wife language for a new frock.

"Now look, Lizbeth. Chicago's a big place. We'll be there at eleven. We're leaving on the three forty-five, which means we board at three-thirty from Union Station, which means you need to meet us there at three. So you've got four hours at the most. But taxi drivers down there see a mark, and they'll drive you all over and charge you for it, and if you walk there's panhandlers and perverts and dope fiends looking to snatch purses. So you'd better get a cab, but make it two-thirty, and don't forget to say Union Station. You don't want to go to the La Salle Street station."

She stared at him with a crooked smile lighting her face. He knew he was worry-warting the way he sometimes did, but he didn't care.

"If you get lost, look for a cop. Tell the cop your husband's with the Milwaukee PD. Tell the cop you need to catch the Milwaukee Road three-forty-five."

She reached over and patted his knee. "Yes, and I even have Mr. Trouville's address on South Wacker, and the phone number."

"You know how to use pay phones?" he asked. "Have you got a dime? It's hard to find pay phones in the Loop. Go to hotel lobbies. Most lobbies have a row of them. If you get mugged, get to a hotel. The desk people can help. They can get the cops."

"If I vanish from the world," she said, "would you remarry?"

He couldn't think of a thing to say to that.

Frank Silva was pretending to stare out the window at the endless string of factories.

The train began to hum, and soon the telegraph poles were flying by. It never was a long trip, and the Milwaukee, St. Paul, and Pacific was usually on time, except when a passenger train got stuck on a siding.

Sonntag began studying the other passengers, looking for faces on Wanted posters, but most of them were students going somewhere for Easter. He couldn't stop being a detective.

Soon enough the train threaded the mares-nest of switches and crossings and elevated tracks and steamed into Chicago Union Station, the cavernous and somehow amazing locus of several rail lines spreading out from Chicago. Lizbeth looked so happy he thought she would start squealing when they reached the huge, echoing main concourse and headed up endless stairs.

"I should have gotten you a whistle," Sonntag said. "A whistle stops a lot of crime."

She patted him on the cheek. "See you at three at the Milwaukee Road tracks. I'll be at whatever track is posted. Right at the gate. Okay? Don't be late." He spotted a crooked grin beginning to spread.

There was a line of Checker cabs waiting. He pulled open the door and she got in, all smiles. "Marshall Field, State Street," he yelled, memorizing the face of the sinister-looking driver.

He and Frank watched the cab grind away, spewing exhaust.

"All right, it's only two or three blocks," he said.

"I've only been here once," Silva said. "When an uncle died."

"Big city."

"I don't know what they do. All these offices. What the hell happens inside of them all day long, every business day? Men sit in offices thinking up ways to screw the world. The more offices, the more screwing."

The Windy City sprayed grit in their faces. They crossed Wacker and headed toward a towering office building.

Sonntag steered him through a marbled lobby to a bank of elevators. They boarded one operated by a Filipino in powder blue livery with a pillbox cap.

"Seven," Sonntag said.

Frank Silva was plainly subdued. This was a larger world than he had ever known.

"I think all these offices are full of crooks," he said.

Everything was larger and better here. The office corridor was wide, marbled, well lit, and even had potted ferns at the elevator bank. The black-and-white checkered floor shone. If Milwaukee was dark and cramped, Chicago was big, polished, and gaudy.

The solid oak door said Armand de Trouville, Special Counsel, in gilt letters.

The key fit. They swung the heavy door open. The office was small, shaded by blinds, with a windowless darkroom adjacent, almost a closet. Sonntag adjusted the blinds so that light flooded the place. There were a few unopened letters on the shining mahogany desk.

What caught Sonntag's eye at once was a black-and-white photograph of a woman, on the desk. A formal photo, a pretty dark-haired woman, twenties or thirties. Taken by Bachrach, New York. He nodded to Silva, who was studying the place. Together they undid the backing and pulled out the photo. There was no legend, no name. Just a photo of a lady. She wore pearls and a fitted dark dress of heavy fabric that rose to her neck. A lovely woman, discreetly dressed.

No date. But a photographer. "I suppose we can take it. I'll tell Bartles we've borrowed it," Sonntag said. "We might be staring at an actual relative of Trouville's."

"This woman's young enough to be his daughter," Silva said. "Or something else."

"It's the first lead we've had," Sonntag said. "Does she look like him?"

"She doesn't look like anybody. But she's wearing some money."

"You know more about that stuff than I do," Sonntag said. "I'd have to get Lizbeth to tell me if the pearls are fake."

Silva was examining the envelopes. "We could take these to Bartles," he said. "One from the building management, one from Illinois Power, and two from attorneys. Like district attorneys."

Sonntag nodded. He clicked the light in the darkroom. The place looked scarcely used. The trays were stacked. Fixer and developer and stop bath bottles lined a shelf. The thick yellow Kodak envelopes containing photographic papers were unopened. A copying enlarger rested on a shiny surface. A drum dryer rested nearby. There were two types of developing tanks on the shelf, one for roll film, the other for plates.

A small cabinet contained negatives, filed in large white envelopes with handwritten labels on them. He opened a few of the white envelopes and saw strips of negatives along with proof sheets. He put them back where he had found them, at least for the time being.

It was time to look at Trouville's two black steel file cabinets near his desk. Silva was studying the appointment book on Trouville's desk.

"Only Mondays," he said. "And some appointments booked ahead. After he died."

"With who?"

"Pretty hard to figure. He used some sort of shorthand."

Sonntag pulled on the handle of the top file drawer—and discovered the drawer was locked. And so was the middle drawer and lower drawer. And so were the three drawers of the other file cabinet.

"All the way to Chicago and we can't unlock the files," he said.

Silva pulled open the desk drawer and hunted through pencils and erasers and blue ink bottles for a drawer key. Sonntag pulled the office key from his pocket, hoping to find a smaller one in the ring, but there was none. Silva tried the other desk drawers, while Sonntag poked around the top and back of the files, and any nearby sill or ledge. His fingers found nothing, not even dust. The office was white-glove clean. Almost spooky clean.

Silva laughed. "No Easter eggs here," he said. "Captain Ackerman will be disappointed. He wants the chocolate rabbit, and he isn't even gonna get a hard-boiled egg."

Sonntag felt stupid. He should have asked the attorney for a file key. The key probably would have been on Trouville's person when he died. The Chicago trip had come to nothing. He wondered if the files in the Milwaukee office were also typically under lock and key. Or whether Potter might have the key. Or whether Trouville kept some files out of Potter's hands. The firm's file cabinets in Milwaukee had opened freely when Sonntag probed them. Here they were locked. But that might be natural, considering that Trouville was here only one day, afternoon really, a week, if that.

"Anything in the desk?" Sonntag asked.

"Office stuff. Ink, paper clips, note pad. Just what are we looking for? Why are we here, ninety miles from home?"

"We're looking for relatives or heirs. We're looking for evidence of crime. Any crime. Crime done to or by Trouville. And I think the captain would be delighted if we could simply fill in the gaps. Where did this man grow up? Who were his folks? What was his name? What did he do? How many of his romantic stories have any truth in them?"

Silva was smiling. "Just thought I'd ask. I thought maybe we're on a junket. You know what a junket is. It's a pleasure trip with a business veneer. But you're serious."

"Ackerman's serious."

"Joe, I'm serious too. There's a crime around here somewhere. The captain's dead right."

Sonntag ignored him. He was tired of hunches.

He headed for the darkroom and opened the file drawer with all the negatives and proof sheets. These at least were labeled and dated. He set a stack of them on Trouville's desk and examined the top one. It was labeled *Bracket Electric Controls Corporation. Anonymous Death Threat. July 1941.* Probably in Trouville's own cramped blue handwriting. Sonntag had seen so much of it that he could spot it immediately. There were strips of Kodak one-twenty negatives within, and proof sheets. A whole roll had been devoted to a block-printed death threat that warned the chief executive officer to pay up. There were enlargements of each letter in the threat, and enlargements of identical letters placed side by side. If an A or B or C were written one way in one word, and another way in another word, these detailed blow-ups showed the differences. These proof sheets simply were the routine tools of a document examiner.

Sonntag paged through more folders, studied more negatives and proof sheets, and found nothing unusual about them. They were simply cases. They supplied the names of clients in some cases but said little about Armand de Trouville.

"He didn't do much here except meet with people," Silva said. "This is where he showed his results to clients, or talked to lawyers about his conclusions. He did his real work in Milwaukee. It's too nice. Too clean. I've been through his desk. You know all the stuff in desks? You know the stuff in your desk at the station? Scraps of stuff. Notes, business cards from all sorts of people, a scribbled address, maybe some stamps, bank receipts, blank checks, wallet-sized photos. There isn't any stuff like that in here."

"So what'll we tell Ackerman?"

"There's nothing here. This was simply a business location for him to meet with his Illinois clients."

"We'll take that picture with us, I guess," Sonntag said. "Maybe Bachrach can give us a name. We got a photo out of it, anyway. We can ask Potter if he knows who's in that picture. She's a pretty lady."

It was another futile day, chasing after Captain Ackerman's obsession.

"Are we missing anything?" Silva said.

"We could talk to elevator operators."

Silva laughed. It was nuts.

They locked up and headed in the wind. The afternoon was young, an hour to go before train time, but they drifted toward Union Station, and then down the steps that carried them well below street level to the cavernous main concourse.

Silva stopped at a news kiosk in the echoing concourse that was selling all sorts of magazines. *Colliers, Look, Time, Life, Argosy, The Nation, Popular Science, Glamour, Vogue, Women's Home Companion, Mademoiselle, Esquire,* and a mess of movie magazines. It was in view of the Milwaukee Road mezzanine, and a good place to wait for Lizbeth.

Sonntag would catch her as she hurried in, no doubt at the last minute, with an armload of packages that would make him sweat out the bills for a month or two. She'd be late, and smiling.

CHAPTER FIFTEEN

The big four-sided clock above the concourse ticked past three. Sonntag checked his Bulova, which ticked past three. The clock inched past three fifteen, and Sonntag glanced at his wristwatch, not wanting to miss Lizbeth when she hurried in from the Loop. He circled the kiosk, where Silva was studying dime western magazines, but Lizbeth didn't show up. He focused on the stair where she would descend from Adams if she had walked, but the traffic was all male. Silva shelled out a dime for *Wild West*.

The great clock ticked three-twenty, and Sonntag checked his watch, and it said three twenty, and now he knew Lizbeth was in trouble. Some cabby had seen she was a mark; or maybe she had gotten confused in the Loop and gone the wrong way. Maybe she had gone to the Chicago Northwestern station. Maybe she'd gone to the Illinois Central hell and gone someplace. Or maybe she had taken sick. Maybe he should call the Chicago flatfoots, give them a description. He couldn't remember what she was wearing. Purple, maybe.

A loudspeaker squealed and a male voice announced that the Milwaukee Road Twilight Express was loading on track fourteen, to Milwaukee and St. Paul, departure three-forty-five. And still no Lizbeth. Chicago was a big place, a hard place, a mean place. They picked on visitors. The big clock ticked past three-thirty.

"She lost or something?" Silva asked. "I could go up there and look for her." He eyed the long stairs.

121

"Check the taxi stand over there; maybe she's paying off a cabbie."

Still no Lizbeth. Trouble, big trouble, a cop's wife vanished in the Windy City.

The clock ticked three-forty.

She came steaming toward him from the Milwaukee Road concourse.

"Where have you been?" she cried.

"Waiting for you!"

"I've been at Track Fourteen, just as I said I would, waiting for you! Right at the gate, just like I said. Forty minutes!"

Silva hurried up and they raced for Track Fourteen, alongside the orange coaches, through steam and heat, and boarded at the first step stool.

Joe Sonntag was feeling about an inch tall.

She was carrying one of those flat, floppy clothing boxes, which she put in the luggage carrier above the seat, stretching on tiptoes, scorning Sonntag's offer to help. It said Marshall Field on it in green. She pulled off her tan cloth coat, staring at her two detectives, who were sheepishly settling in the ratty maroon seats across the aisle from each other. She took the window seat.

He had done what any good detective should never do. He had assumed she would be late. He had assumed he and Silva would get there first. He had assumed they would catch her in the concourse. And worst of all, they had ignored what she told them earlier. She would meet them at the track, right at the gate. It was worse than that: he was a lousy husband making assumptions about his wife.

He wanted to apologize, but all he could manage was a swift pat of her hand as she settled next to him. A moment later they heard the clank of step stools being dropped in the vestibules, and then the train effortlessly glided through the darkness of

122

Track Fourteen and then into brightness.

She glared at him, frost in her eyes. She knew exactly what he had been thinking; that she couldn't handle herself in a big strange city. There was nothing to say, so he slouched deeper into the cushion and began studying the faces of other passengers, looking for signs of evil.

It sure hadn't been much of a day. A lot of payroll had been wasted on nothing. He and Silva had poked and probed and guessed, but what did it matter? So what if Armand de Trouville hadn't left a will and had no relatives and had buried some of his past in a smokescreen? The man was a straight arrow, had contributed more to crime detection than the whole of J. Edgar Hoover's FBI, and had modestly sought neither fame nor fortune from his pioneering. So why was Ackerman wasting cop time on it?

Hunches. Those damned hunches wasted everyone's time. Someone in the station would get a hunch, somehow simply knew who did what, and then the whole department would be in an uproar for weeks. Usually it was a beat cop or a detective, but this time it was the day captain. Sonntag knew he'd had a few hunches of his own, obsessions was a better word, in which he saw what no one else saw, and everyone else was a blind fool because they didn't see it. That's what Ackerman was doing. He saw a crime somewhere in this, and all the rest were fools not to see it.

Sonntag sank into the seat, feeling alone and bleak. Silva had his snout in the western pulp, and was blotting up fast draws and ranch massacres. Lizbeth was studying the tawdriness of Chicago's west side as the coach rolled past gray houses, shacks, factories, junk-filled backyards, and fenced parking lots full of grimy delivery trucks. Chicago worked at being ugly.

But once the train escaped the northern suburbs and the view changed to cornfields and barns, she relented.

"What's that picture?" she asked.

Sonntag turned it over, showing her the handsome black-and-white Bachrach photo of a young woman. She studied it, and Sonntag was sure she was evaluating it with some private and female knowledge.

"It's recent. It says 'Bachrach '46' in the corner."

"We're hoping it's a relative."

"Who's Bachrach?"

"New York photographer, society photographer. I'll make a photocopy of this and send it to him and see if he can identify her."

"She's around thirty, I think. Did Armand Trouville have a daughter?"

"None that we know about."

She grinned. "You never know," she said. "Do you have one?"

"I forget," he said.

"It says here that Wyatt Earp held off an entire lynch mob alone in the middle of a Tombstone street, armed with a shotgun," Silva said. "They wanted to hang Johnny Behind the Deuce. He must have been nuts."

"People are always inventing stories," Sonntag said.

"He got into a fight with some outlaws that maybe killed his brother, and he routed them," Silva said. "There were bullet holes in his clothing, a lot of them, but not one bullet struck him. And maybe he killed Curly Bill, who was never seen again."

"Don't take it seriously, Frank," Sonntag said.

"But stories become reality. Trouville's stories about himself are the only reality we know. Maybe the captain's caught in the myths about Trouville."

"I'm going to try to tell him that tomorrow."

"I've got a whole bunch of car thieves to work on."

"I've got some cold cases worth more time."

Silva went back to reading the magazine, and Lizbeth was

watching the farmhouses sail by, so Sonntag closed his eyes and concentrated. He needed something to tell the captain, something that would shut this down, something that would free him to work on more promising things. It was simple: there was no crime here.

At twenty after five, they scraped to an abrupt halt in the Milwaukee Road station, almost as if the engineer had overshot. A shudder ran through the cars. They were waiting in the aisle, and had to cling to the seats. But moments later they were out of the fusty old brick station.

"Mañana," Silva said, and hurried off to catch a Cudahy streetcar.

"Would it be okay for me to send you home in a cab?" he said. "There's one thing more I'd like to do today."

She looked disappointed. "You don't want me along or something?"

"I want to have Trouville's assistant ID this photo here."

"And that's so dangerous you don't want me along?"

Defeated, he steered her toward a Checker cab and directed the cabbie to the boardinghouse, which was only a dozen blocks away.

Minutes later, he paid the cabbie his seventy cents and steered her up the stairs.

Potter answered the knock at once, and looked them over.

"A social call?" he said, seeing her.

"Sorry to intrude on your dinner hour, Mr. Potter. We just need a minute. This is my wife, Lizbeth. This is Harley Potter. We're just back from Mr. Trouville's office on Wacker Drive, and brought this photo. Can you identify her? Is she a relative of his? Maybe this'll finally put us onto his family."

Potter glanced briefly at the framed photo. "Sure, I know who it is. And it's not anyone related to him. That's Marcie Van Cleef. High society, as they say back east. Remember the case?

Biggest one Trouville ever had."

"I remember her!" Lizbeth said.

Sonntag was slow to reach it, but there was some big deal a couple of years earlier . . .

"That was the kidnapping and the ransom note!" she said.

Then he remembered. The young woman had attempted to extract money from her rich mother by faking a kidnapping. The mother and daughter were at odds, and the mother had threatened to disinherit the girl. Then the girl vanished, and ransom notes began arriving, each carefully printed in grade-school block letters; each on entirely different paper or stationery. Each directing the mother to send money to a certain overseas bank account. Each threatening to mutilate the girl by a certain date if no money arrived.

The New York cops had called in Trouville after a local questioned document examiner made no headway, and Trouville had taken Potter with him and set to work, eventually tracing the printing back to the Van Cleef girl herself.

"So that's his prized case. He keeps a photo of the girl on his desk as a reminder?" Sonntag asked.

"He shouldn't. He didn't solve it. I did," Potter said. "He wasn't getting anywhere with it, just like the rest of the herd, but I pointed out some things about the block letters, like the way the lowercase I was dotted, with a little comma, or even half a circle, and I was the one who told him to get some of Marcie Van Cleef's own handwriting from the mother, and after that I made the link. That photo there, it's nothing but Trouville's propaganda. Clients asked about it, and Trouville did his song and dance."

"You solved it, did you?"

"You bet I did. To be honest, I'm better than he ever was at this game. I solved a lot of his cases, but he never credited me with it."

"You were sort of the invisible partner?"

"Apprentice. He always considered me an apprentice, and he was the Old Master."

"This is a Bachrach portrait. If I write them about it, would they identify Marcie Van Cleef?"

"How should I know? I'm just the apprentice."

Potter was agitated.

"I guess we're invading your dinner hour. Thanks for the help, Mr. Potter."

"Why don't you just let it go? He's dead. He's a legend. I don't know why your captain keeps pushing on a non-issue."

"Sure, sorry," Sonntag said.

The door swung shut rather swiftly, and Sonntag and Lizbeth beat a retreat.

There wasn't a cab in sight on Wisconsin Avenue, so they hastened to Wells Street and caught the next car west. It wasn't often that Lizbeth got to see him cling white-knuckled to the seat ahead when they crossed the viaduct.

"I've just got a hunch about him," she said.

"You too? You've got a hunch, and Silva's got a hunch, and Ackerman's got a hunch, and I don't have a hunch."

He didn't tell her about his hunch that this time the streetcar would tumble off the viaduct over the Menomonee River valley, and they both would perish. Somehow, though, his hunch didn't pan out, and they soon were on solid ground and approaching the stop at 56th Street.

She smiled wryly at him, not needing to be told a thing.

They reached their house in time for a drink and a late supper, and he was glad to hit an easy chair. He wondered how Trouville had managed a Chicago trip once a week.

"You want to see my dress?" she said. "Go make drinks for both of us." She headed for the bedroom before he could reply. He mixed her Manhattan and his whiskey and carried them into their small living room.

She appeared just then, in a cream linen spring suit, which flowed simply over her lithe form. God, she was a doll.

"You like?" she said, doing a little twirl.

"How much did it cost?" he asked.

That wasn't the right thing to say.

"I'd like it better if it was off," he added. He was no stranger to hot water.

"We'll see about that, buster," she said. "You gonna take me out to eat?"

Well, he thought, *at least this bum day wouldn't end badly.*

CHAPTER SIXTEEN

Captain Ackerman exuded sweetness and light. Even the stink from his dog-turd Tampa cigars seemed pleasant. The captain listened patiently to Joe Sonntag's Chicago update, and nodded sagely. Sonntag had seen him like this only once or twice before, and it meant the world was coming to an end.

"We've checked everything out, and that's it," Sonntag said.

"What do you mean, that's it? You've hardly started."

"Trouville died a natural death; no heirs have shown up. There's no crime in sight."

"No crime? Sometimes I wonder about you, Sonntag. You're losing your drive, losing your curiosity. Maybe you should retire."

Sonntag braced for the worst, and it soon came tumbling in.

"There's a felony in this thicket," Ackerman said. "If you won't sniff it out, I'll put others on the case. But I'll give you a couple more days. You and Silva, you'd better start showing some moxie here, and I'm going to give you Eddie Walsh and Boris Dragovich. You'd think with four detectives on the case we'd solve it."

"Solve what?"

"The homicide."

"Who got killed?"

Ackerman simply gummed his cigar and shook his head. "I guess I'll have to intervene. I like to let the detectives work the way they want, and let them do their job, but in this case I'm going to give you a list. Follow that list. Report to me each evening. By tomorrow evening, I want evidence of a felony. By the end of the week, I want the felon behind bars."

Sonntag knew it was going to be bad, but this was new turf for him.

Ackerman smiled. He rarely smiled, but now he beamed and chuckled and lipped his cigar.

"Number one. Interview that doctor, what's his name? Schwartzkopf. Something like that. Put Dragovich on it. I want to know why that pill-pusher was so eager to get the exam out of the way. Trouville arrived dead at a pretty young age. Sixty-eight. Maybe he croaked all by himself, but maybe not. He pushed that resident, Mauss, into doing a cursory exam. Have Dragovich find out how long that pill-pusher's had Trouville for a patient. Whether they've got any business relationship. Whether there's been any bad blood between them. How long he's been supervising the resident, Mauss, and whether there's been any trouble. Stuff like that. Tell Dragovich to get ahold of Trouville's medical records. I want to see whether he was diagnosed with diabetes."

"If Schwartzkopf is willing to surrender them."

"This is a homicide investigation. Get the records.

"Number two. Put Eddie Walsh on this. I want to know why the attorney, Bartles, cremated the body so fast. Why was he in such a rush? Was he covering something up? What was Bartles's relationship to Trouville? Was he Trouville's personal lawyer? What did Trouville employ Bartles to do? How come Bartles never drew up a will? How come the probate court assigned Bartles to the estate? Does Bartles know Schwartzkopf? Or that resident? If so, get the history. Did Trouville ever talk to Bartles about his diabetes? Or the treatment?"

"So where's the homicide?" Sonntag asked.

"That's for you to find out, and you'll grind your nose on it until you solve it."

"Do you want Walsh and Dragovich to tell these people there's a homicide investigation going on?"

"Certainly. Make 'em nervous. Make 'em spill the beans."

"So now it's a homicide investigation? That's the official word?"

"You bet."

"Even without a homicide?"

"We'll find one somewhere. Now, Potter. Put Frank Silva on it. What was Potter's motive? What's in his medical record? How come he can't sleep? Have Silva look into that medicine cabinet again. What does Potter think of Trouville? He's said that Trouville took all the credit. He's said that he's just as smart or smarter and solved some of Trouville's cases, but was still just an apprentice. So maybe Potter's bitter? So maybe Potter figured out how to take over the business? Tell Frank Silva to put some heat on Potter. This is now a homicide investigation, and Silva can put that to use. I want a motive. Tell Silva to come up with a motive."

Sonntag was grinning. "Motive for what?"

"For whatever," Ackerman said, lipping his gummy cigar. "And now, you. You're my top dog. Here's what you're going to do. It's what you do best. You're going over to Trouville's office and look at cases. You're going to look at every case where there was money. Lots of money. Where someone wanted an inheritance and Trouville's work stopped it. Where someone drafted a fraud of a contract that would have gotten him a pile of cash, but Trouville stopped it. There must be fifty angry crooks that got outsmarted by Trouville. Half of them must have been itching to kill him, get revenge, hire a hit man, whatever it took. You're going to get names of losers. And then start looking at the losers. You're gonna call them all, and have a cheerful talk with 'em, and let 'em know Trouville's dead and buried. That's worth the price of a ticket."

"I'll check out all the paid killers too, I suppose. The whole bunch that were chasing Trouville around to bump him off. Twenty, fifty killers waiting to bump him off."

"You think you're being cute, Sonntag, but you're in for a surprise."

"I guess I will be."

"And there's more for you, Sonntag. You're going to find out who Trouville was. He was an etcher named Bolivar Newman. That's one version. It just happens there's some etchings by Newman floating around, so that might be the line to follow. Was he an art student in Paris? Where's the art? Was he in the French Foreign Legion? Was he a pilot in the Lafayette Escadrille, or whatever that flying circus was called? Get the facts. If Trouville was a master criminal, find out who he murdered."

"Who he murdered?"

"No man invents stories about his past if he has nothing to hide, Sonntag."

"Crazy people do all the time."

"Sonntag, Trouville wasn't crazy. He was the brightest light in crime detection. And that brings up another angle. Reputation. Maybe someone was envious. Maybe someone couldn't stand it. There was Trouville, fame spreading far and wide, and someone hated it, and raged at Trouville. Find out!"

"I need more resources, Captain."

"You've got them! Name it."

"Well, Captain, if we can track down every etching done by Bolivar Newman, we've got an account of where he's been. But I need someone to visit art galleries, collectors, dealers, museums."

"You name it, you've got it."

"These dealers may not be in Milwaukee, Captain."

"Well, try long distance. I'll okay it." Ackerman shifted the yellow cigar from one side of his gummy mouth to the other. "Now one thing, Lieutenant. Just because I'm giving this top priority, I don't want your men wasting the hours away in coffee shops. You tell them that if they're caught gabbing in coffee shops, I'll dock them for it."

"They already know that, Captain."

"Good. I want the detective bureau focused and productive."

"I'll tell them."

"All right, have at it. Now, I want evidence of homicide by tomorrow afternoon, and I want the case closed by Friday. And don't whine. Don't tell me you're waiting for a break. The Seabees never waited for a break. Their motto was Can Do. We didn't win the war waiting for breaks. Remember the Seabees. Can Do."

"Captain, we'll bring in so many suspects that you'll have a choice. You point the finger and we'll lock him up. We'll fill the tanks, fill the cells, ship the overflow over to Madison."

"Now you're talking!"

"Theirs not to reason why; theirs but to do or die."

"What are you talking about?"

"The Charge of the Light Brigade."

"Sonntag, don't confuse the issue. This has nothing to do with Wisconsin Electric Power."

"It's Tennyson, Captain."

"You bet it is, lots of tension around here."

"Into the valley of Death rode the six hundred."

"That's a lot of volts, Sonntag."

Ackerman exhaled. The brown smoke plumed from each nostril, like some ancient fire-eating dragon, and settled upon the captain's desk.

Sonntag careened back to his carrel and collected the victims. Silva was grinning. Dragovich and Walsh stood purse-lipped.

Walsh specialized in juvenile crime, such as school vandalism, while Dragovich dealt with narcotics primarily.

"Here's the deal," Sonntag said. "We're going to prove that Armand de Trouville was murdered. Or maybe not." He doled out the assignments one by one, and discovered his men were enjoying the prospect. They hardly ever got an open-ended expense account.

"Any questions?"

"Why is this a homicide investigation?" Walsh asked.

"Because the captain says so."

"I mean, why? What does he think? Who did what to who?"

"I've given up guessing, Eddie. All right, report to me at the end of your shift. We have until tomorrow to discover the homicide. That's what he says. We'll blow this open by the end of the week."

"Discover the homicide?" Dragovich asked. "Say that again?"

"Enjoy yourselves," Sonntag said.

"Is anyone a doper? Is this doc I'm going to talk to a doper?" Dragovich asked.

Boris Dragovich was an earnest, world-weary, graying bachelor cop who was getting thicker every year. Put him on a narcotics case and something turned him into a bloodhound. Put him on anything else and he would have trouble reciting the alphabet.

"Hey, Boris, forget talking to the doc for a while. Go with Silva to talk to the apprentice in Trouville's firm, Potter. He's got a sleeping problem."

"A doper?"

"Some prescription barbiturates in his medicine cabinet. See what you think."

"Ah, now we're onto something," Dragovich said. "I can read dopers."

"From now until Friday, you're the Trouville Taskforce.

Friday we're off the hook."

"What hook?" Walsh asked.

"Captain Ackerman wants a perp charged by Friday."

Walsh started chuckling. "We're the four stooges," he said.

"Any of you want help, call in," Sonntag said. "I'll get it to you. And if you need a car, Ackerman's okayed one."

"He's okayed a car? For us?"

"He said whatever we need, we get."

"There must be a felon around somewhere," Walsh said.

Sonntag watched them pull on raincoats against the constant April showers, and begin their fool's missions. The Trouville Taskforce was going to get some egg on their puss.

He hiked over to the First Mariner Building and along its gloomy stairs and halls until he reached Karl Kessler's torture chamber. Agnes was guarding the reception area.

"Need the key, Agnes."

"Why, Lieutenant, it's good to see you. I think I have it around here somewhere. Mr. Bartles is cleaning out the office. We had some deliverymen come and pack up all of Mr. Trouville's files yesterday. Mr. Bartles called to say he's going to vacate. You know, so the estate doesn't keep paying rent."

"No files in there? Did he say where?"

She shrugged. "Nope. Here's the key. Be sure you return it. It's such a problem when I have to start phoning for it."

"Sure," Sonntag said.

He let himself into the half-emptied office. The movers had hauled away the file cabinets and had taken the lab equipment. It must have taken them hours to pack it safely. The library was packed and gone. There wasn't much left but the furniture. He smiled. Ackerman would think Bartles was messing around with a crime scene instead of closing an estate.

Sonntag settled in the swivel chair where Trouville had died. The desk had been cleaned of all the clutter people accumulate.

There was only the tempered glass desk topper. He stared at the dried rings and dried spill where coffee had dripped onto it.

He rose suddenly, made his way next door and found Agnes typing dental bills.

"Agnes, tell me again what happened the morning you found Trouville. He was slumped over the desk?"

"Yes. Mr. Potter had just come in, and found him, and tried to waken him, and came to me and asked if I could waken him."

"He arrived first?"

"He'd just come in. He was still wearing his coat and hat. He was terribly agitated, of course. It was a terrible thing. There was Mr. Trouville, cold and gone to his reward. We knew he was gone. Then we called for an ambulance."

"You thought Trouville had just died?"

"Why yes, what else were we to think? We learned later that he'd died hours earlier and had been there like that all night."

"Had he made coffee?"

"No, he was slumped over his desk. They make the coffee each morning on a hotplate in the lab; they have a nice shiny pot with a basket in it, and that hadn't been started."

"Was anything spilled on the tempered glass desktop?"

"I couldn't say, Lieutenant. But I think there was something."

"There was no cup or mug? I mean, Trouville wasn't holding anything in his hand? Or set it down?"

"No, I'm sure of that. No cup, nothing that Mr. Trouville had been drinking."

"The cups were all in the lab?"

"Oh, yes, sir. Mr. Potter keeps them washed and ready each day."

"I'm going to take that glass with me, Mrs. Winsocket. Tell Mr. Bartles I have it and I'll return it shortly. I want to know what was spilled on it."

"Why, yes, of course, sir."

Maybe it's a crime scene after all, Sonntag thought. Who could say what fluids had dried on that glass?

CHAPTER SEVENTEEN

Tech Corporal Martin Luther Schmidt studied the tempered glass desk topper as Sonntag watched. The uniformed corporal wore rimless wire glasses, but was amplifying those with a large magnifying glass.

"Is that enough?" Sonntag asked.

"I doubt it."

"I want to know what's spilled on that glass."

"There are some rings where someone set a glass or cup that spilled a little, but the other puddled material is probably saliva."

"Can you tell what's in the saliva?"

Schmidt sighed softly. "There's not much to work with."

"Trouville was found dead, over the desk. In this chair. The captain wants to know how and why. Saliva on that glass would likely be Trouville's."

"What are we looking for?"

"Whether those dried rings on the glass are coffee or what?"

"What else could they be?"

"Barbiturate?"

"Why that?"

"Trouville's business partner uses it."

"I have to take this to a lab. Maybe they can do something with some swabs, but I doubt it. Maybe they can use a spectroscope. They burn the stuff and read the flame. Elements burn different colors, and that shows what's in the stuff. But there sure isn't much to work with."

"I've heard of that. Who'll do it?"

"Lab at the Milwaukee Technical Institute."

"How long? Captain Ackerman wants results, like, yesterday."

"It'll take them a while to figure out the best approach, try a sample, and then run various tests. But I'm not saying it's going to come to anything."

"What'll it show?"

"Such and such elements are present."

"Can that eliminate other chemicals?"

"Theoretically. Let's say—hypothetically—that they come up with chlorine, sulfur, and phosphorus on that glass, and let's say coffee has none of those, but has carbon and sulfur and potassium. Then you've learned something. I'm inventing that as an example. I don't know what coffee has in it off the top of my head."

"Okay. Do your best."

Corporal Schmidt pulled on gloves and lifted the heavy glass the size of a desk blotter, encased in its leather frame, and hauled it away. Sonntag pulled out his notebook and recorded the time, place, object, and purpose.

He hiked back to the First Mariner Building and returned the key to Agnes. "We've got the desk topper."

"What would you want that for?"

"Beats me," he said, smiling. "It has some saliva on it, which might tell us what made Mr. Trouville so sick."

"I thought it was heart trouble and diabetes," she said.

"That's what I hope it is."

"He could be a cutup," Agnes said. "He once had a sheep's eye dinner with Bedouins. That's what he told me."

"Here we are in Milwaukee, talking about dinners in African tents. Cutup. That's a good word for the old rascal."

"He was a cutup, all right."

Back at the downtown police station he found a message to

139

call Stan Bartles, which he did at once.

"Is there something I'm not understanding, Lieutenant?" Bartles asked. "Some reason the police department is examining the Trouville estate? Putting it all under a microscope?"

"Yes. One of our top brass thinks something's not right," Sonntag said lightly. That was true enough.

"Such as?"

"We've been asked to look into the hasty way the death certificate was issued and things like that."

"What things like that? I entertained a detective named Walsh this morning who was wondering who decided to have the body cremated; why the decision was made, and he also wanted to know if I knew the physician, Dr. Schwartzkopf. Certainly I know him. And I made the decision to have Trouville's remains cremated. What of it? What's going on and why are you people sniffing around?"

"One of our superiors, sir, suspects that Mr. Trouville's death was not accidental."

"Homicide? Are you telling me this is a homicide investigation?"

"Yes, sir. And speaking of that, I need to know where Mr. Trouville's case files were taken, and I need your permission to look at them."

This evoked only silence, which Bartles finally broke. "You know, sir, if you come to me with a court order, then I'll supply the files to you. There had better be probable cause. I don't take kindly to wild goose chases. Probable cause, Lieutenant. Good afternoon, sir."

Sonntag held the silent phone in his hand. That would be the end of any cooperation from the trustee overseeing the estate.

That was the best of the afternoon. After that, things headed south.

Boris Dragovich was next to call, this time from a pay phone near the hospital.

"Hey, Lieutenant, you've got a steaming mad doctor threatening to file complaints."

"I guess we do," Sonntag said.

"He said he doesn't like being second-guessed by know-nothings. He said if you want Trouville's medical records, you can go to court for them, because he's not handing anything over. The records are private, and they don't belong to cops, and he'll make a public stink about it."

Sonntag started laughing. "I should have seen it coming."

"You done with me?"

"While you're there, see if there are some official hospital records. You know, DOA records. What was done, who did it, all that stuff. Just tell the administration you want to look at them. And take good notes."

Boris sighed. "Jaysas," he said.

Next on the phone was Silva. "Don't ask how did it go. Don't ask stupid questions," Silva said.

Sonntag laughed. "Let me see. Our man Potter was upset. 'Why are you asking me that stuff?' he asked you."

"Yeah, and his career's in ruins. He knew the files have gone into storage, the lab equipment was packed up and hauled off. He's mad at Bartles. He wants Trouville's files. He wants his own reports and notes. He wants the evidence in those files that he did a good job, and now he can't access it. He wants to be able to show his work, and his reports, to future customers."

"What was his mood?"

"Sullen. A lot madder than he was letting on. He started complaining. Ever since his mentor and friend died, he's been living in sheer misery. He has no future. He can't sleep. He doesn't know how he'll support himself."

"He's got the GI Bill, doesn't he?"

"I didn't ask. It turned into a torrent. All he wants is recognition. Then he could work in the field. The only credentials he has are lying in a warehouse. Now his notes and research, the stuff he did for Trouville, are all tied up where he can't get them."

"What about us?"

"He was pretty cautious. He says he just doesn't understand why we're sniffing around. Is something wrong? Would it help if he comes to the station and talks? I said sure, stop in and we'll talk. That only upset him even more. He's one upset gentleman, Joe."

"Did you talk about sleeping?"

"Oh, a little. I told him I can't sleep worth a damn some nights. He told me he got some Phenobarbital, but he hates it. It's better to lie awake all night than get hammered by that stuff. I told him I count sheep, and he didn't even smile."

"What do you think, Frank?"

"Oh, I don't know. My hunches have all croaked. He's probably okay. He's mad at us, but I don't have any sense he's hiding anything."

Boris Dragovich called a half hour later. "Hey," he said. "I talked with that resident. He's done, packing up, going back to Madison. Mauss is his name. He's puzzled about us. How come we're poking around? I asked him to run through what happened when they brought Trouville in. Mauss checked for vital signs and found nothing. The man was dead. Body temperature indicated he'd died the previous evening. So he collected the stuff Trouville was carrying and put it in a paper sack. I asked him what. He said some loose change, a wallet, which he used to confirm Trouville's ID. There was a driver's license and Social Security card. The wallet had twenty-seven dollars, which Mauss recorded. There were keys, some pocket change, his glasses, a Gruen watch, and some papers in the breast pocket of the tweed sport coat Trouville was wearing. So I asked what the papers were. He didn't remember much, but one was a handwritten letter, stamped and ready to drop in a mailbox. There was a folded paper with writing on it. So I asked Mauss if he'd read the folded paper. He just glanced at it, to identify it for the inventory he was making. He didn't read it. There was also a ring, so I said what kind, and Mauss thought it was a class ring, one with an insignia on it, an oval stone incised—that's the word. Incised in it. I asked Mauss if it was Masonic, you know, that stuff. He said no, some initials. So I asked what hand, and Mauss said the right ring finger."

"What happened to the stuff?"

"Mauss said it was turned over to Bartles, who came for it, saying he was the trustee of the estate. Bartles signed for it."

"So then what?"

"Mauss began looking for wounds, lacerations, punctures, blood, all that."

"Stripped him?"

"You have to if you're determining the cause of unexplained death."

"Clothing go back to Bartles too?"

"Yep, he took it all."

"Did you ask Mauss if he could remember the initials on the class ring?"

"Here's the funny thing. Mauss did. He said the bigger letter in the middle was N, and the letters on either side were B and T."

"Bolivar Newman."

"Huh? What are saying?"

"One of the many names and identities Trouville talked about sometimes. Bolivar Newman was an etcher."

"What's that?"

"Type of art, a little like engraving."

"So maybe Trouville was wearing his identity all along?"

"Maybe not. Newman sounds like a made-up name. How does it sound to you?"

"Yeah. So I asked Mauss if Trouville was a doper. Needle tracks all over hell. And he said no. So after they took the stuff off the body, he started inspecting Trouville, mouth first. There's a lot a mouth can tell a doc, but beats me just what. Anyway, he was poking the mouth around when Trouville's own doc came in, and sort of took over."

"Schwartzkopf did the exam?"

"No, he had Mauss continue but told him what to do and what to conclude, and it went real fast. Schwartzkopf said he knew the history, and it was a cardiac arrest. That was too fast for Mauss, who didn't like it. He said his name's on the death certificate and he wished it wasn't. Heart failure. Diabetes."

"Did you ask him what he thought?"

"He thought Trouville looked too blue. No oxygen. He wanted to learn why Trouville seemed to suffocate."

"Suffocate?"

"Yeah. He said the air passages were okay, but people suffocate for lots of reasons."

"Such as?"

"We didn't get into that. Sorry, Lieutenant. He seemed glad to talk to me, not like Trouville's doc. Like maybe he wanted someone to know he got pushed into signing the death certificate before he was good and ready."

"Boris, this is good. I'll get those effects, but it won't be easy. I want that ring. I want those papers and the letter. Bartles is royally ticked off and thinks we're showboating. I may have to get a search warrant or whatever it takes. And that means I'd better be able to persuade some magistrate there's probable cause, and that means we may have a case."

"Jaysas, Joe, what do we have to take to a judge? Not even a rat's ass."

"Boris, let's rule out a heart attack. With that ruled out, what would you say did happen?"

"Was Trouville depressed?"

"I know what you're saying. No one's suggested it. Potter thought Trouville was wrestling with disease, but was cheerful enough. His main worry was blindness. But he was seeing okay at the time of his death."

"Would some poison show up in the ash? After cremation?"

"Good question, Boris. I'll ask our tech guy. Maybe we can get the ash from Bartles and have it tested. Like for toxic metals."

"Do you think Bartles would volunteer Trouville's ash?"

"Not without a court order, I'm afraid."

"Are we done? Am I off work?"

"Yeah, Boris. And thanks. You've helped a lot."

Dragovich laughed. "If you say so."

CHAPTER EIGHTEEN

Captain Ackerman was glowing like a neon pawn shop sign, and as an act of benevolence had let his yellow cigar die.

"I told you so, Sonntag. You didn't believe me."

"What did you tell me, Captain?"

"There's a homicide in the woodpile."

"I thought it was a felony in the woodpile."

"Same difference. See what one day of serious investigation's done. We've uncovered a giant conspiracy. They're all hiding something. Trouville's doc was rushing the death exam. Bartles the attorney rushed Trouville into the cremation oven to hide something. That young fellow in the firm is seething with resentment, and somehow wiped out Trouville. You've got to find out why, and why the whole lot are in on it. Maybe the funeral parlor's in on it. Throw the net wide, and collect all the fish, Sonntag."

"In on what, Captain?"

"My God, how did you get to be a lieutenant detective?"

"Just an accident, I guess. But maybe you can steer me to a murder."

"It's there all right, Sonntag." The captain scratched a match with his thumbnail and relit the stogie. A fine offensive plume soon spiraled out of his lips, forming a perfect smoke ring that collapsed on his desk. No one on the force could match the captain's smoke rings. Some cops swore that the captain could blow horizontal rings, that would settle like a doughnut on a desk, but Sonntag had never witnessed it.

"We've got a few things to look at," Sonntag said.

"You bet you do. Bring in Potter for questioning."

"He's puzzled by this and said he wanted to come in. I told him okay, come in."

"Go drag him in by the ass. Give him the third degree. And I want two of you on him. Do the good guy/bad guy on him until he spills."

"Spills?"

"He resented his boss and put him six feet under."

"I guess you know a lot more than I do about it," Sonntag said.

"You bet I do." The captain loosed a fine smoke ring that rotated its way toward the floor. "Now we're going to get a court order forcing Bartles to cough up the stuff on Trouville's body that the resident collected."

"Bartles isn't going to surrender it. He said you'd better show probable cause. He'll do what the court requires."

"We can show that. No big deal. I'll get it started."

Sonntag smiled.

"Here's what you're going to do, you and the Trouville Task-force. You're going to spend this day on Bolivar Newman, whoever he was. You're going to find every etching he made, which would tell us where he's been, and then we'll know a lot more about Trouville's past. And you're going to talk to the mortician about that cremation. Who ordered it done fast, and why. And we're going to keep on Bartles. And you're going to rattle Harley Potter until he spills all the beans in his head."

"Anything else?"

"Yeah, I want this thing broken by sundown."

Sonntag grinned.

Ackerman blew a smoke ring at him.

The Easter egg hunt was entertaining, if nothing else.

Sonntag retreated to the bullpen and collected his Trouville Taskforce.

"Okay, Eddie and Boris, you're going to be art collectors today. You're looking for the etchings of Bolivar Newman. He's done a lot of them, some in Paris, a few here in Wisconsin, and who knows where else. They're signed and should be dated. There's galleries that have displayed and sold these works of art. There may be interviews with him in the papers. We're looking for a life; for an artist who lives somewhere, did his etchings somewhere. This person might be the same as Trouville. You've got descriptions of Trouville, so you can describe him to art dealers, but they'd probably know him as Bolivar Newman."

"What's this have to do with anything?" Walsh asked.

"It has to do with the captain's Easter egg hunt."

"And what are you and Frank going to be doing?" Boris asked.

"We'll going to have a long conversation with Trouville's apprentice, Potter."

"For what? What's he done?"

"Beats me," Sonntag said. "But the captain seems to know. All right, that's your day, and by the way, the captain says he wants the case broken by sundown. His words."

"That's what they tell vagrants in westerns. Get out of town by sundown or face the music," Walsh said.

Sonntag grinned. The farther along this egg hunt got, the more he was enjoying it. There was something infectious in Ackerman's hunches, and what better way to squander a spring day?

"Ackerman wants me to work with you on Potter?" Frank Silva asked.

"Yeah, for what it's worth."

"Joe, what do you think?"

"I've stopped thinking."

"Is the captain losing his marbles?"

"I hope so," Sonntag said.

He dialed Potter, and reached the young man at once.

"Hey, Mr. Potter, this is the lieutenant. You still up to a conversation here? We'll pick you up."

"I sure am. I want to get to the bottom of this," Potter said.

"We'll pick you up in ten," Sonntag said.

"I'll be out front."

Sonntag and Silva requisitioned an unmarked cruiser, fired it up, and headed for the boardinghouse near Marquette. True to his word, Potter was waiting at the door, and swiftly hopped in.

"I sure hope this gets settled," he said.

"We do too," Silva replied.

The bullpen with its glaring lights and uniformed cops seemed to subdue Potter, who settled uncomfortably in a wooden chair at Sonntag's desk, while Silva and Sonntag sat close at hand. Over in the next carrel, a cop was booking a frumpy drunk driver, who bawled about her rights. She smelled of vomit. Down the row, a stinking vagrant was whining about fascist cops.

"Coffee? Doughnut?" Silva asked.

"No, I want to get right onto this," Potter said. "For days now, officers have been coming around, asking questions. Making me feel uncertain, and I'm worried. I don't know what's happening. I don't know why I'm sort of being examined by you day after day. I want to know what's happening and why you people seem to dog me. What have I done?"

"Good questions, Mr. Potter," Sonntag said. "We're aware of some irregularities in the death of Mr. Trouville. That combined with the absence of a will and a somewhat mysterious past has gotten the attention of the force."

"Is this a criminal investigation?"

149

"Not exactly, but we're checking things out, and it could become one. We have no evidence of a crime—at the moment."

"A fishing expedition, then!"

"I'm afraid you're correct, sir. We're calling it an Easter egg hunt."

"Is that legal?"

"There's enough irregularity to make it worth a hard look, Mr. Potter."

"Well, I'll tell you whatever you want to know. I'll cooperate any and every way. There's nothing private or secret about my life."

"That's good," Silva said. "Maybe you could just tell us about it. In your own words. That's the best."

Silva is very good, Sonntag thought.

"Well, you already know most of it. I guess what you want to know is what happened that morning. I mean, when we found him."

Sonntag nodded. "Good as any to start with."

"I got there about eight, as usual. Sometimes when we had a lot to do I got there early. But I got there at eight and there he was. It's a small place. A reception area, his office and the lab. You've been there. There he was, slumped over his desk. I hurried there and he looked really out. I mean no movement. I shook him, and he was just cold and sort of, nothing. Nothing there. I shook him again, and he just flopped. I couldn't believe it."

"Lights on in the office?" Silva asked. Good question.

"I don't remember. I don't think so. Just window light, through the blinds. I didn't know what to do. You don't think in times like that. I finally got Agnes Winsocket next door, and she stared, and patted him, and tried to take a pulse, and kept saying 'my goodness, my goodness,' and finally she said we'd better call for help. So I got the operator and said we needed an ambulance, and one came, and they saw Mr. Trouville was dead already, and they took their time, like the sense of urgency was gone."

"What did you think was the cause?"

"I thought it might be a diabetic coma. He had blood sugar problems."

"Insulin coma?"

"I don't think he took insulin. I would have known that. He was always on a very severe diet. No this, no that. I wouldn't know one coma from the other. Too much insulin, too much blood sugar. I just wouldn't know."

"What did Mrs. Winsocket do?" Sonntag asked.

"She just wrung her hands, and fought back tears, and kept blinking as they took him away on a stretcher."

"Did you think he had just died?"

"I didn't even think about it. He was gone. That's all."

"Were you surprised to learn that he'd been dead a while?"

"I didn't think about it. He often worked at night. He would dictate letters and give the belt to Agnes. I guess I should have realized he was cold. I didn't touch him except to shake him. Agnes touched him. It sure was a sad moment."

"Yeah, it must have been," Silva said. "Say, you change your mind about a doughnut? We get a box of them every morning from the Policemen's Benevolent Association. Coffee?"

"Sure, both, that would be nice. I ate, but I'll take one."

Silva headed off, leaving Sonntag to ask questions.

"It was a real loss," Sonntag said. "Some of us knew him and his work. I've been learning more from the obituaries. Not the ones in the big papers, but the ones in technical journals and newsletters. Do you know that Trouville was one of the giants in all the forensic sciences? They called him a wizard. A genius. A pioneer. Things like that."

"Certainly I did. That's why I joined his firm. It was the

chance of a lifetime and I took it."

"So I guess that leaves your future in a limbo, eh?" Sonntag asked.

"When he died, Lieutenant, I thought all was lost. I was beside myself. But now I'm more optimistic. I know nearly everything Armand knew. I can hang my shingle and get ahead."

"What would you tell your clients?"

"That I learned the art—it's not a trade, it's an art, and science, from the best man in the world."

Silva returned carrying two ceramic mugs of coffee and some doughnuts in waxed paper. He set them on the desk and Potter helped himself to a glazed one.

"Thanks," Potter said. "It hits the spot."

"We're really glad when someone comes in and just wants to help out and clarify things. Just like you're doing."

Potter loosed one of his rare smiles. "I'm still sort of at sea about this. I don't know what the problem is, and that's half the reason I came in."

"Well, you see," Silva said, "there was something funny about the death certificate. Trouville's doc sort of took over from an intern and next thing we knew, Trouville's body had been cremated and the funeral had taken place. Some of the higher-ups around here began wondering about stuff. You know anything about that?"

"No, not much. Except both the doctor, Schwartzkopf, and the lawyer, Bartles, really admired Armand. He was their prize. It was like having Albert Einstein as a friend and patient. I guess they just wanted everything to fall into place. You know, a reputation so big in his field it should have made the front page of the *New York Times*. I mean, Trouville was major league, he was World Series. So sure, they were protecting him, making it all smooth as could be."

"Protecting him from what?" Sonntag asked.

"From Trouville's, well, the mysterious side, the side with all the stories he told, the side he invented. If he invented his past, maybe his reputation wouldn't stand up, and maybe even his testimony would have to be reconsidered."

"You're saying that Trouville's yarns about his early years might undermine his work?"

"Yes, and his reputation."

"And his closest friends, lawyer and doctor, may have hurried things along deliberately—so nothing damaging would arise?"

"I—I'm just guessing, Lieutenant. That's what crossed my mind."

"Hey, really candidly now, do you think Trouville's reputation was justified?" Silva asked.

"Yes—and no. He earned every word in those obituaries. But there's more. I was solving cases and no one was giving me credit. I solved the one about that society gal who arranged her own kidnapping. I traced those notes back to her. I did that, but Armand took credit and never gave me the time of day. That's why I have mixed feelings."

"I'm very glad to be told about it, sir," Sonntag said. "This has been very helpful, believe me."

"I think maybe I did some good," Potter said. "I'd like to get the truth out. All of it, including everything there is to say about Armand."

"You've heard all his stories. The Foreign Legion, all that stuff. Would you mind writing all that stuff down? Just a few notes. Like he said he was in the Foreign Legion in the first war. And he met Bedouins in Africa. And he went to that art school in Paris. All that. The more stories, the better. Okay?" Silva asked.

Potter thought a bit. "That wouldn't be easy. The stories sort of varied, you know."

"Well give it a try, okay?"

Potter made his way with a homework assignment.

"Frank, you're a genius," he said.

"Don't start that," Silva said. "Don't do Ackerman on me."

CHAPTER NINETEEN

They watched Potter head through the door and into the sunlight.

"Still an Easter egg hunt," Silva said. "No chocolate bunny in that basket."

Sonntag was still processing the lengthy conversation, his mind plucking gently on some things. "Not much new," he said. "Except the idea that the doctor and lawyer were covering up something, working in concert."

"Sure, you can spin that into something. Even if there's nothing there," Silva said. "What next, Joe?"

"I'd like for you to write down your impressions of the interview. I want to give Ackerman something to chew on. I'll write mine also."

"You think Potter was angry enough about being slighted to kill Trouville?"

"Stranger things have happened," Sonntag said. "He does brood on it, doesn't he? But there's everything against it, including all he's hoped for in his own career. Without some sort of okay from Trouville, he might not get far."

"Do you like him?" Silva asked.

"A good question. I don't dislike him."

"Yeah, that's a good way to put it. I wouldn't warm to him very much. He's not someone I'd share a beer with."

"Lots of people like that," Sonntag said. "What have we got?

A hasty death certificate and funeral. What's he told us about it?"

"Something interesting, if you're conspiracy-minded. The doc and lawyer know each other and got very busy very fast."

Sonntag was amused. "That's about par for conspiracies."

"I still think there's something there. Not what Ackerman thinks. Not even a crime. Maybe something else." Silva shrugged. "Oh, well, if Ackerman wants us to look, we'll look."

A guy in a khaki war-surplus Eisenhower jacket showed up. He was carrying the tempered glass desk cover wrapped in white butcher paper. "You Sonntag?" he asked. "I got this. And here's the report."

"You from the Technical School?"

"Yeah, student. Applied lab chemistry. They gave it to me."

"Uh, they gave it to you?"

"As a student project."

"And what did you do with it?"

"All there in my report. I tried scraping the residue off and doing some basic tests. I tried swabbing it up with water and cotton. I tried lots of stuff. My instructor gave me a B-plus."

"You got a B-plus? How come they didn't give you an A?" Silva asked.

"I messed up a little, polluted some samples. One with rubbing alcohol, and the other with gasoline."

"Were there any good samples?"

"Not much to work with," he said. "You'll see."

"And you signed this?"

"Gary Stolper."

"You get paid for this?" Silva asked.

"Nope, but it counts toward my final grade."

"Was this reviewed by the faculty?"

"Yup. They were pretty tough on me, too."

"And their names are on it?"

"Nope, but you can call them. Just ask for the chem lab. I gotta go, okay?"

"Let me look at the report," Sonntag said.

He pulled it from a manila envelope. It was half a page long, and briefly described three tests. But he turned to the conclusion. Results were inconclusive due to the small amount of residue on the glass. The tests did not rule out coffee. The tests did not rule out any barbiturate or sedative. The dribble elsewhere on the glass was saliva.

"Yeah, you can go," Sonntag said, handing the sheet to Silva.

The applied chemistry student beat it out of there.

Silva read the whole deal and laughed. "So much for that," he said.

"I could have wiped my finger in it and tasted it and decided whether it was coffee," Sonntag said. "No chocolate bunny here. I guess we'll have to show this to Ackerman, and you know what's going to happen."

"Yeah, and I'd like to be in Racine or someplace when it hits the fan," he said.

"He's going to say, 'Why didn't you send it to the FBI? They've got the best lab in the country.' And I'll say, 'Captain, you wanted it yesterday, or maybe the day before, or maybe twenty minutes after we delivered it,' and he'll say, 'I don't know about you, Sonntag. You're just not in the game anymore. You blew the evidence. A felony was right there in that spill, and you blew it, and now some crumb-bum gets away with murder.' "

Silva was grinning. "Give him a cigar, and he'll cool down."

Sonntag found the captain whittling a pencil with a pocket-knife.

"I suppose you're bringing me bad news," he said.

Sonntag laid the test results on the captain's desk. The captain read slowly, depositing slivers of pencil wood on the report. Then he read it again and shook the slivers off the paper.

"I should have been more patient," he said. "The FBI's got the only lab that could get something out of those spills. I got a little eager." He looked up at Sonntag. "Sorry, I got carried away."

Sonntag said not one word.

"There's nothing worse in a cop station than a hunch," Ackerman said. "A cop gets a hunch and that hunch cries for an answer. For validation. A cop with a hunch wants answers right now, by any shortcut, so the results will prove that the hunch is right. I still have a hunch. There's something real whacko here, something being covered up. And I've got to sit in this chair and squirm while my best men dig everywhere, and do a good job of it, to see whether my hunch is just me being nuts or whether there's something to it. I just paid a price. Some evidence ruined."

Was this the day-shift captain of the Milwaukee police? Sonntag slowly processed all that, doubting that he could persuade Silva that this exchange actually happened.

"We talked to Potter," he said.

"I saw you talking to him," Ackerman said. "I did my best to stay away."

"Mostly we rehashed things. He seemed eager to cooperate, and talked freely. He said yeah, he was resentful. Trouville was taking all the credit for stuff that Potter had done. He said he thought the world of Trouville's skills, but thought his own matched them. He broke a major case, but his boss took the credit."

"Envy can be a homicidal motive," Ackerman said quietly.

"Yeah, but Trouville's death ruins Potter's chances. That's a new field, and there's no diploma to hang on the wall. Potter's utterly at sea."

"Killers don't plan things out," Ackerman said.

"That's the other thing. He says the lights were off when he and Agnes Winsocket found Trouville. And there still is no sign of homicide. Nothing. Zero."

"It'll show up," Ackerman said.

It was spooky the way he said it.

"We asked him a lot of other things, and the one thing that sticks in my mind is that he said Trouville's doc and lawyer knew each other and both were eager to defend Trouville's reputation."

"There, you see?" Ackerman said. He set down his pencil and jackknife, lit up a dead stogie, gummed it and sucked until the tip glowed orange. "An unlawful conspiracy," he said.

Sonntag began to crawl deep inside of himself, under his spare manhole cover.

Ackerman started laughing. "Sonntag, you've got a nut telling you what to do."

"I've got Walsh and Dragovich talking to art dealers and art professors. Maybe they'll come up with something about Newman."

"AKA Armand de Trouville," Ackerman said, blowing noxious brown smoke at Sonntag, which curled around his suit like a cop patting down a suspect.

The lieutenant knew that when he got home, Lizbeth would take one sniff and tell him he'd been talking to the captain—and she was always right.

"Yeah, one more thing," Sonntag said. "I want to see what was taken off Trouville when they brought him into the hospital. The intern, Mauss, inventoried it, along with an orderly. Trouville's own doc looked at it, and the attorney took it. There were some things worth a look. A wallet with driver's license and some bills; a ring with initials incised in a stone; an envelope ready to mail; a folded sheet of paper, change, pocket knife."

"Bartles won't give it to you?"

"Over his dead body. He's ticked off about this whole investigation."

"You want a search warrant. And what do we tell the judge?"

"You got a hunch," Sonntag said.

"So we wait a while. When we get a probable cause, I'll see to it," Ackerman said. "You keep working on the Newman angle, and we'll have cause enough to get the warrant."

"What's your hunch?" Sonntag asked him. "I mean, exactly."

"There's a conspiracy to keep something big from the cops," Ackerman said.

"Who are the conspirators?"

"Trouville's doc, his attorney, and maybe Potter, maybe people unknown." Ackerman sucked, blew brown haze, and winked.

That proved to be the end of the day. Sonntag read Silva's assessment of the Potter interview, typed his own, and folded up shop. Neither Walsh nor Dragovich reported in. He cleaned the wax paper out of his black lunch bucket, emptied the last of the coffee from the thermos, and headed home. Another day, another Easter egg hunt, he thought. No chocolate rabbits.

He stepped into a fading April afternoon. This had been the first day he had ventured to work without the trench coat, relying on his scratchy suit from Irv, The Working Man's Friend to keep him warm. That and an old gray fedora with a stained rim where his hands had held and mauled it for scores of hours.

There wasn't much crime in Milwaukee. Who could explain it?

He cut over to Wells Street and waited for the Number Ten car to stop, which it did with an acrid screech of iron on wheel. He settled into the last remaining yellow wicker seat, and absorbed the mixed odors of rush hour, as shop girls, factory workers, clerks, and teachers headed back to their bungalows.

When they eased out on the Viaduct over the Menomonee

Valley, he closed his eyes and white-knuckled it.

"You all right, sir?"

An elderly woman with blue hair across the aisle was addressing him.

"I will be if we survive," he said.

"I lost my son in the war," she said. "The island of Guam. He was a sapper."

"I'm sorry."

"And my husband when his car stalled on the Milwaukee Road tracks. He was killed by the Hiawatha. It took the Jaws of Life to free his body."

"I'm so sorry."

"So I know how you feel," she said.

That diverted him from the lurking doom when the streetcar would leave the tracks and tumble to the bottoms far below. But next he knew, the land was rushing up and the car was rolling on solid ground again. He pulled the cord and got off at 56th Street, and hiked over to 57th and then south to his house, which needed paint and a shingle where one had fallen.

Lizbeth was in the bathroom. There was light under the door. He pitched his hat onto the hat rack and waited. He heard water, lots of water, and finally she emerged, looking unhappy.

"You're home on time for a change," she said. "I haven't even started dinner."

"I'm in no rush. I could pour you a Manhattan."

"The water heater quit," she said.

"Quit? No hot water? Did you call the plumber?"

"Of course not. How do I know what's in the bank?"

"Maybe it just needs a new element."

"Maybe I need a hug," she said.

He was glad to cooperate. He liked to feel useful.

"Chop suey?" he asked. They often went to a Chinese joint on North Avenue, especially when she'd had a tough day.

"You'll shower in cold water," she said. "Have you been talking to the captain?"

"All afternoon, I think."

"Go get something on. I'll hang your suit outside on the clothesline."

He ditched his suit, moved his wallet and change into some corduroy slacks, and gave her the suit.

"You must have been in his office all day," she said, sniffing the fabric. She hung the pants on a clasping hanger, and then the coat, and took them outside, where a gentle breeze would freshen them. *In the morning they'll smell like hops,* he thought.

"Do you want me to call the plumber?" he asked.

"I'm quite capable of calling the plumber. If it's not the element, and if we need a new one, should I tell him to go ahead?"

"Yeah, but get the cheapest one."

"What's the captain up to?" she asked.

"He's got a hunch that there's a huge criminal conspiracy keeping the cops in the dark about what happened to that little genius, Armand de Trouville, who really died an unnatural death even though he was sixty-eight, diabetic, and had heart disease."

"Why does he think that?"

"He has no reason, apart from some irregularities in issuing the death certificate."

"I have the same hunch," she said.

"You and Ackerman and Frank Silva," he said. "Next it'll be the Pope."

"It's just a feeling," she said. "I'm going to have chow mein tonight, and we're going to have a close look at your fortune cookie, okay?"

After dinner, they cracked the cookies.

Hers read: "Follow your instincts. Your hunch will come true."

His read: "Timing is everything. Wait for the right moment."

He was disappointed. He wanted one that said, "Tell Ackerman to drop dead."

CHAPTER TWENTY

The Apple Galleries catalogue was a find. The Galleries, with well-appointed shops in New York, Chicago, and San Francisco, had produced a catalogue featuring the etchings of three artists, Bolivar Newman among them.

"Where'd you get it?" Sonntag asked Walsh.

"Foster's Fine Art, on Water Street. They didn't know much about Newman, but the owner dug it up. He has piles of these things, and remembered it."

"We hit every art joint in town, I think," Dragovich said. "I'd prefer some good tattoos. I'd like a mermaid on my biceps."

"Did anyone know much about Newman?"

"Oh, sure, there are some etchings done around the state, and they sell one now and then. But Newman did just a few of those. The real stuff's in Paris. You'll see. He spent a lot of time between the wars there."

The Apple catalogue, on glossy white stock, contained illustrations of seventeen Newman etchings, all familiar Parisian scenes ranging from the Louvre to the Eiffel Tower. They had been pressed in editions of two hundred, and were dated from 1919 to 1939.

"They sold pretty well?" Sonntag asked after studying them. They looked rather ordinary to him.

"Yeah. See all those figures? Most etchers do an etching of a building, all squares and angles. Maybe add some trees. But not Newman. He's got men and women and children running through most of these."

"Foster told you that?"

"Yeah, the owner drilled us on that stuff."

"Did he have any of the etchings?"

"Yeah, he had several. They're all numbered, like one hundred seven slash two hundred. That means it's the hundred seventeenth out of two hundred. After that the plates wear out, and the quality goes down."

"So Newman was in Paris until nineteen thirty-nine?"

"We asked that. The answer is not necessarily. An etcher can work from photos anywhere. If he lived here, as Trouville, he could have done these right here."

"What about the others? The ones he did around here?"

"Mostly buildings. Bascom Hall at the university in Madison. Stuff like that. Foster says they were commerce, not good art. Newman was looking for some moolah."

"This fits with what we know or guess about Trouville. He came here in early nineteen thirty-six—from somewhere. He liked to hint it was Chicago. But maybe it was France. And he didn't have many cases. No one ever heard of document examiners. He must've been hungry. Is this good art? I wouldn't know a good etching from a dollar bill."

"Yeah, the Paris ones. All those fine lines, they create the illusion of light and shadow," Walsh said. "And the figures. Etchings are notorious for not having people in them, but Newman put them in."

"Who are the other artists in here?"

"Some Frenchie named Delousse, and a woman artist named Edna Raphael. She's American."

"Did you price any of these?"

"Foster said the French ones can go for two hundred, the Wisconsin ones for half that. And both Delousse and Raphael can go for more sometimes. In other words, Newman was not top dog."

"And these galleries you stopped at, they sell Newman?"

"Now and then. He's not a hot item."

"Do they sell the others?"

"One gallery sold a couple of Raphaels. She does river scenes."

"Where does she live?"

"New York. She's doing watercolors now."

"Eddie, call her and see what you can learn about Newman."

"What should I tell her?"

"You're a cop. Newman may have died. We don't know. Did he have any other names? You figure it out."

"What did he do before that? Before 1919?" Dragovich asked. "Before the first war. Where was he during that war?"

"If I can locate her," Walsh said. "I like flirting with operators."

If she was there and had a phone, the odds were pretty good, Sonntag thought. Eddie Walsh was a ladies' man, though heaven alone knew why. Mostly because that's what he thought of himself.

"Hey," Eddie Walsh said, shoving his Panama back a notch. "You mind telling me what we're looking for?"

"I ask myself the same question," Sonntag said. "Trouville died a while ago. He led a mysterious life. He told lots of stories about his youth, but they seem to be inventions."

"So what?" Walsh asked.

"So the captain's curiosity got the best of him," Dragovich said.

"There was some odd stuff when he died," Sonntag said. "A hurried up cause-of-death exam. No heirs, the trustee in a hurry to close the estate. It makes me curious, like the captain, but we're not thinking alike. I'm thinking where's the crime? And he's thinking get the crooks."

"What was irregular again?"

"A young resident, Mauss, was doing the cause-of-death, but Trouville's own doc, Schwartzkopf, more or less took over."

"Mauss found nothing?"

"You mean wounds or trauma? Nothing. No punctures, no wounds. No sign of strangulation or anything like that. I don't think it was murder, no matter what the captain thinks."

"Why would the older doc intervene?"

"There may have been medical requirements. Like a senior doc supervising a resident or intern," Sonntag said. "But maybe not."

"So why are we tracking down Trouville's early life?"

"Ackerman's curious. I am too, but it hardly seems a cop matter."

"No, Joe, I gotta hunch about this," Walsh said. "This here's a deal, and we're going to get to some spot where we're glad we're digging in. Just a hunch, but we're aiming at something big."

Sonntag laughed. "You too, Boris?"

"I never get a hunch until I've had three beers," Dragovich said.

"Okay, what needs doing?" Walsh said.

"Eddie, you start flirting with operators until you reach the Raphael woman and maybe get the story on young Newman or whatever his name was. Boris, you start in on Trouville's social life. What did he do for friends? I want to know every club or organization or professional society he belonged to. You might talk to Agnes Winsocket. She's the dental receptionist who handled Trouville's secretary stuff. She'd know. After lunch I'm going over to the funeral home. See whether there was anything funny about the way Bartles handled that stuff."

"You want to eat at the Automat?" Walsh asked.

"I brought mine," Sonntag said.

They drifted off. The bullpen was pretty quiet, except for Lydell Swan's corner, where he was booking a couple of purse snatchers. They were a skinny pair, one dressed in fake janitorial costume, the other dolled up in a fancy suit and flowery hat. That was a good catch. The pair had operated around women's restrooms in department stores, snatching purses from stalls that were in use. The victim never even got a glimpse of who hooked her purse from the stall. From the looks of things, that would come to an abrupt stop. *Two or three years in Waupun,* he thought.

Sonntag pulled out his black lunch bucket and opened it. He poured hot coffee from the thermos bottle into its top, and tugged at the wax paper of the sandwich. Chicken salad today, which pleased him. Lizbeth made a fine chicken salad, with a little saffron in it. There was something else down there. He recognized a fortune cookie in a paper wrapper. She must have been plotting something. It'd probably say Happy Sun Yat Sen Birthday.

"Join you?" Frank Silva asked.

Sonntag nodded and gestured toward the other chair. Silva brown-bagged it, awarding himself a beef or pastrami sandwich, which he prepared every morning, and an apple.

"We going somewhere this afternoon?" Silva asked.

"Funeral home. Trouville died one evening, declared dead the next morning. The next afternoon there was a visitation; he was cremated that eve, and the service was the next Monday."

"What's wrong with that?"

"Oh, nothing much. Except the usual thing would be to notify relatives and heirs; death notice in papers, including Chicago where he had an office. Try to collect family before the funeral. Bartles didn't go that route."

"I just got a hunch," Silva said.

"Try my fortune cookie," Sonntag said. "Lizbeth's little surprise."

"Seriously, we've got to follow what the fortune cookie says," Silva said. "I've got a feeling. Don't just kiss it off. If it says do something, we got to do it. Sometimes you got to believe in fate."

Sonntag grinned and bit into the chicken salad.

"Why would Bartles push the whole burying so fast?" Silva asked between bites.

"He probably wanted to play golf."

Silva stared, not processing that.

"People with no heirs, people like that, no one cares. Get it over with and go play golf. I've watched it a few times. The executor, whoever, jams it through, and it's done. Funerals, memorials, all that—it's for the living, for the bereaved. You get a little guy like Trouville in a funeral home, and he'll be out in a few hours, out and buried."

"Is there a crime in it? Am I missing something?"

"The crime of not giving a damn, that's all. That's what I think has got the captain stirred up."

Silva was young. He hadn't been to a few hundred funerals, like Joe Sonntag. There were funerals and there were funerals, and they all said something.

"So Bartles could play golf?" he asked.

"Or go muskie fishing. Or take his ladies to dinner. Or buy a round of drinks at the Brown Deer Country Club."

"I was on the streets handing out socialist tracts. The only thought I ever had about the country club was that the rich bloodsuckers hung out there."

Sonntag downed the Maxwell House, washing the crumbs out of his teeth, and then snapped his lunch bucket together. That's how it went, day after day.

Silva crumpled the brown bag and wax paper and pitched it.

They headed into a damp afternoon. Madsden Mortuary was only a few blocks north, up near Schlitz.

"What are we looking for?" Silva asked.

"Ask Captain Ackerman. He's a funeral expert. He knows more about funerals than a mortician's convention."

"What kind of man is Madsden?"

"You know the Fred Allen radio show? Allen's Alley? And the mortician in it, Digger O'Dell, The Friendly Undertaker?"

"Yeah. The one who comes on, meets someone, and says real slow-like, 'You're looking fine . . . very natural.' And the audience laughs."

"That's Madsen. He has an eye for business."

They arrived in the middle of a visitation, and this time the place was jammed. Some society lady. Sonntag spotted Dorothy Parnell of the *Sentinel*. The place reeked of perfume.

"This is a jewel thief's paradise," Silva muttered as they passed a pair of gals wearing a lot of ice.

"Well, let's give it a try," Sonntag said. He didn't see Madsen around; just the help, smiling unctuously at everyone.

"Where could we find Mr. Madsen?" he asked one of the help.

The gent in the black suit looked him over, not missing the attire bought from Irv, The Working Man's Friend, and then pointed to a distant door.

The perfume diminished with every step. Sonntag knocked.

Madsen himself opened and recognized the detective.

"Lieutenant?"

"Got a minute?"

"I always have time for my friends on the force. Come in. Have a seat. You've braved the fierce weather to see me."

Madsden slid behind a desk that was polished to an aching glow with lemon-scented wax, and lifted a quizzical brow.

"Yeah, thanks. We're looking into some irregularities with

Mr. Trouville's death certificate. Maybe it was whacko."

The eyebrows lifted, quivered, and settled slowly. "Something wrong?"

"Maybe. We don't know. Could you tell us what happened? Whole thing? Who contacted you? Who set it up? Especially about the timing? Was there a hurry?"

The caterpillar eyebrows quivered a little, and Madsen's hands steepled and unsteepled.

"Why, officers, it seemed perfectly fine. We were called by Mr. Trouville's attorney to come for the deceased that morning, and we did so promptly. He gave us a photocopy of the certificate, and we made some arrangements right there, at the hospital. Were the arrangements satisfactory, sirs?"

"What was the deal?" Silva asked.

Madsen winced. Deal obviously wasn't the right word. "The simplest arrangements that we offer. Death notices in both papers, visitation the next afternoon, cremation of the beloved that evening, a memorial service on a following weekday morning. That's our basic package, sir. No frills, but death with dignity and honor and attention to the grieving."

"Why the rush?" Sonntag asked.

"He did seem a bit rushed. I advised against it. Give the family time to collect. But he said there was no family, and we should complete the sad mission as fast as we could."

"He give any reason?"

"He said the estate had few resources, sir. So we did our best, and I personally saw to a floral arrangement. I knew the deceased slightly, having met him in one of my service clubs, The Optimizers."

"Trouville was an Optimizer? The outfit that meets at the Pfister dining room twice a month?"

"He didn't attend much, sir. But yes."

"What do the Optimizers do?"

171

"We promote progress, sir. Progress toward a better world. We hear luncheon talks about the front lines of science and faith and technology, and try to spread the good word."

"Did Mr. Trouville have many friends there?"

"Most often, he came to talk. He kept us abreast of his pioneering. His life's work, you might say. Once in a while he illustrated with cases. We always enjoyed his talks. We're busy men, but he could give us a good story in fifteen minutes. He would talk about fake wills, or forged stock certificates, just delightful little peeks into his work, and the hurly-burly of the world of schemers and crooks."

"Did he tell the one about the New York society gal who kidnapped herself to try and get some bucks out of her mother?" Silva asked.

"Oh, he certainly did. He was proud of that one, detective. That girl was scheming to get herself a fortune."

"I didn't see many of those gentlemen at the visitation," Sonntag said. "Where were the Optimizers? Don't those gents support one another?"

"Well, it was all rushed. We barely got death notices into the papers. It takes a bit of time for word of a departure of a loved one to filter out."

"How come, I mean, why so fast?"

"The attorney, sir. Court-appointed, since there were no heirs. He set the time."

"How did anyone know there were no heirs?"

"He seemed to know, sir. Within an hour or so after the hospital released the remains, Mr. Bartles had obtained trustee status from the probate court."

"You know of any reason for that? For, say, cremating the remains and getting it over with?"

"It's not unusual, sir. I hesitate to say why. But mostly because there's no one close to the deceased, and people have other things to do."

"Did Mr. Bartles say so?"

"Well, I do remember an odd comment. I shouldn't share it with you, but I will, of course. He said, if I recollect correctly, that the sooner we laid Mr. Trouville to rest, the better for his reputation."

CHAPTER TWENTY-ONE

They tarried under the mortuary's green striped awning while a fierce thundershower laced the streets.

An elderly gent in a trench coat, dripping rain, approached.

"Is this the place for Mrs. Justin Case? Juanita?"

"Guess so," Silva said.

"Nobody knows anything," the gent said, and dripped through the doors.

"There's that name again," Sonntag said. "How would you like to be named Justin Case?"

"Beats Sterling Silva," Frank said. "The skunk next door calls me Sterling. I'll get even one of these days."

"I think we got this thing laid to rest," Sonntag said. "There might be a misdemeanor floating around somewhere, but the only crime in sight is entirely in Ackerman's head. If there's no relatives in sight, everyone just highballs the burying."

A gust of rain shot spray at them. Sonntag was tempted to retreat. A crack of thunder almost persuaded him, but he didn't want to mix with the mourners of Mrs. Justin Case.

"You know what? This whole thing was about Trouville's reputation. The deceased wasn't giving Potter any credit, and Potter was pretty steamed up and probably threatening to say a few things in public, and both Trouville's doc and lawyer thought to put out the fire and get the man buried, and Potter would pack his bags."

"Yeah, but there's more," Silva said. "I got a hunch there's lots more."

"I doubt it," Sonntag said. He was tired of shadowy intuitions.

"What were the lawyer and the doc covering up?" Silva asked. "Why'd they hurry the death exam? What harm was there in letting that resident do it right? Why'd they cremate so fast?"

"Frank, all this is just ordinary haste by people who don't care a lot. No heirs, no fortune, the state pockets the money; they want to get the man buried and get on with life. Bury Trouville and it'll all go away."

"It doesn't explain what happened, Joe."

The gusty rain slackened, and Sonntag plunged in, crossing Juneau and heading toward Kilbourn. The scratchy suit from off the south-side pipe racks was taking a soaking, but he didn't care. The bullpen at the station was going to stink of wet wool.

"I'm gonna tell Ackerman it's done, over, solved. The worst I can come up with is a possible misdemeanor if that death certificate wasn't done right. What else is there? You gonna argue that Potter killed his boss? The doc gets rapped for his haste, and it's done."

"Something killed him, and not the way the death certificate says."

"I used to believe my hunches too, Frank. We're running in circles. We haven't got a fact that amounts to a hill of beans. So we're playing hunches and making guesses. We got better things to do. There's a car theft ring, and we haven't a good lead. We've got some cold homicides. It's time to let Ackerman know where his hunches led. To a few dozen hours of wasted time for the PD."

"We'll see," Silva said.

There was the usual smell of urine around the station doors. Sonntag could never figure it out. It wasn't a place where drunks would piss. They swung inside and were greeted by the stink of Ackerman's yellow five-cent stogies. Why did rainstorms bring out the stink in everything?

Eddie Walsh was waiting, looking pretty smug.

"Here's my notes," he said. "I had to sweet-talk the girls from here to Manhattan, but we found her. She's deaf and living with a daughter in Forest Hills, out on Long Island, but we got her. Edna Raphael in person. She said yeah, she lived in Paris, and those were great times, and she knew Hemingway and that crowd, and she made etchings. She returned to the States before the war. And yes indeedy, she knew the little guy, Bolivar Newman, with a moustache, but she always thought that was a fake name, and she wondered who it was. He spoke good French, but he was a Yank, and he was also a rival. They were competing with their etchings, and she thought his were inferior to hers; she didn't think his had much, what did she say? Perspective. His were too flat-looking, and a good etching takes you into it."

"When did she meet him, Eddie?"

"After the war. He showed up out of nowhere, and lived in a loft on the Left Bank, the Latin Quarter, with the rest of the bohemians. She lost track of him after she returned to the States, and didn't know anything about him until the Apple Galleries catalog."

"Did he ever call himself Armand de Trouville?"

"She thinks that was somebody else."

"Someone else? You mean she knew two short men, one with a French name?"

"She wasn't sure, and I couldn't squeeze her for more, Joe."

"Did you tell her the man here called himself Trouville? But hinted at a life long ago as the etcher Bolivar Newman?"

"Yeah, and that just confused her. She must be over seventy. Older than Trouville, or whoever we're looking at."

"Did she ever hear of anyone being a document examiner?"

"Ah, I sort of approached that, and she said, you mean a palm reader? And I said no, a guy who looks into forgeries and handwriting, and she asked if I was talking about fortune tellers who read handwriting and tell you if you're sick or happy or just suffered loss."

"I guess she wouldn't know things like that, Eddie."

"She said it fit. The man she knew would be a good document examiner."

"Did she say why?"

"Temperament. Newman's eye for detail."

"Anything else?"

"Yeah. She said Newman or whoever it was, he was real quiet about his past. He never talked about himself, or his family, or the States. She saw him most often at the Café Les Deux Magots, or whatever that place is. He was one of the bunch of Americans. He had an attic room on Rue Jacob, about four floors up."

"Did you think to ask her about any of Trouville's stories? Like being in the French Foreign Legion?"

"Yeah, I did. And bingo. Newman told her once he spent the war in the Legion."

"So maybe Newman and Trouville are the same," Sonntag said.

"I think so, Joe. But who knows where he was during that war, and when he was younger. Remember, he was born in 1881. There's a lot of missing time in there."

"Good job, Eddie. Write it up."

"Hokey-dokey. I got to talking to the long-distance operator in Philly, and she invited me to meet her mother. Then I got to talking with another and she wanted me to meet her husband."

"Did Edna offer anything else?"

"Yeah, she said I'd blush between my ears if she told me any more."

"Give me something for the captain. He's like a hungry bear waking up in April."

"Looks like Trouville had a wild side," Silva said.

"He wasn't handing out tracts on street corners," Sonntag said. "We're inching closer, but this man is a mystery."

Walsh drifted back to his upright Underwood and began some one-finger hammering on the keyboard. Cops hated to type, and he was no exception.

There was a note on Sonntag's desk asking him to call Dragovich, who was off-shift.

"Yeah, I got some good stuff, Joe," he said. "That Agnes, the dental lady, she said Trouville's whole social life was service clubs, like Kiwanis and Rotary. He was always trotting off to those outfits. Lunches. Those people eat lunch and have meetings afterward, and usually hear a talk about something or other. So I began checking, and Trouville was a member of three or four, and I got to asking around and finally got ahold of a soft drink bottler named Earl Sylvester, out in West Milwaukee, Rotary president, and he knew Trouville as well as anyone. He called Trouville colorful. So I said, what's that? And he said, like, he had a new story about himself every time he showed up. Mostly about being an artist in France. Did you know he was in the French Foreign Legion in Algeria?"

"He was for a fact, or he said he was?"

"He told Sylvester he was."

"Did he make etchings?"

"Yeah, in France and England. He said he made the etchings in London and used the name Bolivar Newman."

"In London?"

"He said his father was a chancellor to the King, and he spent his boyhood playing tiddlywinks in Buckingham Palace,

178

usually with a prince or two."

"You kidding? Trouville said that?"

"That's what the soft drink man says."

"You pursue that any? I mean, playing in Buckingham Palace?"

"Hey, I don't even know where that is. Where's Buckingham?"

"Anything else, Boris?"

"Yeah, one thing. All those Rotarians—man, what a sanitary bunch—they didn't take Trouville seriously. Like he was the local Tall Tale Teller. But they knew he was the world's foremost document examiner, so they just swallowed their spit and smiled."

"How come?"

"Hey, the rest of those gents, they hardly been outside of Milwaukee. Some army ones been all over, but they're home-grown businessmen, insurance salesmen, and here was Trouville talking about eating sheep with Bedouins and the tough life in the Foreign Legion. And all the scum in the legion. So sure, he was like a peacock in with the robins. How did beertown get such a peacock, eh?"

"Good question. Did you ask Sylvester?"

"Trouville liked to fish. We got into fishing. Trouville trolled the seas. He fished for shark. He's cast lines for swordfish. He's gone after tuna. At least he said he did. Maybe that's some more of his yarns."

"Boris, Trouville's more of a mystery than ever. You got any ideas about it?"

"Either he was a liar, or else he had something so big and bad in his past he was smokescreening. You know how to hide a past? Invent about fifty of them."

"Like what? What was he hiding?"

"Damned if I know, Joe."

"Keep on this tomorrow. Find some more Kiwanis or whatever."

"He was a member of the Milwaukee Athletic Club, too."

"Trouville was? Try there. That's a different breed of cat."

"He took clients to dinner there."

"Ackerman will want to know if he ate asparagus with or without hollandaise sauce."

"I'll find out, Joe."

Sonntag settled into his oak swivel chair and stared at the phone, a black stalk with an earpiece hanging from it. The phone had only deepened the mystery of Armand de Trouville. He glanced at his Bulova and saw the shift had ended. Maybe he could catch the captain.

"You're late, Sonntag. Now you're going to keep me overtime," Ackerman said. "Now I'll reach my lousy little bungalow ten minutes late, and my wife will have my ass for letting her delicious dinner overcook on the stove."

Briefly, Sonntag outlined what had been unearthed that ordinary day by four detectives in the Investigations Bureau.

"I knew it! Trouville was a confidence man. You see? My hunch was right!" Ackerman said. The yellow cigar wobbled and danced and its tip turned orange.

"Ah, Captain, you got any evidence? One hard fact?"

"Not yet, but it's all coming together."

"All right. Go get some warrants. Who do I arrest? For what?"

"It'll take another day, Sonntag. Tomorrow we'll nail Potter for homicide, and that doc for falsifying a death certificate, and we'll nail that lawyer for tampering with the evidence. Both of them accessories after the fact."

"What? You nuts or something? Show me a crime! Just show me one!"

"Cool down, Lieutenant."

"I'm tired of this. I'm tired of wasting my time, the time of my good men, on your crazy whims. Get yourself another sucker to do your Easter egg hunt. So you're late for dinner now. What's that, a first?"

Sonntag was seething. He was so hot he didn't care what he said.

The captain didn't blink.

"Go buy Lizbeth a Chinese feast, Sonntag. See you tomorrow," Ackerman said. He rose, clapped his duty cap on his head, and plunged through the door. The funny thing was, the room suddenly seemed forlorn without him.

Sonntag watched him go. Maybe he'd buy Lizbeth a meal. He was tired of Chinese. Maybe steak and mashed potatoes. Maybe he'd buy a porterhouse, medium, with all the sides, and some ice cream to top it off. He was tired of chewing old bones.

CHAPTER TWENTY-TWO

Sonntag sat in the armchair, staring at the wall. The *Journal* in his lap remained unread.

Lizbeth emerged from the kitchen. "Want a drink?"

He shook his head. She vanished into the kitchen again, and he heard the clatter of pots and the refrigerator door opening and shutting. When she emerged from the kitchen, she was not wearing her white apron.

"Get in the car. I'm driving," she said.

"Where are we going?"

"You'll see."

"What about dinner?"

"I put it back in."

"I'll drive," he said.

"No, you'd have a crack-up."

He could barely stand to sit in the passenger seat while she drove the old prewar coupe. He didn't trust women drivers. Only men should drive. So far, she had eluded disaster, but only because he was there to shout at her when trouble loomed.

Sulkily, he clapped his fedora over his graying hair and climbed in. She slid into the other side and started the car, inexpertly leaving the choke on too long. But the engine smoothed out. She eased the clutch out, and the engine died. She refused to look at him, started up, and this time maneuvered the Hudson down the driveway.

"Where are we going?" he asked.

"Oh, Tulsa maybe."

But on Hawley Road she turned north.

"Dinner somewhere?"

"No, you'd be impossible to eat with," she said.

"Well, I'm hungry."

She ignored him and pushed northward past North Avenue, and then Center, until she reached Capitol Drive. There she turned west.

He slouched sullenly in his seat, to let her know he was a long-suffering captive and a victim of her crazy whims. She'd probably stop at some fly-by-night women's handbag seller and ask him whether the patent leather one was better than the fake burlap.

She pulled the headlight switch because twilight was advancing. He thought it was too late. She should have turned on the lights in their driveway. She concentrated on driving, which was a good idea because people were zipping by at twice her speed. Some big crazy man in a green Lincoln Zephyr sailed past.

He considered bailing out at the next stoplight. He'd show her a thing or two about body-snatching. But she pushed west until there were empty lots and some four-plex apartments under construction. And then she screeched to a halt in front of a brightly lit outdoor place of some kind. It was a miniature golf course. There was a caddy shack, where one bought tickets and got a putter and a golf ball, and then a mess of tiny fairways, concrete with green felt pasted on top.

"What's this for?" he asked.

"For your wife," she said tartly.

She laid two quarters on the counter and got two putters and two battered golf balls and two scorecards. She handed one set to him, a queer smile on her mug.

"Ladies first," she said.

The first hole was a matter of timing. Just ahead of the pocket was a small Dutch windmill with rotating white blades that blocked the shot every few moments. One had to time the shot to get past the blades. She studied the thing for a while, lined up her putter, and when she deemed the moment right, she tapped. The ball sailed through, narrowly missing the windmill blade, and stopped an inch from the pocket. She whooped, walked over to the green, and tapped the ball home.

Then she stood leering at him. They both knew what was about to happen.

He'd show her a thing or three. He squinted ahead, studied the speed of the rotating white blades, studied the lay of the fairway, and thought he could ace it. He tapped it at exactly the right moment. It rolled steadily toward the momentary gap, but then he swore the blades speeded up and the ball conked the blade and died.

She was pretending to study the sunset.

He got a four.

"I don't have a pencil," he said, which was a fib.

"Just as well," she retorted.

The next hole was fiendish. It involved a banked left turn. If the putt was too weak, the ball would end up in a sand trap. Too strong and it would ride over the top into a water trap. And the pocket was on a tilted green.

She waggled her shoulders, wiggled her hips, and swung too hard. The ball raced up the banked turn, poised a moment, and they heard a splash.

He ended up in the sand trap. She won the hole because he tried to putt his way out, and ran up five strokes. She just took the penalty and went on.

The next one was simplicity itself. It was a long fairway that declined the entire distance, only to rise slightly at the end. The pocket was on a little plateau back there, surrounded by drop-off cliffs. He thought he could ace it, and almost did, and his ball ended up sliding back into the gulch. She ended up rolling past the pocket and off the cliff. But he putted the ball up and in.

He was starting to get pretty smirky. If she thought she was Babe Didrikson Zaharias, he'd show her a thing or two. He bore down, squinted at each challenge, hefted the putter like an old pro, lined up shots by sight, lined them up in reverse from the pocket to the ball, and started getting real fancy.

"Hey, speed things up a little, okay?" yelled a pair of zoot-suit kids behind them.

"Be careful who you're talking to, punk," he retorted.

Now she was getting smirky. She didn't do any of that stuff. She just eyed the hole, the ways a ball could go wayward, and tapped the shot. The miserable truth was that her shot was as good as his, or better. And they were neck and neck.

The punks, stymied by Joe's deliberate playing, turned kibbitzers and began making smart-ass comments.

"If I got a dime for every minute he wastes lining up a shot, I'd be rich," said one, who was just sprouting his first chin-whiskers.

Sonntag refused to let them rile him up. Maybe he'd just nab the pair for disturbing the peace.

A half hour later, they emerged from hole eighteen, which was an incline and drop-off shot. By then there were half a dozen parties behind them, half of them making acid remarks, which Sonntag ignored. He was going to win, and he'd do whatever it took, and if that meant lining up his shots, then he'd line them up.

Lizbeth leaned on her putter, looking bland.

"Well, what's your score?" she asked.

"I didn't keep score," he said. "You did."

"Mine's eighty seven," she said.

"Score isn't important. What counts is getting every shot

perfect," he replied.

They deposited the balls and putters at the shack and headed for the coupe. He'd just let her drive. Pile it up. That's what she'd do.

"Where you going?" he said when she continued east on Capitol.

"Mexican," she said.

"Are you sure that's safe?" he asked. "I mean, foreign food like that?"

She didn't reply.

She led him into a place full of bright colors with sombreros hanging on the walls, and gaudy serapes too. How could anyone stand to eat in a place full of primary colors?

"I'll order for you," she said.

"I'll get sick," he said. "Don't do this to me."

She ordered green enchiladas for both of them. A caramel-skinned *senora* in a scooped white blouse brought a bowl of salty chips, not bad unless they were poisoned by that sauce that came with them. Man, she was an eyeful.

Lizbeth was grinning.

"I had a fight with Ackerman," he said.

She dipped a chip into the hot sauce and was obviously relishing it. He feared he would have to carry her to the emergency room. She started wolfing down chips like they were the main course. He thought he'd better tell her the story before she collapsed. Chilies were obviously dangerous to one's health.

"I told him to go to hell," he said. That was an exaggeration, but he wasn't going to admit it. What he dreamed of doing and what he actually did were always two different things.

She downed more chips.

"You know where hunches lead cops? To injustice. I've seen it a few times. Some cop has a hunch. So we all go digging and scraping and we find some dirt, or we think we do, and then some poor bastard's hauled in, charged with something, and sent up the river, and the only thing wrong is that he's innocent, and he's a victim of some cop's itch to throw someone else into the slammer."

She dipped a chip into that red stuff and handed it to him. He bit gingerly on it, let the red stuff scorch his teeth, and finally ate it. If he croaked, no one would care anyway.

"There's no such thing as conscience in that place. I mean, if I begged off from an investigation because it offended me, I'd get my ass kicked. Ackerman's going to send some innocent people up the river, you can count on it, and everyone in there's gonna feel real proud. The PD doing its job, right? Some poor devil will spend his life's fortune trying to prove his innocence, and the months and years will go by and he'll never get out of Waupun, no matter what. That's what cops can do to an innocent man."

She dipped a chip into the sauce and handed it to him. It had more stuff on it, and went down hot in his mouth. He was hot, and the stuff was hot.

"What am I a detective for, eh? To keep peace on the streets? To put away the thugs? Sure. But also to do justice. I've got to make sure the innocent are safe. If one innocent person gets sent up, I've failed. How do I tell Ackerman that?"

She handed him another chip, dripping with hot sauce. He downed it, feeling the fiery chilies work down his gullet. She handed him another chip soaked in that stuff, and he pretty near swallowed it in a gulp.

A *mamacita* showed up with two plates. My God, she was pretty. There weren't any pretty foreigners like that in Milwaukee before now. Sort of Indian-looking. Great cheekbones. The plates had long greenish tan things on them, and rice, and some dark beans. She smiled and set them before Joe and Lizbeth. He stared at that stuff suspiciously. It looked like something he should not eat, would never eat, couldn't eat, and would regret eating.

So he ate. New flavors. He recoiled and came back for another bite. Good stuff. He couldn't even pronounce the name. *Enchilada.* It sounded like some city in Mexico with a red-light district a mile long.

She poured some of that hot red sauce over her stuff, so he did too. It might burn his tongue out, but by God he would show her he could take the heat. He chomped away, feeling the liquid lava pour down his throat, and feeling a little sweat rise on his forehead. Whatever this stuff was, it would purge the bile out of him, and he was ready for a sweat. He was in his fifties and he was a good cop, and this stuff was building a fire in him.

She dabbled with hers, like maybe she wasn't sure about it, but in spite of all her dainty eating she managed to reduce the beans and rice and those long things to rubble.

"I like it better than the Greek," she said.

He was awed. This stuff was an aphrodisiac. They'd probably outlaw it when the public figured it all out. No wonder the Mexicans were so prolific. He was getting sweaty and finished fast so he could get some air.

She paid. She had taken something out of the cookie jar.

They stepped into the April evening, and he wiped his brow. The air was cool and still and sweet. The scent of lilacs was on the breeze.

"Joe," she said. "Just reverse it. Instead of looking for something to hang on those people, look for things that get them off the hook. That's what you're there for. Turn Ackerman's investigation upside down."

He stared, absorbing that.

How the hell could any cop have a better wife? He held her hand all the way to the coupe and chauffeured her into the driver's seat, and closed the door carefully so her skirt wouldn't be caught, and let her drive him all the way home without scolding her even once.

CHAPTER TWENTY-THREE

Sonntag clutched the black stalk of the phone, and waited. Then the operator over at the law office came on:

"Mr. Bartles will be with you in a moment, sir."

Sonntag waited. And waited. It was intended that he wait. Bartles wanted him to cool his heels a while, waiting, waiting.

Finally, the attorney came on the line. "Lieutenant? You need something?" His voice was iceberg cold.

"Nope, don't need anything, sir. I just wanted you to know that we're still plugging away at finding out if Trouville had any relatives."

"Well, there's no need, Lieutenant."

"He was born somewhere, had two parents and four grandparents, and maybe some siblings and aunts and uncles. We'd like to find them for you, and help you get that estate settled."

Bartles didn't respond at first, and when he did speak it was with that measured tone of someone plotting out every word of every sentence.

"First, Lieutenant, let me thank the police department for your extraordinary diligence. I must say, I've never seen anything like it. Needless to say, your purposes have awakened my curiosity. Why this particular estate, and not the thousands of others for which there are no heirs or will? Now, let me say, sir, that in the absence of any criminal malfeasance or anything of that sort, this unusual quest is entirely unwarranted.

"Let me put it to you this way. Suppose Armand de Trouville

left no will and concealed his roots because he wanted it that way? Suppose he drew a veil over his origins because they embarrassed or disturbed him? Suppose he was ashamed of his family, and wished to have nothing to do with them? Suppose he died the way he wanted to die, something of a mystery to the rest of us. Isn't that his absolute right? Has a man no right to his own privacy? If he chooses to draw a veil, must we tear it aside?"

"I guess you're saying you'd prefer we stop looking, sir."

"I would prefer it. Absolutely. It seems a matter of, well, decency, that we respect Mr. Trouville's wishes. If he had intended that heirs be discovered, he would have left word."

"I understand, sir. And I'll convey your wishes to Captain Ackerman, who's pushed this investigation."

"That would be exactly the right thing to do, Lieutenant. And I'd be glad to tell him so myself, if that's what it takes."

"Just out of my personal curiosity, sir, do you have any idea why Mr. Trouville has kept his past so quiet? Or why he's used other names? Like Bolivar Newman for his etchings? We found a catalog listing his work, and most of it was done in Paris between 1919 and 1935."

"He's as much a mystery to me as he is to you, Lieutenant. No, I can't say."

"Okay, that's fine. Once you get curious about a life like that, you sort of want to keep digging," Sonntag said. "You probably have the secret buried among his effects, and that's the way it's going to remain."

"I have all his effects, and they are inventoried and stored, awaiting an heir or disposition of the estate, sir."

"Including the things taken from his body at the hospital?"

"Absolutely."

"Dr. Mauss said there was a stamped and addressed letter. Could that have been intended for a relative?"

"No, Lieutenant. That letter was addressed to the author of a book he was reading. I've not opened it; it's not my business. But the letter was addressed, I recollect, to a certain Gilbert Merchant, the author of a work on the history of counterfeiting he had on his desk."

"Had he dictated it?"

"No, the envelope was hand-addressed, and I could see enough through the envelope to know the note was in longhand. It's for his heirs to open, if they appear."

"If his stenographer, Mrs. Winsocket, didn't type it, I guess it's pretty personal," Sonntag said.

"Absolutely, sir. Now, if you'll excuse me, I have clients waiting."

"Of course. I just wanted to update you on the investigation. And I'll let Captain Ackerman know your wishes."

Sonntag hung the black receiver on its cradle.

Gilbert Merchant. Sonntag vaguely remembered the book, along with some professional papers, on Trouville's desk.

He dug up the number of the Milwaukee Public Library, and soon was talking to a librarian.

"Have you a copy of a book on counterfeiting by Gilbert Merchant?" he asked.

He waited a few minutes, and then she returned to her phone. "Yes, Lieutenant. It's called *Making Money: A History of Counterfeiting.*"

"Hold it for me please. I'll be there in ten minutes."

"Ask for Estelle," she said.

He eyed the weather through a grimy woven-wire window, saw sunshine, and decided to head right out. Silva was off on another visit with Harley Potter, and Walsh was trying to track down Trouville's prescriptions. That wouldn't be hard. Who knew where it might lead?

He ducked out. The hike would stir up his grumbling body.

The city was quietly going about its business. Cars stopped at stoplights. Streetcars ground to a halt at stops every other block, doors flapped open, people got on and off. A few toted umbrellas. He glanced upward but saw only blue sky, but in this place everything could change in five minutes.

The library had a welcoming quality about it, imposing and dignified, and redolent with the smell of books. He liked that smell. He stopped at the heavily varnished desk and eyed a handsome blonde of indeterminate years.

"Estelle, please. I'm Lieutenant Sonntag, and I talked to her a few minutes ago."

"I'm Estelle, sir, and I have your book right here."

She handed him the volume. As far as he could remember, it was the same as the one on Trouville's desk, but now with library binding. "You can sign for it on this sheet, just name and Milwaukee PD and phone number. We just need to know where it is, and you'll need to renew in two weeks, just like you had a card."

He did as instructed.

"Will this help you solve something?" she asked.

"Probably not. At least not a crime. But it'll maybe give me some insight into someone."

"I'd like to write a mystery, you know, like Rex Stout, in which a librarian solves crimes by researching books," she said. "Maybe I'll call her Goldilocks Holmes. Or Samantha Spade."

"I'd read them," he said.

She dimpled up, and he suddenly realized librarians were the best-looking babes in the world, better than movie stars because they had smarts. If there was one thing he'd learned from a long life, it was that dumb isn't pretty, not even if the face is as good as Ingrid Bergman's.

"Then I'll write the first one just for you. You're the expert," she said.

He grinned. "I just want to poke around in this. I'll get this back real soon."

"I'll be waiting," she said.

"Don't wait long," he said, flashing a smile.

He headed into sunlight, thinking he should spend more time flirting in libraries.

No sooner did he reach the bullpen when Ackerman landed on him.

"Where you been? You're supposed to stay in contact all the time."

"Library. Got a book to look at. About counterfeiting."

"What's that got to do with anything?"

"The book was on Trouville's desk when he died. I just got to wondering about it."

"You're reduced to that, are you?"

"Have a look," Sonntag said, thrusting it at the captain.

"I can't read," Ackerman said. "Comics, maybe."

They both laughed.

Sonntag settled in his carrel, studied the contents, and noted it was a chronological history of paper money, with chapters on the employment of currency as a medium of exchange, paper money issued by banks rather than governments, paper money backed by gold or silver, inflation, and then the more interesting stuff. The history of counterfeiting. How artists and engravers and people with back-room presses turned out fake bills, dollars, rubles, pounds, francs, pesos, you name it. There were chapters on how it was done, how the fraud was detected, defenses such as numbered bills, how counterfeit money was distributed, what denominations were most likely to be counterfeited, and much more. There was also a rogue's gallery of great counterfeiters, pictures of some, and their fates, if known.

Pretty good stuff. Maybe he'd even read a little of it. Maybe get Lizbeth to look through it. She had an instinct, and would probably give him some ideas about why a document examiner like Trouville would be reading the book.

The phone jangled. He wished the phone company would use quieter bells. His phone clanged like an ambulance. He held the ear piece to his right ear.

"Eddie here, Joe. I got a little something from Trouville's drugstore, Epperson's, up on Downer. Talked to the pharmacist. He said he was always glad to help the cops. Trouville wasn't taking much, but he did have a prescription for digitalis. The heart stuff. He said that an overdose is real dangerous. You want to watch out. It can cause heart failure. I said that's interesting, because that's what Trouville died of, and he said he didn't think Trouville would do that to himself. No one loved life more than that little guy."

"Anything else?"

"Yeah, I've poked around Potter's pharmacy just for the hell of it. Over in the Wisconsin Tower. Potter had two prescriptions—an old one for a liquid barbiturate and a new one for Seconal, both for sleep problems. The new one was dated last March."

"Seconal, like the suicide pill?"

"Yeah, the suicide capsule. Take ten, and it's *adios.*"

"Go talk to Potter if you can. Just to update him on our investigation. Ask him about a book on counterfeiting on Trouville's desk. It's called *Making Money.* What would Trouville be doing with that? I mean, what's the connection? What does a document examiner get from a book on counterfeiting? Technical knowledge? I'm just curious, is all."

"Yeah, that's interesting. That fellow's eager to help us."

"Ask him if Trouville ever talked about his ailments. What he was taking for them. Stuff he complained about. What he said about his ticker."

"Go at it sort of roundabout?"

"You bet. Aches and pains. People love to talk about their pains."

"Gotcha. I'll phone in or get it to you tomorrow."

Boris Dragovich phoned in from a booth at Milwaukee Hospital.

"Talked to the orderly about the Trouville case," he said. "His name is Arty Fillmer. Got that? Arty Fillmer. He doesn't remember much. It was just another DOA coming in. There was no rush. Trouville was long gone. Mauss picked up all the stuff on the body, and Fillmer copied it down. The class ring, bills and change and wallet, glasses, and whatever was in the breast pocket. So I asked him about that. What about the letter? What about the loose sheet with writing on it? He didn't know nothing. He said Schwartzkopf came in, real testy-like, and demanded the sack of stuff taken off the body, and disappeared with it. He went into an alcove there and looked it all over, and didn't pay any attention at first to Mauss. Then he put it all into the sack, and put the sack aside, and began telling the resident that there wasn't a need to go further; he knew the history. Trouville had died of heart failure. Put it on the certificate."

"Schwartzkopf didn't even examine the body?"

"Not if Fillmer's telling me true."

"Is that unusual?"

"Yeah, the orderly, he never saw anything like that. Usually death examinations are real slow and careful, at least when someone's brought in off the street. It's cut and dried when someone dies in the hospital, or when a doctor's been attending. But not off the street, like this one."

"Any reason, you can see?"

"Oh, hell, Joe, I don't know. That's just the way it all fell out."

"Thanks, Eddie. It's quitting time. I'll see you tomorrow.

We'll see if there's more to this Easter egg hunt, okay?"

Walsh laughed. "That's up to the captain," he said.

Sonntag didn't feel like braving the Wells streetcar and the Viaduct, so he decided to walk home, over fifty blocks. It would take most of an hour. And he'd be late again. But he wouldn't fall to his doom off those rails this fine April day. He collected the book to give to Lizbeth to read, and headed west, congratulating himself for not getting on the streetcar, then thinking he was a coward.

CHAPTER TWENTY-FOUR

Lizbeth hefted the library book, puzzlement upon her.

"What's this for?" she asked.

"I want you to read it."

"I have to reheat the meatloaf."

"Not now, not all at once. We have it checked out for two weeks."

"Big deal," she said, and hurried to the kitchen, where she knew and understood the world.

"You want a Manhattan?" he asked.

"Not if I'm going to read books. Why are you bringing me a library book?"

"I don't have brains enough to read."

"Ha!" she said. She was rattling around the kitchen, firing up the burners, and being thrifty with the paper napkins.

"I'll change my mind," she said. "I can't read unless I'm looped."

He set to work, noticing that she was turning the burners as low as she could to allow for some happy hour, or at least a happy half hour.

He poured some Old Crow over plenty of ice, added the vermouth, added a dash of bitters and a bright maraschino cherry, and handed it to her. Then he poured some whiskey over ice, splashed it with some tap water, and steered her to the cramped living room that a real estate agent would call cozy.

She settled across from him. He didn't pick up the *Journal* or dive into the Green Sheet, as he usually did.

She sipped a moment. "How come?" she asked.

"That book was on Trouville's desk, along with a couple of professional journals. In Trouville's breast pocket when he was found was a stamped, addressed letter to the author of that book."

"What did it say?"

"The estate's trustee, Trouville's lawyer, says he doesn't know. It's unopened, and shouldn't be opened. It belongs to the estate."

"I'd sure like to see what's in the letter," she said.

"I guess I would too. But it'll probably deal with technical things. If there was anything Trouville loved, it was technique, process. All that."

"This is about counterfeiting?"

"That's one thing that Trouville deals with to some extent. Forgery can include documents, stock certificates, all sorts of things that might involve printing or engraving."

"He was an artist?"

"Trouville may have done some etchings under some other name. I don't know the details, but it's two different deals. An engraver cuts tiny lines directly into the plate used to print copies. He uses engraving tools to cut into the plate. An etcher coats the printing plate with wax or gum or varnish stuff, uses tools to cut through the coating, then uses an acid bath to cut into the plate."

"So what do you want me do? Is this part of your investigation?"

"Oh, just read it. He was reading it. He obviously wanted to contact the author. He'd written a letter to mail just before his heart attack. It was handwritten, hand-addressed. Not a business letter."

She sipped her Manhattan, hefted the thick book, and sipped again.

"This book spooks me," she said.

"It's just a book."

"No, this is a big deal. This book is the biggest thing to happen since you started in on this. This book sends shivers through me."

He raised his glass. "Here's to your shivers, kiddo."

She glared at him and swallowed a slug of her drink. "What's it about?" she asked.

"Oh, mostly paper money, how it started, how it's used, how governments make it, and how crooks have tried to duplicate it and get rich."

"Okay, I'll read it. Maybe it'll help my art. I do the wrong kind of art. I like tempera. Maybe this will inspire me to start painting again."

"This isn't a big deal," he said. "I have to return it to the Milwaukee Library, but take a look if you can."

"It's a big deal. I just know. I have a hunch. Only you're going to have to explain it all to me."

"More hunches!" He laughed.

They had a dinner of overcooked meatloaf, overcooked asparagus, potatoes that started up whole and ended up mashed, and store-bought cookies. It was as funny a meal as he ever remembered. He thought he would walk home from work more often. Fifty-five blocks was nothing.

The next morning Captain Ackerman dragooned him into his smoke-soaked office.

"You're dodging me," the captain said.

"Nothing new to report, Captain."

"What do you mean, nothing new? You checked a book out of the library. You've got my best investigators looking at prescriptions. What's that all about?"

Nothing escaped the captain, it seemed. Sonntag wondered who the snitches might be.

"Lizbeth is reading the book about counterfeiting. The title on Trouville's desk."

"I have a hunch she won't find a thing. You've run out of leads, Sonntag. Where's your imagination?"

"Bartles asked me to tell you, sir, that this persistent inquiry into a man's past violates his privacy. And he said that there's something not decent about it. And he said that unless there's suspicion of a crime, it ought to be stopped."

"He said that, did he? He's right, Sonntag. It's indecent. I'm itchy to know what that little genius did before he showed up in Milwaukee. Maybe he worked for Al Capone."

Sonntag decided there could be no reply to that, so he just stood at the captain's desk and waited for the moment to pass.

"It's only a hunch," Ackerman said. "But it sure itches. It's like a bedbug in my brain."

"You want to let it go? There's other stuff."

"No, I don't want to let it go. I have a right to be irrational." He laughed. There was something infectious in Ackerman's laugh, so Sonntag joined him.

"Okay, you've got three or four detectives still chasing Easter eggs. You want to pull some off? Pull me off? I'd like to dig into that car theft ring."

"Nope, not yet. That's the fun about Milwaukee. Crime is all slow-motion."

"Okay, you want to send me somewhere? You got any leads for me? For Silva? For Dragovich and Walsh?"

"Hey, you're the sleuth. Get out your magnifying glass and start looking," the captain said. "And don't spend hours in coffee shops. I swear, the department loses thousands of work hours in every coffee shop around here."

201

"Not to mention chasing Easter eggs, Cap."

Joe Sonntag returned to his desk, wondering what the hell to do. How could anyone cope with a captain who went nuts if any cop had a cup of java on duty, but was ready to waste whole work-weeks of valuable time on a stupid hunch?

He hit the free doughnuts, poured a mug of Folger's, and hunkered down at his desk, wondering how to look busy. Maybe he could type up a lengthy report for Ackerman. Fill time. Maybe he could quietly start work on something else. That spring, crime had oddly taken a vacation, but he knew it wouldn't last long. With some hot days, there'd be plenty of hot cases, including a few new homicides. The summer rush began after Memorial Day and didn't quit until frost steered hooligans into their rooms.

Maybe he could look at some long-distance records.

He called his pal Monica Devine at Wisconsin Bell. Monica was an investigator's wet dream, a supervisor who loved to help and found ways around obstacles, some of them a little edgy.

"Monica, babe, this is your old doormat," he said.

"Joe! I haven't heard from you in a week! Are you still alive?"

That was how it always went. He usually did call her several times a month.

"I am, but I'm in the doghouse," he said.

"Well, I love dogs," she replied.

"Say, could you dig up some LD for me? Last two or three years?"

"That's easy. Is this a criminal deal? Are we dealing with a warrant and stuff?"

"Nope, it's sort of a missing person case. No, that's not it. We're trying to find a dead man's heirs and family. There's no crime. They guy left no will and no heirs have shown up. I'm hoping he talked to some family somewhere. He's kind of a loner."

"That's no fun. I prefer to solve a good murder."

He gave her Trouville's name and office phone number, and a brief rundown of the quest to find his heirs.

"I'll call you."

"Let's just try the past twelve months. And could you tell me where those calls went? I mean, the name of the person Trouville called?"

"Including secret wives and mistresses?" she asked.

"Yeah, and mobsters and confidence men."

It took her only half an hour. "He didn't use long distance a whole lot," she said.

"Well, lay it out, or would it be easier for me to come over there?"

"Nope. Trouville averaged only half a dozen long-distance calls a month, it looks like. Most of them went to lawyers. He talked to lawyers in California, Illinois, Tennessee, New Jersey, Massachusetts, Arizona, all over."

"Were they long calls?"

"A few. Most were like five minutes."

"Who else?"

"Law enforcement. District Attorney offices here and there."

"Anything else?"

"Companies. He talked to someone at typewriter companies, Smith-Corona, Underwood, Woodstock. And Parker Pen over in Janesville. He talked to the Kimberly Clark paper company in Green Bay. He also talked to Eastman Kodak."

"Any remaining calls, just people, not firms or companies?"

"A few to Illinois. I don't have those names, but I can get back to you."

"Yeah, those are the ones I'm most interested in, Monica. Calls to residences. The rest look like business calls. But we're hunting for relatives."

"I'll get back to you," she said. "There's a few of those. Is he someone important?"

"He's a dead genius," Sonntag said. "He pioneered a whole new science."

"I wish I could pioneer the science of pay raises," she said.

"I'll bring you a doughnut sometime," Sonntag said.

She cackled and hung up.

He knew she would bring him, without his asking, a typewritten transcript of all of Trouville's calls. Anyone in Trouville's shoes would be talking to lawyers and prosecutors and typewriter companies.

That's how it went that afternoon. She found calls to homes or apartments, and said she'd bring the names of the people Trouville called.

It didn't look very promising, but what the hell.

Eddie Walsh sat down beside him.

"I had another talk with Harley Potter," he said. "I told him we've still not connected with any relatives. I asked him whether Trouville ever took trips, vacations, not business. And Potter mostly shook his head. The little guy worked nonstop. He was so absorbed that he continued to rework closed cases, seeing if he could have done them better. That meant he didn't travel much. He always told Potter that the train to Chicago was all the railroad he needed. But when he did travel, he liked to go in style. His favorite was the Twentieth Century Limited to New York, but he liked the Super Chief out to LA just as much."

"What did the man do for relaxation, Eddie?"

"He didn't relax. He was driven. If times were slow, he would enroll in linguistics courses. Different places use different words. If you're from the South, you use words and phrases, all that stuff, that don't show up in the North. California's got its own way to talk. I didn't know that. I knew about the South. Groups got their own tongue. I guess it helped him pinpoint a forgery sometimes. He also studied the way people use letters. Like the

European seven, with the bar across it, or the Scandinavian *O,* with the slash. He just blotted that stuff up."

"Sounds like that little guy never slept."

"Yeah, well Potter and Trouville were always talking about sleep. Trouville would get himself knocked out because his mind would race all night. Potter, his mind didn't race but he just would stay awake, like on a permanent coffee jag. So they discussed drugs, like barbiturates, and even swapped some to see what would work."

"Anything there?"

"Yeah, maybe. Trouville tried some Seconal, didn't like it. It scared him. Potter says that stuff's safer than other barbs."

"Is this leading somewhere?"

"Nah, it's just a couple of single guys who need a couple of women, is how I figure it."

"Anything else?"

"Yeah, I'm tired of looking for Easter eggs. You think you can spring me?"

"I tried this morning, and I'll try again."

"I'll see ya, if I show up."

Sonntag smiled. Maybe this thing would wear itself out. Even that mule in the front office with his yellow cigars would quit pretty soon.

He checked his black lunch bucket, cleaned out some wax paper, emptied the thermos bottle and rinsed it and fitted it into the top, and signed off. He was done with another beautiful spring day in beautiful lakeside Milwaukee.

He was tempted to walk again, but took the Wells car instead. Lizbeth was a good sport, serving late dinners more than half the time.

She greeted him at the door with a hug and a huge smile.

"Fix me a Manhattan. I read this book all day. I know who Armand de Trouville was," she said. "It's in here."

Chapter Twenty-Five

He figured that was worth a big hug. No perfunctory peck tonight. So he clasped her tight, and saw that she didn't mind it a bit, and hugged right back, even if the potatoes were boiling.

"Okay, babe, spill the beans," he said.

"Fix me a Manhattan first," she replied.

"You'll get snockered," he said.

"Beats vacuuming the house," she said.

She turned down the heat under the potatoes and he collected the stuff to make her a cocktail, and pretended not to be curious about her sleuthing.

Soon enough they settled on the couch. She smiled, clinked his glass in a quiet salute, and sipped. "I could read all this stuff and bore you for an hour," she said. "You want to be bored?"

"Spill the beans or it's the third degree," he said.

She laughed. She was enjoying not telling him. "I'll need a few sips to get up to speed."

He saw how this was going to unfold, and resigned himself to his impatience. She loved to find clues and help him. Sometimes she really did help him, just by throwing light on something he hadn't considered. Sometimes her armchair sleuthing was just guesswork. But she had been so valuable over the years that he kept her abreast of everything, especially where there was a mystery about what happened, or who did what to whom.

"The book's got a lot of technical stuff, bank paper, engraving, inks, a history of paper money, a history of each country's paper money, like the pound or the franc. I sort of skimmed that. I headed toward a chapter called Rogue's Gallery, which was all about the best counterfeiters in history. Including one from Cicero, Illinois."

That sure got his attention. He sipped his Old Crow, knowing she'd get around to it. She was backgrounding him, and that was necessary.

"This book, it's copyrighted this year, nineteen forty-nine. I mean, it's new."

"I didn't bother to look," he said.

"So here's this chapter about the rogues, and it says that the biggest, most famous, and most mysterious counterfeiter of all time, bar none, was a young man named Hermes Debussy. And he never counterfeited a dollar. He produced brilliant five-pound notes that the British couldn't tell from the real Mc-Coys, and he produced hundred-franc notes that completely fooled the French. Hermes Debussy printed himself several fortunes, and completely eluded capture by France or England for many years. He was so good he could even process certain types of paper to appear more like bank note paper. And he was a master engraver, a genius—that's the author's word—a genius in every way, from his skill at duplicating a bill using his engraver's tools, to a genius at getting the ink colors right, and putting them on paper just so. That author said there's never been anyone even close to matching Debussy."

"That's a familiar name," Sonntag said.

"Yes, and the same family. Hermes was a cousin of Claude Debussy, the composer, but Hermes grew up in Cicero, the son of a prosperous coal and ice dealer. He spent his early years delivering sacks of coal for parlor stoves and ranges, or carrying ice into homes that needed it for their ice boxes."

"So?" He was growing skeptical by the minute.

She saw it, sipped, stirred her red cherry around in the amber fluid, and let him stew a while. She was plainly enjoying this all to hell and gone.

"Well, guess what, kiddo? Hermes got tired of delivering ice, and wangled a trip to Paris, and a got few bucks from his dad, and started in at the, what do they call it, the École des Beaux-Arts. And he took up engraving. And got in touch with his Debussy relatives over there. And guess what? His engravings were the finest they had ever seen. This was around the turn of the century. He was born in 1881. He made a name for himself, and began to sell a few. And with a little prosperity, he visited London, and traveled around Europe, always trying to sell his engravings, which he produced in small editions."

"I see the handwriting on this wall," Sonntag said. The Old Crow tasted mighty fine.

"He studied papermaking, and other fields, such as mezzotints and etching, and made use of the academy's equipment and whatever the faculty could teach him. And here's the deal. Somewhere along the way he began working on the five-pound notes, and the hundred-franc notes, and did nothing with any of these plates until he had perfected the whole thing. Meanwhile, he was simply a very busy student in his early twenties, considered a young master. But little by little, he was manufacturing millions of pounds, millions of francs, and stashing them somewhere, probably his attic garret five floors up from the streets of Paris. I've got to go turn off the potatoes."

She handed him the half-emptied Manhattan glass and vanished into the kitchen of their little bungalow. In a moment, she returned, collected her drink, and settled in.

"But you can figure out the rest of the story," she said.

"Actually, I'm having trouble with that."

"Okay, J. Edgar, here's how it ended up. Hermes ran into the usual problem. How do you put such a ton of money into circulation? He had several million pounds, or francs, up in his attic, and no good way to get rid of all that stuff. But he knew one good way, and that was to exchange pounds in Paris, and francs in London. So on his London trips he would play the rich Frenchman exchanging francs for pounds, and in Paris he'd turn into an Englishman and exchange pounds for francs. It worked for several years, because he never went beyond what was plausible for a wealthy young man to be carrying. He never told a soul, never had a confederate. He also found a ready market for his stuff among gold and silver dealers who were more concerned about whether the gold and silver was real than whether the paper was real. Pretty good, eh?"

"But he got caught. They usually do," he said.

"Yep, the French finally figured out that composition of the paper used on the phony franc notes didn't match the official paper the government used to print them. They alerted banks and exchanges, and suddenly Hermes Debussy's money machine came to a quick halt. They raided his attic and found millions and millions and millions of loot."

"So he was off to jail?"

"Yes, until the world war. He lived a terrible life in jail, and then the French badly needed every man they could get to fight the Germans, and they raided their own jails. If a criminal was deemed valuable or reasonably reliable, he was posted to the Foreign Legion, outside of France in Algeria. Some of the criminals were eligible for freedom after the war was over, and that was the last anyone knew of Hermes Debussy."

"End of author's story?"

"Yep."

"And you think the Cicero kid was Trouville?"

"Yep."

"And what do you connect?"

"His age. His height. Debussy was short and dapper. His training. His skills. Engraving and etching are similar. Trouville's stories about joining the Foreign Legion. North Africa. Going to school at the Beaux-Arts. Two languages, English and French. His wild story about his father being a chancellor at Buckingham Palace. And he mentioned Cicero, didn't he?"

"You're pretty smart, kiddo."

"So Debussy went straight. He became an artist. But that didn't earn much. So he used all his skills to pioneer a new field. If he was a genius in Paris, he died even more a genius here."

He sure had to hand it to her. "You're onto something, kiddo."

"Not me. Captain Ackerman kept saying there was a felony in that woodpile."

"Maybe he'll be satisfied with this, but I doubt it. He likes to get it all nailed down. And we haven't answered where Trouville was from the first war until nineteen thirty-six when he came here."

"Yes we have. He was back in Paris with a new name, Bolivar Newman, doing etchings of Paris landmarks," she said. "He had to make a living, and etchings were the way."

"Maybe," he said. His innate skepticism was at work now. Was Trouville this man? Might he have borrowed a past from someone? The more Sonntag pondered it, the less sure he was of all of this. Still, Lizbeth had made the first breakthrough. And right in their parlor.

She abandoned him to his musing and pulled a casserole from the oven. She always added stuff to the uninspired recipes and he had come to accept the dish he always thought was boring. No paper napkins this eve. She had rolled linen napkins into napkin rings and placed them at each setting.

She carted her Manhattan to their dining table, and smiled at him. Her face was suffused with a glow he rarely saw in her anymore. All the years of raising boys, struggling with a cop's pay, coping with Will's polio death, and sheer years of scrubbing and cooking had drained her face of that. But this night she glowed, and it was because she had, at least to her satisfaction, unlocked the thing that had knotted up the investigations bureau for days.

It's a good beginning, he thought.

Almost by unspoken agreement, they didn't talk of her discoveries that evening. But then, in bed, they did talk of it again.

"I'll get ahold of Stan Bartles in the morning. Maybe there's some heirs after all, down in Cicero. There might be some Debussy names there. Maybe the mystery's over. The estate will end up somewhere."

"He won't like it," she said.

"Is that another hunch?"

"Nope. How would you feel if you learned that your client Armand Trouville, the little genius, had a past?"

"I don't know that lawyers think that way. He might just be relieved to find some heirs and end the mystery. Settle the estate."

"I think he would just dismiss the evidence and not bother to look for Debussy heirs."

"Why do you say that?"

"I don't know. Reputations are all we have. Trouville's reputation was all he had. A good name is worth more than anything else."

That put Sonntag back on a line of thought he had pursued all evening, even while listening to Amos and Andy and Fibber McGee and Molly. What did that book do to Armand Trouville? It was on his desk the night of his heart failure. Had he read it? Did anything in it apply to himself? Was he Hermes Debussy? Did he think the book would destroy him? Was the publication of *Making Money* the beginning of the end? Had his whole life, lived honorably since the end of the first war, now come to disaster?

He tried to picture Trouville reading that book. If the connection wasn't there, and he wasn't Debussy in an earlier life, then there would be little to seize his heart and kill him.

And then there was something else. If Trouville had a past, what did that do to all the cases he had resolved? Over the years, there were scores of cases. Sometimes he testified in court, sometimes he simply supplied his expert opinion to lawyers. Sometimes he was a witness in criminal cases, involving forgery or fraud. Other times he testified in civil cases, such as lawsuits involving estates. What of those? His expertise had resolved litigation involving tens of millions of dollars. What would happen if it were now revealed that this little genius was also a genius at counterfeiting pounds and francs, had spent time in a French dungeon, and had mysteriously vanished in the wake of the first war? Would all those lawsuits be reopened? And what did the attorney Stan Bartles think of that?

He sensed it was all speculation. There were coincidences aplenty, but so far no solid link between the youthful counterfeiter and Trouville himself.

"I know what you're thinking," she said.

"Another hunch?"

"Nope. What happens to our genius if he's the kid from Cicero?"

"I guess we'll have to let the cards play out."

"You don't need to tell the captain right away."

"I have to tell the captain."

"You could look into it a little. Maybe there's no relatives alive. Then you could just drop it."

"I do what I have to do. If his reputation is ruined, it can't be helped. I think he was facing that very thing, and that's why he had the heart attack. I think his heart attack was his way out.

He saw this thing, this exposure, heading his way like an express train, and it was more than he could bear. I think a lot of heart attacks come just when life's impossible for someone."

"If that's what happened," she said.

CHAPTER TWENTY-SIX

He took Lizbeth's advice and thought to nail things down first. That meant Cicero. He contacted Illinois Bell information, and asked if there were any Debussys in Cicero, and was finally rewarded with a number. A Dominique Debussy lived there. He placed a person-to-person call, and was soon rewarded.

"Yes, my father was a coal and ice dealer, Lieutenant," the lady said.

"By any chance do you know of a Hermes Debussy?"

"Ah, may I ask what this is about?"

"We're simply trying to help an estate."

"Is there, shall we say, something wrong?"

"Not that we know of. We think maybe a sixty-eight-year-old man who died in Milwaukee recently might be Hermes. He left no will and nothing that might point us toward a family."

"That would be the right age, sir. What was his name?"

"Armand de Trouville," he said.

"That certainly isn't one I've heard before. What has this to do with me?"

"I don't quite know. I guess that's what's so tough about investigating something or someone."

"Hermes was my brother, Lieutenant. And he went to France long ago, and we never heard from him again."

There was something in her voice that suggested she was holding things back.

"You've lived there in Cicero all your life?"

214

"Yes. I taught Latin."

"And what did your brother do?"

"He went to school in Paris. My dear sir, surely this conversation is leading nowhere."

"Was he rather short, and a natty dresser, Mrs. Debussy?"

"I never married. No, he dressed dreadfully. He was the despair of the family."

"Do you have any photos of him?"

She hesitated. "I've put them away."

"I was hoping we might see what you have, and compare that to the man here who died. There's a small estate involved, you know. We're looking for heirs."

"Why would the police look for heirs?"

"Well, Miss Debussy, the man who we knew as Trouville was kind of a hero of ours. He did more for law enforcement and the investigation of certain crimes than anyone else."

"Crimes?"

"Trouville was a document examiner. He could spot forgeries, fake wills, things like that. We're just wondering whether he's the same fellow, and changed his name for some reason."

"I'm sure it's not the same man. Hermes was an artist."

"What sort of art?"

"It's not the same person, sir. I'm sorry to disappoint you."

"We would sure like to see some photos if you can lend them. We'll get them back. And of course, if there's a connection, you might receive something of his estate."

"This is very strange," she said.

"There's some information about Hermes in a book called *Making Money*," he said.

"Is that so?" she said, bristling. "Well, you've struck out."

She had obviously read it. The family black sheep. The conversation stopped.

He left contact information with her, and thought maybe she

would come around in a few days. He intended to call her in a week or so.

There had to be a bridge from Cicero, Illinois, to Armand de Trouville. All he had to do was find it. He slouched in his desk chair. In the next carrel, Eddie Walsh was booking a numbers runner. Beyond that, Mono Spina was collecting info on a hit-and-run from an elderly couple. Joe was their boss, but he rarely gave them direction. They went through their days doing what needed doing. They didn't need to please him. *We all have bosses,* he thought. His was Captain Ackerman, who was still running this Easter egg hunt. *One of these days,* Joe thought, *I'll be free to do something worthwhile.* He wondered how it was in private business. Everyone had a boss there, too. They would be as mean and crazy as bosses in government, but at least they had to put working people to good use or lose money. They couldn't afford to devote paid labor to crazy pursuits. He wondered how many bosses in private business smoked yellow five-cent stogies.

He headed into a blustery day and walked to the First Mariner Building, piercing its gloomy dark corridors lined with pebbled glass doors, until he reached Dr. Kessler's torture chambers. He found Agnes Winsocket perched at her desk like a tormented bird.

"Oh!" she exclaimed, and glanced at whatever was in her Underwood.

"Mrs. Winsocket, how are you?" he asked.

"Oh! I wasn't expecting you, Lieutenant." She seemed rather displeased to see him for some reason.

"We're still trying to find some heirs," he said. "Or some history, so we can track him down."

She seemed oddly ill at ease, with her shoulders hunched over her desk.

"Just one question. Did he ever talk about Cicero?"

"The Roman?"

"No, the city south of Chicago."

"Goodness, I don't remember."

"Did he send any letters there?"

"There might have been some. They should be in the files."

"We think he had family in Cicero. Ever heard of the name Debussy?"

"The opera singer?"

"That's close enough."

She pondered it, almost afraid to speak. Dr. Kessler appeared.

"You want something, Lieutenant?"

"We're still looking for heirs," he said. "Did he ever talk about Cicero, Illinois?"

"Al Capone's little town. Crookedest town in Illinois. That fits. Trouville was probably a mobster."

"Why do you say that?"

Kessler grinned. "I know one when I see one. Now, Sonntag, I'm glad you dropped by. Let you in on a little secret." He turned to Agnes. "That letter typed yet?"

"Almost," she said.

"It's addressed to the Trouville estate. I'm filing a claim against the estate for eleven thousand dollars. That's the amount of Agnes's labor he confiscated, over and above the agreed upon one-third of her time. He actually consumed two-thirds of her time for eleven of the years he's been here, depriving me of her labor. I've calculated it closely. He paid me a thousand dollars a year, and he consumed two thousand a year of her time. This letter's going to Bartles, the trustee. If he resists, it'll end up in court."

"Is there that much in the estate, doctor?"

"We'll find out, won't we?"

"How did that work? Mind telling me?"

"It's simple. Agnes was over there so much I had to have my dental hygienist, Dandelion, deal with patients, bill people, etc.

217

Sometimes I had to leave a patient and handle matters here in the waiting room. Trouville was stealing time from me and not paying, and now I intend to be paid."

"I suppose if there are no heirs you'll have a better chance," Sonntag said.

"I suppose so. But heirs won't slow me down."

"What if heirs show up?"

"They won't," Kessler said. "Count on it. It'll be my claim against an estate without heirs."

"What if Mr. Bartles defends the estate?"

"I know a few things about Trouville."

"Such as?"

Kessler smiled cheerfully. "Guess you'll have to wait and see, won't you?"

Agnes looked frightened.

There wasn't any more to be gotten there. The almost-typed letter to Bartles was rolled around the platen of her typewriter.

"Send me a copy," Sonntag said.

"No," Kessler said.

"What do you know about Trouville?"

"He couldn't tell the truth if he tried."

"How do you know that?"

Kessler smiled. "Put me under oath sometime. Then I'll talk for a week."

"Maybe we will," Sonntag said.

Well, that was interesting. Sonntag hiked back to the station, trying to make sense of it. It looked a little like a blackmail job to gut Trouville's estate of any loose cash. But so far, at least, there wasn't a felony lurking in the shrubbery. Kessler spotted an estate without heirs and decided to help himself.

Reputations mean a lot, Sonntag thought. Trouville may have gone to elaborate lengths to protect his. He was known as the impeccable expert. But what if he had a past? If he had something to hide, he was vulnerable. If his reputation were destroyed, would all his cases be reopened? Would lawyers file motions to vacate all those decisions based on his evidence? If a crook was testifying as an expert of impeccable reputation, what then? Would the history books be rewritten?

The station was quiet, almost as if Milwaukee had given up crime for the spring. Maybe it had. The budding warmth was too delightful to inspire robberies and berserk rages and ice pick murders. Silva and Walsh and Dragovich were all working on other stuff. He had quietly released them from his Easter egg hunt because there was nothing for them to do. Ackerman would give up eventually, and that would be the end of it. But this nutty quest could tie him up for another week, or two, or worse.

He settled in his swivel chair, feeling low. Or maybe it was spring fever.

He pulled out a legal pad and tried to put together a list of Trouville's stories about himself. Student in Paris. Raised in Quebec. Huguenot stock. Foreign Legion. Eating meals in Bedouin tents. Flying in the Lafayette Escadrille during the first war. Chased out of Chicago by the Mob. Working as an artist under the name of Bolivar Newman. What if they were all true? What if they were so improbable that they seemed to be fanciful stories, at least to the sober citizens of Milwaukee, yet were all based on truth, if not precisely true? Most people talk of their pasts; why not Trouville?

The man had died with a book on his desk. And there was an unopened letter in the estate addressed to the author of that book.

Ackerman bloomed beside him, a wall of blue trailing brown smoke.

"You've been dodging me," he said.

"When I have something to tell you, I'll tell you," Sonntag

replied. He was ready to dish back whatever was about to be dished at him.

"Where've you been? What's the long-distance call you made?"

"Maybe Trouville had another name. Maybe he was born Hermes Debussy, in Cicero, Illinois. Maybe not. I found a sister there of Debussy. A Latin teacher, never married. She was reluctant to send me any photos. She hadn't been in contact with him for years. She didn't want to talk."

"So who's Debussy?"

"World's best counterfeiter."

Ackerman's yellow cigar crackled and glowed. "So what's the deal?"

"Debussy printed pounds and francs early in the century and landed in a French lockup before the first war. During the war the French put some of their criminals in the Foreign Legion. They needed soldiers and most any crook would do, at least outside of France. They let him go when the war was over. After that, Debussy vanished. He never returned to Cicero. He never counterfeited again as far as anyone knows. All that stuff's in a book called *Making Money,* which was on Trouville's desk when he had his heart attack."

"That's the man. Now you got him."

"The hell we do."

"I knew there was a felony in there somewhere."

"You want to connect Debussy with Trouville? Be my guest."

"What did the sister say? Was Debussy short?"

"Yes, and dressed carelessly."

"Why won't she send a photo?"

"Debussy's a black sheep in her family. I'm guessing that's why. It's a closed book and she's not going to open it."

"Take the train down there and have a look."

"I don't think she'd let me through her door."

"Why'd you spring Silva and Walsh?"

"This is a dead end, and I haven't a thing for them."

"The hell this is a dead end. Put them back on the case. This is my Easter egg hunt, and by God, you're going to find every last egg, bust them all open, and eat them. Here's what you're going to do. You're going to find out what this Debussy did after the war. You're going to get a description of him and compare it to Trouville. And you're going to find out who killed Trouville and why."

"A heart attack killed Trouville."

"That's what the death certificate says," Ackerman replied. "But not what happened."

How do you argue against that?

Ackerman was chortling. Sonntag was wondering whether he ought to resign. He was awfully tired of the game. He wondered how many people walking the earth had bosses as crazy as Captain Ackerman. He wondered why he didn't clean out his desk and scram. He wondered how Ackerman had ever made captain. He wondered whether he'd put in enough time to retire. He wondered who was going to get hurt. He wondered whether to stick around all afternoon. He wondered what he'd tell Lizbeth if he came home in the middle of the afternoon. He wondered if he could get a job selling vacuum cleaners door to door. He sure couldn't sell anything to anyone, least of all his boss.

CHAPTER TWENTY-SEVEN

Frank Silva found him staring at the window.

"You planning to jump?" he asked.

Sonntag brushed him off.

"Don't open the bucket. I'm taking you to lunch. Lizbeth's sandwich will keep."

"I'm fine. Save your change."

Silva lifted the black lunch bucket from Sonntag's desk and motioned.

Sonntag found himself traipsing toward Wisconsin Avenue, with Silva firmly leading the way. Milwaukee was as quiet as a confessional. They turned into the Automat on Plankinton and Silva got some coins from the change lady and handed Sonntag some quarters, dimes, and nickels.

"Treat yourself," he said.

"Frank—"

"Shut up and eat."

Sonntag eyed the little windows that ran primly in rows, each with a coin slot and handle. Drop in the coin, open the door, pull out what you want. There wasn't much. Crummy salads, a decaying sweet roll, bowls of turgid gray soup.

He chose a chicken salad sandwich with wilting lettuce for two bits, some Oreo cookies for a dime, and a little carton of milk for a nickel. Water was free.

The place was too well lit. It was so light and bright it made his eyes ache. Blue-haired women with shopping bags and new permanents, old men with nothing to do, young mothers with their scattering broods surrounded a few tables near the street. The tables were all chrome and orange Formica. Silva aimed toward the rear, as far from the rest of the lunch crowd as he could get, finally settling on a four-top table in a corner.

"Well, thanks, Frank," he said.

"You're not going to quit," Frank said. "You're going to stick."

"I didn't know I wear things on my sleeve."

The sandwich was already turning dry, but it was serviceable. Not up to anything Lizbeth would make. But hell, he'd eat sawdust if that's what Silva wanted him to eat. This was supposed to be a treat.

Silva was eating some thick gray chicken soup, and Sonntag wished he'd opened that door instead of the sandwich door.

"I heard it, Ackerman and you," Silva said.

"It's nothing. Just a cold case. He's stubborn."

Silva spooned more soup into himself, and dabbed a thin paper napkin to his lips.

"It's no case. There's been no crime that anyone can finger."

"Yeah, and nothing but a few hints there ever was one," Sonntag said.

"And when you try to shut it down, beg off, he tells you to get your ass to work and solve it. What fun."

"He's a good man, Frank."

"Yeah, that's the trouble," Silva said. "This isn't just a cold case. A cold case is an unsolved crime. This time there's no crime, so there's no cold case. You're being pushed into finding or creating one. No wonder you're blue."

"I'm not a bit blue."

"I've been watching you wrestle with Ackerman for days. You're blue. You're shot. You're being a good cop, doing what he asks as best you can. But that needs to change."

"Don't say anything you'd regret, Frank."

"I know what I see. I also know there's no good way out for you. I also know I grew up in a different world from you, and I learned a few things from it. There are times to dig in your heels, no matter what the rule books say."

"Frank—don't."

"It's time for you to go on strike."

"Strike?"

"A sit-down strike. He'll keep on pushing you, and you'll simply sit at your desk and ignore him."

"I can't do that."

"Mohandas Gandhi does it."

"I've been a good officer all my life. I accept a chain of command. I need to give orders myself, and I expect them to be followed. I might not like what I have to do, but if I'm asked, I do it. I'm sworn to do it. I'm a sworn peace officer, Frank, and that's that."

"Just get nothing done. We'll all get nothing done. We'll all join you in getting nothing done until it dawns on Ackerman that he's off base, and backs away from this."

"No, Frank. Part of my job is loyalty. Part of my heart. And to make sure that every man-hour on the force is well spent. I can't betray my superiors."

"Even if what he wants is destroying you? And us? Listen, Joe, I haven't been a radical for nothing. Sometimes when things are bad enough, you strike. You get hauled off in a paddy wagon and booked. And the papers pick up on it, and people begin to think about things, and maybe some good comes of it, down the road. We've got strikes going all over town. There's a lot of blue-collar people like you and me who are walking picket lines and risking getting beaten up by cops, losing out to scabs, going broke, because a strike is the only way."

"Is this why we came to the Automat?"

"Yes it is, Joe. Let Ackerman roar and demand all he wants,

but I want you to ignore him, work on other stuff, pull us off this loony case. Just ignore him. That's the only kind of strike I'm suggesting. Go deaf whenever he starts in. I also want you to find yourself again. Ackerman's crawled into your head, and the more you let him, the worse you'll feel. Who are you? Sit back and remember who you are. You're a good officer. Okay, I've got this off my chest. Maybe I should keep my trap shut. I'm younger, and you're my boss, and if I'm in trouble for this, then that's the way it is. So yes, that's why we're at the Automat."

"I'm not blue, Frank."

Silva simply smiled and kept on spooning.

Sonntag stopped chewing on his sawdust sandwich and stared.

Silva was grinning. "Well, I tried. Okay. If you won't go on strike, then at least put the monkey on Ackerman's back where it belongs. Tell the captain we need whatever was in Trouville's breast pocket, and right now."

"A handwritten note and a stamped, sealed letter."

"Yeah, tell the captain that's the next thing we got to look at."

"Why do you think that?"

"The letter's addressed to an author of a book about counterfeiting. I figure it's just a fan letter. Trouville liked what the guy was saying. It was handwritten, hand-addressed. The other? The folded sheet? I don't know. Maybe it's important, maybe not. But we need to see it."

"We'd have to compel Bartles to surrender it, and that won't be easy. What do we tell a judge? What's our probable cause? What crime?"

"Tell Ackerman to think of something. He's the one who's looking for grubs under the rock. Or give it to the DA."

"Who's a pal of Bartles."

"Okay, Joe, lay it out to Ackerman and let him run with it. This investigation will now be his baby. Tell him he's got to take the next step, get the DA in and go to court for a warrant and try for a look at what was taken off of the body."

Sonntag drank his milk, and ate the last of the Oreos. He liked Oreos, even if Lizbeth disapproved of them. She always said she could do better.

"Throw the ball to Ackerman?" Sonntag said. "I'll be darned."

"Hey, the Automat's food is real good," Silva said.

They hiked back through a spring drizzle. Sonntag wasn't ready to jump out of any windows. Silva was cheerful.

No sooner did Sonntag settle at his desk than Captain Ackerman boiled out of his office.

"You're late. Where you been?"

"Captain, we got to talking over the big case. Your big case. I'll tell you what we need. We need to get Bartles to cough up whatever was on Trouville's body. And it's not going to be easy. Bartles isn't inclined to hand it over. I tried. So, Cap, now you can talk to the DA about putting the squeeze on Bartles. Go to court and get the order. And good luck."

Captain Ackerman digested that, puffed, exhaled, and blew rings. He stared out the window. "Tell me again?" he said.

"We need a warrant."

"The DA's going to ask me why."

"Because you have a hunch, and we are conducting an Easter egg hunt."

Ackerman's agate eyes flared and dimmed. He sucked his yellow cigar. He leaked noxious fumes.

"I'll talk to him. I'll get the warrant. Just watch me. Meanwhile, you connect Hermes Debussy to Armand Trouville. Follow the dotted lines, and fill in the color."

"Just like that."

"Just like that," the captain said, and vanished. Sonntag

watched him vanish into his office, where he would continue to smoke himself into a Virginia ham.

For the first time in many days, Joe Sonntag was enjoying life.

The bullpen was mostly empty. The beat cops were out; not a detective was in sight. He grabbed his lunch bucket and headed for the nearest uniform.

"You want a lunch? I've got one," he said.

The beat cop shook his head.

Over at the State Street side, Sonntag spotted a cop booking a kid. The kid was thin, grimy, clad in war surplus olive drab, and sullen.

"You want a sandwich, kid? Cookies?"

The kid stared and nodded.

Sonntag unhooked the cover of the lunch bucket and handed the kid the wrapped egg salad sandwich, and the chocolate chips. "Good stuff. My wife made it," he said.

The kid tore at the paper and began wolfing the sandwich. The beat cop stared. The half-completed form in the typewriter told the story. Vagrancy, minor in possession of cigarettes, public urination. There probably would be a few more.

The kid looked as if he hadn't eaten for days other than what he could steal.

The beat cop nodded slightly, and Sonntag slipped back to his desk.

He dug out the directory and looked up the Schwartz bookstore over on Wisconsin Avenue and reached a clerk.

"I want to talk to an author. How do I do that?" he asked.

"You'll need to reach the publisher, and see whether they'll connect you. Some authors don't want to be bothered, Lieutenant."

"Okay, the book is called *Making Money,* and it's some guy

named Gilbert Merchant that wrote it. Merchant, like a businessman."

"I'll need to look that up in the catalogs. May I call you back?"

"You bet. I'll be here for a while, ma'am."

The kid had demolished the sandwich and cookies. Sonntag poured some of Lizbeth's coffee into the cap and sipped. It was good. This spring day was just fine.

Ackerman had vanished and was probably putting a half-nelson in the district attorney.

The lady at the bookstore called back.

"Yes, Lieutenant. It's a Doubleday book. Here's what you do."

He got the number, which was in New York, and thanked the lady.

More long distance. Lots of long distance even if the department frowned on it. Sometimes a cop had to pay for it if someone higher up didn't like it.

But Sonntag figured he had Ackerman's okay, and that would be enough.

He dialed. "Operator, station-to-station long distance, New York." He gave her the number, and she busied herself connecting phone companies together. Finally, the phone rang, a distant clamor, and a last exchange of information.

"Long distance calling Doubleday. Go ahead, sir."

"Yeah, this is Lieutenant Sonntag, Milwaukee police, calling. You put out a book called *Making Money,* and I want to talk to the author."

"Just a minute, sir, I'll connect you to the editor."

It took only a moment, for a change.

"Garland Keenan here."

Sonntag let the man know what he wanted.

"Merchant? Sure, I think you can talk to him. It should be

easy, sir. He's in Milwaukee beginning a new book."

"Here?"

"Let's see, Pfister Hotel."

"Right now? Today?"

"Far as I know. He took the Twentieth Century Limited to Chicago, and then coach to your town."

"What's he going to do a book about?"

"You've got a genius there, Lieutenant. Apparently someone who's created a whole new field. Merchant wants to do a biography. The fellow's the most important man in the whole field of documents. I don't remember his name, but I gave him the okay. We're plenty interested."

"Ah, would this man be Armand de Trouville?"

"You got it! I'm not surprised."

"Ah, I guess I'll head for the hotel, sir. How long has he been here?"

"Oh, a day or so."

"I have some sad news for Mr. Merchant, sir. Trouville perished a few days ago."

There was a long pause. "The dickens you say," the editor said. "And we paid for the trip."

"A heart attack. He was in poor health."

"Is that who you wanted to talk to Merchant about?"

"Well, not exactly. The first book had stuff about a counterfeiter named Debussy."

"Well, you two should have something to talk about. Merchant thinks the two are the same man."

Chapter Twenty-Eight

A Pfister desk clerk answered promptly.

"Please connect me with a guest, Gilbert Merchant. Don't know the room."

"Sorry sir, I just checked out Mr. Merchant moments ago."

"Checked out? Did he say where he's going?"

"He canceled here, sir. Why, I can see him out front, getting a taxi."

"Catch him. It's important."

"Of course, sir."

Sonntag waited, heard some noises, and then a man's voice.

"Merchant here."

"This is Lieutenant Sonntag, Milwaukee police. I just talked to your editor and discovered you're here. But you're leaving? Can we have a talk?"

"Is something wrong, officer?"

"No, we're just trying to track down Armand de Trouville's heirs. He left no will. We understand you're doing a book about him."

"Was, Lieutenant. Not now. I came all the way over here to begin the interviews, and discovered he'd died. No one told me. It's very strange. You'd think someone would tell me. Long trip for nothing."

"You're taking the train?"

"In an hour. Milwaukee Road."

"You mind if I meet you at the station? Maybe you could fill us in a little about Trouville. He's a man we all admired."

"It'd be short, sir. I have to make that train. But sure. I'll meet you."

"How do I identify you, Mr. Merchant?"

"Five-ten, sixty, gray-haired, and wearing a black homburg."

"The homburg. That's all I need. I'm medium and look like a cop. See you in a few minutes. Depot waiting room."

He hung up, raced out, found a beat cop, Harry Turk, in a cruiser, and got a lift to the station.

Merchant was waiting there, easy to spot, carrying a black attaché case. His bag must have been checked through.

"You're right. You look like a cop," Merchant said, shaking hands.

"That's what they say," Sonntag said. "Even off duty."

They headed toward a heavily varnished bench that reminded Sonntag of a pew in an echoing cathedral.

"You came out here to start a book, and the subject died?"

"No one told me. We set up the interview weeks ago. I dropped him a note affirming that I'd arrive here in time for a meeting this morning. So I came, ready to take a lot of notes about the man. I found his office dark. The dentist next door said he'd died. Boy, that was a shock. I'm a long way from Connecticut."

"How much time do we have here?"

"Train leaves in thirty minutes, sir. Time enough to answer whatever you're looking at."

"We're looking for relatives, and trying to find out about his life before he moved here in thirty-six. Can you help us?"

"That's a mystery, isn't it? I've got it mostly figured out, and it's a whopper of a story. I was going to lay out what I knew, and see whether he'd cooperate, and if he didn't, too bad for him. There's a book in it."

"I've looked at your other book, sir. You've done a lot of work on crime that involves forgery, printing, currency, counterfeiting . . ."

"Yeah, and this new book would have followed suit."

"How so?"

"He's a mystery man. I really wanted to get a good look at Trouville. I've hardly found a recent photo of him anywhere. I think he was someone else once, and he's ditched one life for another. I think he was a big-time counterfeiter named Hermes Debussy, a guy who grew up in the Chicago area long ago and ditched it for Paris."

Sonntag could hardly hide his curiosity.

"You think Trouville's the same man?"

"Maybe you could tell me that. Have you seen him?"

"Many times," Sonntag said. "I'd know him anywhere."

"Then we can help each other," Merchant said. He snapped open the locks on the attaché case and pulled out some photos.

"These are Hermes Debussy as a young man. Got them from his only living relative, a sister in Illinois when I was working on the first book. Tell me what you see."

Sonntag studied each photo carefully. There was little doubt. He was staring at a young Armand de Trouville. These were early portraits, semi-formal, taken in a studio, an arm resting on a fluted pedestal covered with black velvet, another with a hand tucked into a suit coat, another profile shot, the young man staring upward into an ethereal mystery that shown light into his face. There simply was no doubt. The long nose and triangular head, the bulging forehead and hair combed straight back, the knowing look in the eyes.

"When were these taken?"

"Turn of the century, his sister says."

"I'm pretty sure this is Armand de Trouville."

Merchant grinned. "At last. I've been trying to piece this together for years. I came out here with one thing in mind: I wanted to walk into his office and see the man himself. See if there was a match. It's all a mystery, you know. Debussy vanished after doing hard time in France, and no one knows what happened after that. But he seems to have gone back to Paris, acquired a new artistic discipline similar to what he already knew, and changed his name."

"Bolivar Newman?"

Merchant stared. "You're very valuable to me, sir."

"We've run into blank walls. He's a famous man, you know. He's changed a whole branch of investigation. They think of him as a little genius."

"This lady, she's the spinster daughter of an ice and coal dealer in Cicero, and she knew nothing about anything when I talked to her two years ago. The kid went to Paris to study art, and that's all she knew—until my book came out."

A crowd was collecting at the gate. The orange Milwaukee Road coaches leaked steam.

"She's an heir, the sister. That's what we're looking for. Any chance I could borrow these photos?"

"I can have copies made, Lieutenant."

"Any chance I could borrow just one, this one here?" He fingered the one that most obviously revealed a young Trouville.

"Ah, I'd rather have them copied and sent to you. I can't replace these."

"The sister didn't like the book?"

"No, sir. She didn't like a book that revealed her brother as a master counterfeiter. She won't talk, or even read letters. I've lost contact with her. I can't blame her. A rotten brother like that. My book must have come as a shock to her. But I do have these photos, and they're the only proof I've got."

"They look like a young Trouville, sir. I'm confident of it."

A scratchy loudspeaker announced that Train Two Forty

Three for Chicago was ready to board, and would leave in ten minutes.

"Anything else, sir?" Merchant asked, tucking the photos in his attaché case.

"Yeah, your address. We're both chasing the same Easter egg."

Merchant laughed. "My egg just got broken," he said. "Here's a card."

"You'll get copies to me? We'll pay."

"Oh, hell," Merchant said. "Copy this one, and mail the original to me." He snapped open the case and pulled out the one Sonntag wanted. "And be absolutely sure to mail it to me as soon as you can," he said. "In fact, I'd like to see it in my mailbox when I get home."

Sonntag nodded. "I'll do it. And here's my card. One last thing. You can identify this as coming from the sister?"

"Look on the back, Lieutenant."

The name, "Hermes Debussy, 1901," was written on the back in a spidery hand. The photographer, Cyril Blavatsky Portraits, Cicero, Illinois, had also stamped the back of the photo.

"This is a big help, sir," Sonntag said.

They shook, and Merchant hurried off to the waiting coaches.

At last, Sonntag had a link. He was elated.

He hiked the long blocks from St. Paul Avenue back to the station, clutching the photo, which was in a cardboard oval frame. It felt like pure gold. He headed toward the basement, looking for Gorilla Meyers, the technical corporal doing the station's photography. Meyers was in his darkroom, light on.

"Hey, Gorilla, can you copy this fast?"

"Sure. Who's that?"

"Probably a man with two lives, a counterfeiter and a genius."

"Pull it out of the cardboard and I'll put a plate in," he said.

Sonntag eased it out of its soft cardboard frame and set it on the table. Gorilla clamped it into a metal frame, lit the original photo with frosted glass lamps to minimize glare, adjusted the focus of the overhead camera, and shot it, and did it again for good measure, and then the back side to catch the handwriting and photographer's stamp.

"Take it. I'll get the copy to you in a while," he said. "How many copies you want?"

"Three," Sonntag said. "One to file, two for use on the street."

He took the steps up to the bullpen two at a time and settled in his carrel to study the photo a while more. It was one of the formal portraits of its day, taken when a person had to stand very still or end up blurred. But this was a good image. There were very few photos of Trouville anywhere, mostly a few grainy newspaper photos. He had these in a folder, and soon was comparing Debussy to Trouville, using a magnifying lens to help him. The only thing he couldn't say for sure was how tall Debussy might have been. In the portrait he seemed taller than Trouville. But Debussy may have been standing on a box.

He pulled out Merchant's card. The man lived in Fairfield, on the Long Island Sound. Sonntag made notes of his hurried conversation with Merchant. Notes were always useful. Just to make sure, Sonntag thought he'd have a talk with Agnes in Dr. Kessler's office.

There was one thing more worth doing. He phoned Harley Potter, who answered at once.

"Sonntag here, sir. We think we have a portrait of Armand de Trouville as a young man. And if so, maybe we've found an heir. Mind if I bring it over to see what you think?"

"Sure, any time. You want to meet me at that outdoor patio next to the campus?"

"Suits me, long as it's sunny. Ten minutes?"

It wasn't sunny; it was overcast, so he grabbed his trench coat and hiked toward the university. He felt good. This business was almost over. What the captain really had wanted all along was to fill in the blanks, and now it was pretty much sure that Trouville had started life as Debussy. He found Potter in tennis togs, sipping coffee, not quite warm in the gray.

"Glad you could make it, sir. We've been trying to find something, anything, to give Trouville a family, parents, grandparents, siblings. Did he ever talk about Cicero, Illinois?"

"Yeah, he did, Lieutenant. He was fascinated that it was Al Capone's refuge from the Chicago police. He knew the town, too."

"That fits. We think he was born Hermes Debussy, a son of a coal and ice dealer there. Now I'll show you a portrait, and see what you think. Is this a young Trouville?"

Sonntag slid the portrait from the manila envelope and laid it before Potter.

The young man studied it closely, turned it over, read what was on the back of the cardboard frame.

"Sure looks like him, but I wouldn't swear by it. Lots of people look alike."

"Same jaw line, same bulging forehead, same eyes, don't you think?"

Potter seemed uneasy. "Where'd you get this?"

"Merchant. That's the author of the book on counterfeiting that was on Trouville's desk. He came out here to start another book, a biography of Trouville. He said Trouville was one of the authentic geniuses of our times. But also a mystery. And he was set to begin some interviews with Trouville, only to find out the man had died."

"Really? A book?"

"He said that Trouville's work was among the most important things ever to happen to crime detection."

"Yeah, but what about this portrait?"

"He believes, and I do too, that this young man from Cicero is the same as Trouville."

"How did he, you know, reach that?"

"You read that book?"

Potter nodded.

"Then you know that Debussy was the most successful counterfeiter in history, until the French got him. He was jailed there, but released to serve in the Foreign Legion, and after that war he vanished."

"He was probably Newman, selling very commercial etchings. If you knew him well enough he'd talk about his years trying to make a living with etchings."

"New Man, yeah."

"I don't know what I hang around here for," Potter said. "Now there's nothing left."

"What's the deal, Potter?"

"I can't step into the shoes, or buy the practice, of a crook."

"But he's not a crook. There's no evidence of anything like that following the first war."

"In the field of the expert witness, Lieutenant, any blemish is fatal. In court, the opposing lawyer says, 'Is it true you were born Hermes Debussy? Is it true you were convicted of counterfeiting? Is it true you served time in a French prison?' And after that, nothing that Trouville says, no matter how compelling, is bought by anyone. And it gets worse. Everything he testified to in previous cases is now suspect, and cases will be reopened. And it gets worse for me. If I were to purchase his practice, as I've hoped, the first thing an opposing lawyer would ask is whether I learned by trade from the counterfeiter and jailbird."

"I guess Gilbert Merchant really opened a can of worms," Sonntag said.

"Worse than that," Potter said. "Reputation is all an expert witness has."

CHAPTER TWENTY-NINE

There was that thing about Ackerman. When you saw him coming, you didn't see a person in blue; you saw a blue wall. This time the wall spread blue from right to left, and then Captain Ackerman sat down across from Sonntag.

He seemed subdued, and the cigar in his pocket was tightly wrapped in cellophane.

"I talked to the DA," he said.

"Poker O'Byrne or one of his staff?"

"Poker himself. I told him we needed a warrant for the stuff in Trouville's pocket."

"And he asked why?"

"I told him why. Suspicion of a crime. The death certificate was rushed."

"And what did the DA say?"

"Well, he said, 'Ackerman, you need to take an Alka Seltzer and quiet the rumble in your guts.' "

"So you don't get to serve paper on Stan Bartles."

"Not until I figure something else. You know what, Joe? During the war they called me Ack-Ack. Ack-Ack Ackerman. I always figured if you put enough shrapnel up there, you'd bring down something every time."

"You want more shrapnel?"

"You know, someone might get hurt," Ackerman said. "Didn't expect to hear that from me, didn't you? That's the trouble with shrapnel. It can hit friends."

"Well, you were right about one thing, Captain. There was a felony in the woodpile."

"The hell you say."

Sonntag pulled the portrait from its envelope and handed it to the captain. Ackerman studied it, and read the back.

"So?" he asked.

"That young man from Cicero, Illinois, went off to Paris, to an art school, and turned himself into the best counterfeiter in the world. The French finally nabbed him. They let him out during the war if he would fight in the Foreign Legion. He did, and after that he vanished."

"Where'd you get this stuff?"

"The author of that book on counterfeiting. Gilbert Merchant, Fairfield, Connecticut. He had several photos. I begged this one off him, and I'll return it shortly. Gorilla's making some copies."

"Tell me this deal."

Sonntag did, beginning with the quick interview in the Milwaukee Road waiting room.

"An old photo or two. That's not much of an identification. Lots of people look alike. And this one was taken forty-some years ago."

"Well? You knew Trouville as well as anyone."

"Same person," Ackerman said.

"Potter thought so too."

"What else did he say?"

"Potter? Reputation is everything for an expert witness."

Ackerman mulled that a bit. "Have you got a theory?"

"Merchant gets ahold of Trouville. He wants to do a book. So Trouville reads Merchant's first book, *Making Money,* and realizes that the author's close, very, very close, to exposing his earlier life and record. He wonders how Merchant found out about him, what he knows, what he'll ask in the interviews. If

Merchant figures it out, it's the end. Trouville's life work, which he's proud of, is ruined. He's exposed. Old cases based on his expert testimony are reopened. He's worried. He decides to tell Merchant not to come; no biography. The handwritten letter's in his suit coat, ready to mail in the morning. Don't come. Maybe Merchant will drop it. Maybe nothing'll happen. Maybe life will go on. But it's a worry. He can't sleep. He tries barbiturates, and some of Potter's Seconal. But the worry wears on him. He's diabetic, in perilous health. Then, that night, he worries himself into a heart attack and dies."

"Yeah, but why did the doc and the lawyer turn him into ash so fast?"

"To protect his reputation. The doc saw what was obvious, the heart failure, and hurried the examination. The attorney made some quick decisions, easy to do with no relatives, no wife or children around. Bury him fast and hope his reputation survives."

"Yeah, believe it if you want," Ackerman said.

"So what should I believe?" Sonntag was getting annoyed again.

Ackerman smiled, plucked a yellow cigar out, stripped away the cellophane, and lit up.

"We just haven't found it yet," he said.

"Found what?"

"The homicide."

Sonntag laughed. What else could he do? "Captain, it's time to fold this tent."

"There's still some Easter eggs we ain't found," he said.

Sonntag absorbed that. "You tell me what to do next, okay?"

"Forget the shotgun. Forget the shrapnel. Go after this with a sniper rifle."

"Thanks a heap."

Ackerman smiled, exuded a plume of mustard gas, and

ambled off to his lair.

Sonntag thought he'd write a book about bosses. They higher up they got, the crazier they became. He'd call it *Up Your Ladder*. Maybe Lizbeth would help him. It'd make the best-seller lists. Most everyone in the country had a crazy boss. Anyone in the military had a whole chain of crazy bosses. He supposed that if he ever made captain, he'd be crazy too.

He dialed Stan Bartles, and worked past the cool operator and the cool secretary.

"What is it this time, Lieutenant? Make it fast, please."

"I think we got an heir, Mr. Bartles."

"An heir? Who?"

"Long story. Want it on the phone?"

Bartles thought about it. "I'll listen," he said. "Frankly, an heir is the last thing I expected."

"There's a sister living in Cicero, Illinois. Trouville and her, they were children of a coal and ice merchant down there named Debussy. Like in symphonies. That was his name, Debussy."

"I think I want to talk to you privately," Bartles said. "Can we meet tomorrow?"

"Not now?"

"Come here early tomorrow. I'm in by seven. I start early, leave early."

"I'll see you around seven thirty."

Sonntag wondered what the attorney would say or do, far from secretaries, colleagues, and telephones.

Sonntag spotted Silva, and headed that way. "You got a moment?"

"I'm chasing rainbows," Silva said. "I saw Ackerman looking like he came out of a confessional."

"He confessed, all right. He went to Poker O'Byrne, who told him to take some Alka Seltzer."

"No warrant?"

"Poker needs something, anything, real to take to a judge."

Silva was enjoying all that, so Sonntag finished the story. "I told him it's time to fold the tent, and he said we haven't found the right Easter egg yet. He said he was known as Ack-Ack in the war, but shrapnel can bring down friends as well as enemies. He said to keep on looking for the homicide, using a rifle instead of a shotgun."

Silva was grinning. "And what does that mean?"

"Beats me," Sonntag said.

"You know, I keep having my own hunches, and they are all telling me that there's an Easter egg we missed."

"You, too. Frank."

"We should go over that death. Finding Trouville slumped over his desk in the morning, determining he'd been dead since the previous eve. We've got two direct witnesses, Potter and Winsocket. We've got the time of death from body temperature. What are we missing?"

"Anything that points to a crime."

"What does Ackerman think? I mean, what's bugging him? Sometimes people are intuitive. There's lots of strange things happen. We hear voices in the night. We dream."

"He sees something criminal in the way the death was handled. The death examination. The cremation. He thinks all that stinks, and we should be looking closer. That's fine with me, but so far, nothing's ringing any bells."

"If that's what's bothering him, let's see what we can find out."

"Yeah, it's worth a try. You got any ideas? I'm fresh out of them."

"Let's do some supposing, Joe. Suppose both the doc and the lawyer are deep admirers of Trouville. Suppose they realize he's great and amazing. Suppose they both intuitively want to do whatever needs to be done to protect the man. Suppose they'd move fast to squelch anything that injures Trouville's reputation. Suppose that Potter feels the same way, too. If anything happens that injures the reputation of this genius they'd try their best to cover it up, smooth it over. Suppose we're dealing here with a cover-up of some sort, like the three who know and admire the document examiner better than anyone else suddenly unite to preserve the man's reputation.

"But along comes Merchant. He writes a letter wanting to do a biography. They all rush to buy his previous book, the one on counterfeiting. They read it. And there's stuff in there that matches some of the stories Trouville's been yakking about for years. Studying in Paris. Foreign Legion. Doing some etchings. North Africa. Even Cicero. Why was Trouville always talking about Cicero? So Trouville's health deteriorates. He can't sleep. He doesn't know what to do about Merchant. The man's coming to Milwaukee to start a biography. It's not just Trouville who's worried. His doc knows enough about it to worry. His lawyer knows enough. His colleague, who's told us a lot about the importance of the reputation of an expert witness, he figures it out, too. Their man's in deep trouble. Merchant's coming, and he's got more in mind than writing a book. He comes to this town like the grim reaper, and all of Trouville's friends and colleagues rush to defend him. You know what I'm saying, Joe? Maybe this isn't a crime, like we think of crimes, so much as a cover-up. Protect the genius. Out of loyalty, out of admiration. And in Potter's case, out of financial interest. Where's he if his colleague had a past?"

"Maybe that's what I'll talk about tomorrow morning," Sonntag said. "The three men closest to Trouville have collected around him—to protect his reputation."

"Hey, you're the genius," Silva said.

They smiled. No one had ever before accused a lunch bucket cop of being a genius.

"I'll let you know what Bartles says," Sonntag said.

He collected his black lunch bucket and fedora and headed into a chill afternoon. He hiked down to Wells Street and waited for the orange car that would screech and whine him home. He wondered how many thousand times he'd stood at that corner, braving sun and wind and rain and snow, for the car to stop, collect him, and haul him to Lizbeth.

Milwaukee was a town devoted to science and technology. It made machines. It made shoes. It made beer and tractors and electrical equipment. And somehow it had made, or harbored, a genius in a field little known to anyone else.

The whipping wind rocked the car as it traversed the viaduct, making Sonntag white-knuckle the seat in front of him, but then he was on solid dirt again, and soon he was walking down 57th Street to the bungalow he called home.

He found a note on the kitchen counter. Lizbeth would be late. She was wrapping CARE packages at the church, and might not get in until six. She would have supper in a jiff when she got in.

He made himself a drink, Jim Beam this time, and ice and a splash, and settled into his armchair.

This day had been much like the others on this maddening case, or non-case. And yet, in some odd way, he and the rest had been making progress, working steadily toward something, something as yet unknown.

He sipped, feeling the initial shiver as the drink slid over his tongue.

There might be a crime, he thought. The saddest sort of crime. Some crimes were committed by ruthless or brutal men without a care for others. He had seen all sorts of cruelty, self-indulgence, utter heedlessness, over many years. But the saddest of all crimes were those that rose from love or concern or loyalty. Crimes rising out of the hearts of decent people, who feel compelled to break the law on behalf of someone else. Who hide things from the law, paper over things that go wrong. He had seen a few of those. One of the most common was when a spouse helped a tormented, pain-racked cancer victim to end the torment. It was a crime of compassion, yet it was illegal, and a man who assisted a wife's suicide would find himself spending the rest of his life in Waupun. Those were always the most agonizing, those crimes that rose out of desperate love.

And here were three men who admired the little genius, who may have tried to thwart the crisis that was upon Trouville with the future arrival of the author. And defend his sterling reputation. Sonntag didn't have much proof for what was becoming his own hunch, which was that Trouville's friends and colleagues were covering up a suicide, and trying to bury the man before Gilbert Merchant got off the train.

CHAPTER THIRTY

Sonntag could only wonder why the attorney chose to meet him so early, in the brown quiet of an office that had not yet welcomed colleagues and staff. Bartles led the detective into his conference room, with early light filtering softly through the blinds, and closed the door behind him.

"Well, sir, I'll tell you what happened," the lawyer said.

Sonntag settled into a leather chair; Bartles slid into the chair at the head of the polished table, perhaps because he was most comfortable there.

"The author turned Armand's world upside down," he said. "That book about counterfeiting. It turned out to be one of the greatest tragedies that I've witnessed."

Sonntag nodded. This was heading in the direction he hoped it would.

"We've always known that Armand's past was a little mysterious," Bartles said. "There were all those wild, romantic stories, which I'm sure you've heard. The art school in Paris, the French Foreign Legion, feasting with Bedouins in their tents, flying the Lafayette Escadrille in the first war. It all seemed to be about a man inventing himself. A man is entitled to his privacy, and we supposed it was just his way of obscuring his past. What always counted was that Armand was probably one of the great geniuses of our times, and also a man of impeccable reputation."

"I'm sure his vocation as an expert witness rested heavily on

247

it," Sonntag said.

"It did. No question about it. No one imagined he had lived another life, a life he disavowed, a life he put behind him. As you perhaps know, the Merchant book described a man named Debussy who was the most gifted counterfeiter of all time, a man who specialized in pound notes and francs, and was eventually caught by the French. And freed from prison during the war if he would join the Foreign Legion. And then disappeared.

"Merchant was plainly a gifted researcher. He pursued the counterfeiter from his childhood in Cicero to the postwar years—and then somehow connected him to the man we knew as Trouville. He wished to do a biography of Trouville—he said. You could call that his cover. Actually, he wished to connect the two men: Debussy the counterfeiter and Trouville the genius who pioneered a whole branch of the forensic sciences. You can imagine what Armand felt when he received the request and read Merchant's book, with its vivid description of a hidden early life."

"Despair?"

"Worse than despair, sir. Armand, my old and treasured friend, sank into a terrible depression. His life was over. An expert witness with that sort of background would be instantly discredited, no matter how sound his conclusions, and how expert his research. He was done. Ruined."

"He committed suicide, sir?"

"Well, now, it's my hypothesis that the heart attack he suffered did for him what he was thinking of doing. That the burden he faced was so crushing that his heart faltered, that he couldn't go on with life."

"Are you saying he didn't commit suicide?"

"I'm not saying anything, detective. I wouldn't know. He's dead. I have Dr. Mauss's signed death certificate. I've never discussed it with anyone, or questioned it. I know of no evidence of suicide, sir."

"Well, suicide is an unnatural death in the law, sir, and that automatically involves an inquiry."

"Yes, of course. But to the best of my knowledge, he died of heart failure. Now, as trustee of the estate I have various obligations, chief among them being to find heirs. I've discovered a living Debussy in Cicero and written to her saying that if she can supply evidence that Debussy and Trouville are the same person—photographs, things like that—she might well be entitled to the estate. She never replied. And I've advertised widely, inviting anyone named Debussy to respond. There have been no responses at all, Lieutenant. None.

"Now, it's also my responsibility to preserve the estate as best I can, and I consider preserving Trouville's reputation as a major part of that burden placed on me. Apparently Armand did agree to meet with Merchant. At least, I gather, Merchant traveled all the way from the East Coast to begin some interviews. But by then Trouville was buried, and I take some pride, sir, in hurrying that along. When the author arrived here, there was nothing for him to do. It was over. Merchant probably won't be writing anything more about Armand. I like to think that I've given Armand a final gift, letting him rest in peace, his reputation just as it always had been."

Sonntag listened skeptically, not quite knowing why.

"Did Trouville leave a suicide note, sir?"

For a fleeting moment, Bartles seemed to weigh what he would say. "Yes, Lieutenant, that was what was in his breast pocket."

"We're going to need that, sir. Suicide changes it. Everything taken from the body at the hospital. The letter addressed to Merchant, the folded note, the wallet and its contents, his pen, watch, glasses, ring, change—everything."

"Yes, of course. I do hope, Lieutenant, that your inquiry will permit my treasured friend Armand to rest in peace."

"Did you talk to Dr. Schwartzkopf about the death, sir?"

"I did."

"And did Dr. Schwartzkopf say it was suicide?"

"We didn't talk about that. We both simply grieved the loss of our friend."

"Dr. Schwartzkopf said it was a heart attack?"

"He didn't say anything of the sort. It never came up. I have only Dr. Mauss's death certificate. As I say, my hypothesis is that Trouville was contemplating suicide, but his heart failed him first."

"Dr. Schwartzkopf offered no explanation of the death?"

"Ill health. Diabetes. Trouville's fear of going blind. That sort of thing. He did tell me that at least Armand wouldn't face the prospect of blindness."

"Did he read the note in Armand's breast pocket?"

"If he did, he never said anything to me about it."

"Dr. Mauss, a resident there, said that Schwartzkopf greatly hastened the examination and concluded that cardiac arrest was the cause, and no further examination needed to be done. Do you know why Schwartzkopf hastened the process? Had he read the suicide note?"

"I have no idea, sir, and didn't know it had been done."

"So, you're saying Trouville was contemplating suicide, but died of heart failure."

"I'm not saying that. I'm hypothesizing it. I'm not asserting it. I don't know what happened. I'll leave that to you and your excellent detective staff."

"I'm going to ask you to turn over everything that was on Trouville's person, everything in the list inventoried by Dr. Mauss and his orderly. I'll give you a receipt for it."

"It's here, under lock and key, Lieutenant. I'll get it."

Bartles retreated for a moment and returned with a pocket

folder. He spread the contents on the shining table, along with the inventory sheet. There indeed was the unopened letter to Merchant, the suicide note, the wallet and its contents, Trouville's Parker 51 fountain pen, some keys, and change. The contents on the desk and inventory tallied. Sonntag scratched out a receipt using his own pen and handed it to the lawyer.

"I'll get back to you. There may be more questions, Mr. Bartles."

"I'll answer them all, sir."

Sonntag was out of there before any of the firm's staff showed up, with the evidence tucked under his arm. The door clicked softly behind him. Plainly, it was an uncomfortable moment for Bartles, and raised some questions as to whether Trouville's doctor and lawyer had somehow managed to hide a suicide, which in itself was serious business and might be a crime, depending on all sorts of things. At the same time, the interview confirmed some things. The Merchant book and the author's proposed biography had upended Trouville's life and threatened to destroy it and his work. And the lawyer and doctor, perhaps out of empathy, had tried to forestall whatever the author intended.

It would require a long talk with Merchant.

Back in his carrel he laid out the evidence once again. The wallet, pen, pocket items, ring, watch, glasses, and the note as well as the stamped envelope, still unopened. The suicide note interested him the most. It was carefully wrought, in Trouville's easily recognizable hand, the black words on a white page, brief and to the point.

To whom it may concern:

I have chosen to release myself from the future. Illness, the prospect of blindness, the uncertainty of my health, have taken their toll on me. There is nothing left. I live in torment. I am without hope. I desire only to rest in peace. My decision is entirely my own.

Armand de Trouville

Sonntag read it several times, letting his mind run any way it chose to run. It said nothing of a threat to his reputation, or scandal, or shame. It said nothing of Merchant, or a previous life, or a criminal record. But that may be exactly how Trouville wanted it. Perhaps in the dying, the books would be closed. The only odd note was the last line, that the decision was entirely his own. Who else might have influenced the decision?

Bartles had certainly been walking a delicate line. But for a death certificate attesting to cardiac arrest, he would have been required to make this suicide known to the authorities. Still, without medical evidence of suicide there was no reason to make the note public. This was going to require a long talk with Dr. Schwartzkopf.

Frank Silva loomed over the desk, and Sonntag handed him the folded note.

"I got the stuff from Bartles," he said.

"He covering up anything?"

"I don't know. He says not."

Silva arched a brow. "Very interesting. You gonna open that?"

They looked at each other, uncertain about opening a stamped envelope, and finally Sonntag shrugged and carefully slit open the envelope with his pocketknife. There was a brief letter within, addressed to the author.

Dear Mr. Merchant,

You put two and two together and ruined a man who has struggled to live an honorable life and contribute to the world's understanding of a species of fraud. Now everything is lost. My

*work, my reputation, my life. By the time you receive this, I will
be gone.*

Armand de Trouville

Silva said nothing. Trouville had dealt with the crisis his own
way. Or intended to, if a heart attack had not intervened.
Sonntag thought there were some questions that needed answer-
ing. Had Trouville's doctor attempted to cover up a suicide,
pushing the resident to ascribe death to heart failure? And if so,
what had Schwartzkopf concluded? And what did Bartles know?
And how much had been covered up, for whatever reasons,
including compassionate ones? Suicide was homicide, man-
caused death, and now the police would actively pursue the
matter.

"I think the doc and lawyer were simply trying to protect
someone they admired," Sonntag said.

"That doesn't make it legal," Silva said.

"No, but there wasn't any malice in it," Sonntag said.

"Maybe, maybe not," Silva said. "Hiding what an expert witness did to himself might unsettle some lawsuits."

"There's that," Sonntag agreed. "You want to go talk to
Schwartzkopf? Tell him it's now a homicide investigation. And
then ask him whether he read the suicide note before instruct-
ing Mauss to list cardiac arrest on the certificate." Sonntag
smiled. "He's not going to be a happy doc."

"Especially if his motives were simply to be as kind as he
could be," Silva said. "I'm off."

"I've got some things to figure out," Sonntag said. "Like, if
he actually was going to kill himself, how? There wasn't a thing
on his desk or in that office, at least from our look-see of the
place."

"Sleep medicine?" Silva said. "That's the old reliable."

"Yeah, and he borrowed some Seconal from Potter."

"Offhand, Frank, what do you think?"

"The dead genius didn't want to turn in his genius card. And his closest friends are covering up. Too bad for them. We're going to have to file charges."

"Here's the rest of Trouville's stuff. Do you see anything in it?"

Silva studied the wallet, driver's license, bills and change, keys, the Parker 51, and the letter to Merchant.

"I don't know why he wrote this," Silva said. "Why bother? It only confirms Merchant's suspicions."

"I don't either. People act strange when they're pulling the temple down on their heads."

"Well, let's find out," Silva said. "Are you going to share this trove with Ackerman?"

"End of the day," Sonntag said. "By then we'll have some answers. Frank, hold up. I'll go with you. Let's both see what the man has to say."

CHAPTER THIRTY-ONE

Sonntag and Silva found Trouville's physician in his offices on Wisconsin Avenue. They also found an affable and entirely cooperative man who delayed his patient schedule to give the detectives a few minutes.

"When Mr. Bartles phoned me about the suicide note, I wasn't surprised," Schwartzkopf said. "Mr. Trouville had been agitated and complained of lack of sleep. I prescribed a barbiturate, with some reservations. But I was certain he would handle it properly."

"What did he die of?" Sonntag asked.

"Heart failure, sir."

"It wasn't suicide?"

"Of course not. He had a long history of diabetes and associated cardiac problems. It was plain from the moment I saw him. The pallor was typical. And it all fit the history. Dr. Mauss, the resident, had already done a complete exam for trauma and had found nothing at all. I told him nothing more was needed."

"He thought you were hasty, sir."

"Trouville was my patient. I had his entire history in mind. I wasn't a bit hasty. On the other hand, if Dr. Mauss had jumped to the same conclusions, without knowledge of Trouville's history, that would have been hasty. Most certainly. But that's not what happened."

"Did you read the suicide note at the time?"

"How was I to know there was a note? The personal effects

were in a manila envelope. I don't happen to be interested in personal effects. It wasn't until Mr. Bartles phoned me today that I had an inkling of a suicide note. As I said, I wasn't shocked by it."

"His death was caused by the underlying diabetes?" Silva asked.

"Just a moment," the doctor said. He headed for the reception area and returned with medical records.

"Here. I see no reason why you shouldn't have a look."

There in a neat blue hand were the visits, the complaints, the diagnoses, and the treatments and tests. Blood sugar. Heart trouble. Deteriorating vision. Prostate trouble. The record extended back over many years. The barbiturate prescription was recent. Here was a complete and substantial medical history, and it dealt with a man with advancing diabetic disease and the damage it was doing.

"Had he talked of suicide, sir?"

"No, but he did talk of being under great stress at the moment. That was just a few weeks ago. He wanted something to calm him, to give him rest."

"His associate, Harley Potter, lent him some Seconal. Did you know of that?"

"I did not, and I would have warned my patient away from it. That's tricky stuff. I had no idea."

"Did you even consider suicide when you learned his body had been brought to the hospital?" Sonntag asked.

"Oh, I'm ready for anything, sir. One thing about medicine. You never know. I didn't suspect it, but I was certainly open to it, open to whatever tragedy of life and death that arrived with that ambulance carrying him to us." He paused. "You can imagine how I felt. He was not only a patient, but an admired friend and colleague."

"Colleague?"

"We've done some work together on symptoms of diseases that show up in handwriting."

"What happened to the personal items taken from the remains, doctor?"

"Those went to the administrator of the estate. There's a standard routine for that. The Milwaukee Hospital bursar turned those over to Mr. Bartles."

"It seems odd that no one would have read the note," Silva said.

"Are you saying, sir, that hospital employees should poke through the effects of a dead person?"

Silva shook his head. "Sorry, dumb comment," he said.

That's how it ended. Dr. Schwartzkopf shook hands, and offered further help if needed, and saw them to the front door of the suite.

It would be a long hike to the station, but they both felt like it, and started east.

"So much for that," Silva said. "I simply don't see anything that looks like concealing a suicide."

"And the body's ash," Sonntag said.

"And Ackerman's gonna growl at us."

"You know what, Frank? We're back to the starting gate. Unless you want to list Trouville's early life as a counterfeiter, there's nothing to interest cops now."

"Poor old Captain Ackerman," Silva said.

When they neared Marquette, Sonntag got an idea. "We could stop and tell Potter about the suicide note. If he's still around. I think he's been looking to move."

"Sure, why not?"

They found the boardinghouse, knocked, and discovered Potter, who was in the midst of packing. He was in dungarees and a khaki war surplus undershirt. There were wooden crates and cartons lying about. "Well, this is a surprise," Potter said.

"Yeah, we got a little news," Silva said. "A suicide note. Mr. Trouville's lawyer coughed it up."

"Suicide? Whose suicide?"

"No one's, apparently," Sonntag said. "But it was in your associate's breast pocket when he died. And it seems to have been a heart attack after all."

"Does this change anything?" Potter asked.

"Yeah, it seems to put an end to our game," Sonntag said. "There's not much that we don't have nailed down. That writer tracked down Trouville, and was connecting the dots. That upset your colleague. He died before he could kill himself. Natural death, according to his doc."

"This is all unbelievable, just unbelievable," Potter said.

"He must have been pretty agitated those last weeks, eh?" Silva said.

Potter gazed into space. "The only thing was sleep. He kept complaining he couldn't sleep. But if there was a wolf at his door, he never let on. When you got right down to it, he was as private a person as they come."

"You packing up?" Silva asked.

"Nothing left for me in Milwaukee. I can't afford to open up my own practice. I'd hoped to buy Armand's practice from the estate, and pay it off. But now, who knows?"

"Yeah, who knows?" Silva said.

"Will this suicide note be made public?" Potter asked.

"It's in our files," Sonntag said.

"So it's going to hang over Armand's reputation?"

"I don't see how it'd damage the man's reputation. That's not how he died. Now that book about counterfeiting, that's another deal. That would depend on whether Merchant can connect Debussy to Trouville and prove they're the same person."

"That's just more tragedy," Potter said. "Along comes a writer and he ruins my colleague. Everything gone. Poor Armand. All the years of research and figuring out how to examine questioned documents, and along comes some half-baked writer . . ."

"Yeah, along he comes, and you're caught in the backlash."

"I've got to start over," Potter said. "I'm still trying to figure out what to do. I know I'm just as good as he was, but he got all the credit. I've been thinking of applying to the FBI. Maybe they could use a document examiner."

"Good idea as any," Silva said.

"Is the investigation over?"

"Far as I know, but there's no telling what the bosses have in mind," Sonntag said.

"Yeah, well, thanks for telling me," Potter said. "I'm not surprised."

Sonntag and Silva continued their trek, mostly in silence.

"You know what?" Silva said. "Gilbert Merchant wrecked two lives, not just one. Potter's been waiting in the wings, wanting a chance to shine, and now he's found himself acting in the wrong play, with the wrong star."

"I was thinking the same thing," Sonntag said.

"Maybe it's worth a call to Merchant," Silva said. "Just to find out what he had in mind, writing that biography. It's not common to write a biography of a living subject, you know. Maybe the biography was his pretext. Maybe he really wanted to connect Debussy and Trouville. Isn't that why he had his pictures with him?"

"Yeah, but what's that got to do with anything now?"

"He drove a man to contemplate suicide."

"Is there a crime in it?"

"Probably not, but before we shut down, I'd like to ask him a few questions."

"I have his number."

"Yeah, let me know, Joe."

They found Ackerman looming over their desks.

"Where've you been? Why didn't you report where you were? I was about to raid every coffee shop in town," the captain said.

"Something urgent?"

"What's urgent is that you played hooky. We pay you and you suck java all day."

Sonntag carefully removed his fedora and settled it on his desk, where he kept it handy. Silva winked and sidled away, affecting to look at his mail.

"No Easter eggs anymore, Captain."

"Yeah, so tell me."

"Where do you want me to start?"

"With that stuff in the manila envelope. Where'd you get it?"

Had it all started at dawn this very day? Sonntag realized that it had. Captain Ackerman knew nothing of Sonntag's early visit to the law office, and what was entrained by all that.

"So, have a seat," Sonntag said.

Ackerman stripped cellophane from one of his dog turd yellow stogies and fired up. He plainly would make as much stink as possible.

"I think we've pretty well licked it," Sonntag said. "This stuff was in Bartles's safe. It's what's off the body."

"I know, I looked."

"You looked?"

"You hide stuff out on me, and I come after it," Ackerman said.

He was laughing his ass off. That was the thing about Captain Ackerman. He always smiled when he was massacring protocol.

In an odd way, Sonntag enjoyed it. Dealing with Ackerman always involved blunt-force trauma. There were no nuances. Everything was always on the table.

He told about the visit to Bartles's office early in the day, collecting the stuff, including the suicide note and the unsent letter. And Bartles's quest to find an heir among the Debussys of Cicero. And the interview with Trouville's doctor, and settling the question of whether the doc and the lawyer were concealing a suicide. And a long look at Trouville's medical records, with its history of progressive disease. And checking in on Potter, a young man who saw his hopes shattered by Merchant, and Trouville himself.

"He's quitting us?" Ackerman asked.

"He said he's going to try to take his wares to the FBI, if he can persuade them. There's no sheepskin for questioned document examiners. Lots of luck, I'd say."

"And work for Squeaky Clean Hoover. Now that requires ambition."

Sonntag went over what the day had revealed, while the captain sat bright-eyed, oozing smoke and hellfire. Weeks of investigation had uncovered a lot, and now the lieutenant was able to put it all into a narrative, a story of a wayward young artist from Cicero who turned his talents into a bonanza—until he got caught. And then the missing years, still not well anchored down, and then a new life as a questioned document examiner of sterling reputation. And then the death. No law had been broken, as far as Sonntag could see. The doctor's case was persuasive. The lawyer's conduct was as it should have been. If there had been no suicide, on the advice of one of the examining physicians, there was no need to take the suicide note to the police. Out of respect for Trouville, it would remain private.

And so it was over. No crime.

Ackerman puffed and glared and stared and studied the grimy floor.

"It's over, then," he said. "I've had this hunch, the damnedest hunch, and it was a monkey on my back, and it still devils me. But you've gone as far as anyone could go. We have the story, all but a little bit of it anyway, and you're right. If there wasn't a suicide, there's no cover-up. We won't be tossing the book at any professional people anytime soon." He stood, a wall of blue again. "We'll shut it down. No Easter eggs this time."

Ackerman lumbered off, and the whole world returned to normal.

The case was done. No more looking for Easter eggs or chocolate rabbits.

Almost done, anyway. Sonntag thought he'd give Gilbert Merchant a ring. Maybe the author could explain a few things.

And the weirdest thing of all was this: Sonntag had an itch, hell no, a hunch.

Chapter Thirty-Two

It didn't get any better than this. The case that had bugged him for the past couple of weeks was dead. Sonntag sipped a bourbon and water while Lizbeth boiled the hot dogs. The weather was just fine, and tonight there would be the dogs, good Milwaukee frankfurters, and vinegary German potato salad, the kind she whipped up herself, out on the back deck, in the sun-faded canvas lawn chairs that had comforted their backs for years.

He was glad. Ackerman had finally caved in, and seemed subdued just before Sonntag caught the streetcar. The captain was having trouble with it; there was no reason to keep the case alive, but his instincts were still howling.

Tough, Sonntag thought. *Tough luck.* A cop's gut feelings weren't always connected to reality. Ackerman had played this one for high stakes, invested his whole force in his hunch, pushed his hunch even when one piece of information after another pointed in a different direction. Stubborn old Ackerman.

"So, are we celebrating?" Lizbeth asked.

"Yeah, I guess so."

"You guess so? You mean you're not sure?"

"It's a dead hand, babe. There's nothing there. Even the smooth doc and lawyer managed to wiggle around any questions we had. It was a heart attack. He may have been wrung out, and may have been sick, but he died of natural causes."

"So why aren't you sure?"

He didn't know. She put a pair of wieners on his plate, some buns, a dollop of her ace potato salad, and handed it to him. He added some ballpark mustard, sliced onions, and a thin red line of ketchup, which took a long time leaking from the glass bottle. The dogs had split while boiling, and now oozed savory juices. Why did he always get so happy about something as simple as a hot dog? Lots of things tasted better. Lizbeth's meatloaf was better. But hot dogs rang bells in his belly.

She served herself and continued to work on her Manhattan, which was making her real smiley. Whenever there was an investigation and some insider stuff she could squeeze out of him before she read it in the papers, she got happy.

"Okay, spill the beans," she said.

That was her ritual request to stay current on his cases.

He told her about the early-morning visit to Bartles, how he was perfectly willing to pull out the stuff recovered by the hospital, the suicide note, the letter he opened, the visit with the doc, the stop at Potter's flat, and the rest of it, including his long talk with the captain.

"So Ackerman finally caved in," he said. "If there's a crime floating around somewhere, we don't know where. He got kind of morose. He hates to see a hunch go sour. He let his cigar die in his teeth. But anyway, we're done."

"Except you aren't," she said presciently.

"A call to Merchant in the morning, and I'll toss in the towel myself. I want to read him the letter. I've gone from liking the man to thinking he's a predator. The more I think about him, the more I get steamed."

She sipped, waiting.

"You know, he came here, he said, to start work on a biography of a great man. That sounded good to me. Someone should write a book about Trouville and what he achieved. But the more I think about it, the worse that gets. He also came with some photos he got from Cicero, and that means he didn't have a biography in mind. He was going to expose a man with a past, and probably try to make a sensation of it, and maybe use all the publicity to sell his book about counterfeiting. I doubt that he ever seriously considered a new book."

"That was a long train trip."

"His editor said the publisher sprang for it. He's probably just another predatory writer looking for prey, but I don't know that for sure. This would have been a dandy. Front page stuff. Great yellow journalism. Sell it to Hearst. Get to push his book on the side. Put it on the best-seller lists. Secret revealed. The foremost man in a field closely tied to law enforcement was once the most successful counterfeiter in the world. I just want to read that suicide note and the letter to him. I want to see what sort of man Gilbert Merchant is. Is there one bit of kindness in the man? Maybe I'm stretching the rules, making a long-distance call on a closed case. But I'm going to do it. I just want to know about this guy."

"I think he'll give you a prettied-up answer," she said. "Revealing the sordid truth is the noblest of all callings. Stuff like that. People sure have lots of excuses."

"You're my babe," he said.

"Then you can do the dishes," she replied.

The boys had always done them, when they had boys. But polio had taken Will, and the army had taken Joe Junior, and he figured he was the current kitchen police. He rinsed the plates and drew hot water and added the Ivory Flakes. It never took more than a minute or two anyway.

He caught an early car the next morning, and endured the grinding trip downtown in a light rain. He'd packed the stuff taken from Trouville's body into its manila envelope and put it in the desk drawer. It wasn't evidence anymore. He would return it to Bartles and the estate.

He called when it was about eight-thirty in Connecticut, and the great author would probably be up and caffeinated.

It was person-to-person, and the operator soon had Merchant on the line.

"Morning, sir, this is Joe Sonntag, in Milwaukee."

"Who?"

"Sonntag, Milwaukee police."

"Oh, yes. I remember."

"I sent your photo back. Did you receive it?"

"Yes, thank you."

"I'm still awaiting the photocopies you were going to mail us."

"Oh, I'm afraid . . . is it necessary?"

"I thought we would be trading information, sir."

"Yes. Perhaps I can do that."

"There's some new stuff I want to share with you, as we promised."

"There is? You nail him?"

"Nail him? I don't know what you mean."

"Expose the little crook?"

Sonntag thought the interview was going just about as expected. "We've been able to obtain some things that were in the estate, sir. One of those was a stamped, unopened letter to you. We opened it."

"To me? What did it say?"

"I'll read it. This is in his own hand, not typed. 'Dear Mr. Merchant, you put two and two together and ruined a man who has struggled to live an honorable life and contribute to the world's understanding of a species of fraud. Now everything is lost. My work, my reputation, my life. By the time you receive this, I will be gone. Armand de Trouville.' "

"He killed himself?" Merchant asked.

"No, he died of a heart attack before that happened. Stress, apparently. His doctor was quite sure of it."

"Well, I nailed him. Those pictures. That took a lot of digging, and I scored."

"There was also a suicide note, but he died before he could destroy himself."

"Isn't that something!" Merchant said. "This is the story of the year."

"He was greatly honored here, sir. He pioneered something valuable to law enforcement, and he was widely recognized as a first-rate intellect. A lot of people will be missing him."

"That makes it all the better," Merchant replied. "Little crook like that worming his way back into the world."

"I think his heart was broken, sir. He'd spent a quarter of a century at his new vocation."

"Well, he should have been on the FBI's Ten Most Wanted list."

"How did you spot him, Mr. Merchant?"

"Lucky break and some guesswork. What would an ace engraver do? Enter an allied field. Like etching, an art form pretty close to engraving, but different technique. And there was this etcher named Bolivar Newman, who did a bunch of work in Paris in the twenties, and then did a few in the Midwest. Then, when talking to an art dealer, I found out the document man, Trouville, admitted to doing etchings in France. So all I had to do was nail it down, and when I got the photos I thought I could. But he croaked first. What a lousy break."

"Maybe you were his lousy break, Mr. Merchant."

The author laughed. "Maybe I was. Does that cover it?"

"For the moment," Sonntag said, and hung up.

He headed for the men's room, got a paper towel and some soap, and washed down his telephone. He wiped and wiped the earpiece. Then he retreated to the men's room and scrubbed his hands.

Trouville's stuff lay on his desk. The last, intimate things the man carried with him, the things that formed a life. There was the worn leather wallet, the somewhat battered driver's license. There was a key ring, with the keys to his apartment, office, car ignition, a file cabinet, and another unidentified key or two. There were some crumpled singles and some change. The Parker Pen was a beauty. A lot of Wisconsin people owned and used them. They were known everywhere as the finest of their kind.

Sonntag pulled the pressure-fitted cap off the pen, and wrote with it. The deep blue ink flowed as readily after weeks of storage as it would have the day the pen was filled from one of the Parker ink bottles with the reservoir in the top. Sonntag idly wrote his name with the fine pen, capped it, and put it into the envelope. He would deliver the stuff to Bartles. It belonged to the estate, as long as there was no police usage for it.

Maybe he should do that now. He liked to tidy things up after a case. Get things in place, or back to owners. It was part of being a good detective. He made sure all the others in his unit did the same.

He spotted Silva, settling in for the morning. "Hey, I'm going to take this stuff back to Bartles," he said.

"You sure that's not evidence?"

"I'm never sure of anything," Sonntag said. "But we can't hang onto stuff. It's not ours. That's the rule."

"Even the suicide note?"

"It wasn't a suicide."

"I'd sure like to squirrel it away on our evidence shelves," Silva said.

"I know what you mean," Sonntag said. "I'll be back in a bit."

He remembered it was raining, and he would need an umbrella and one of the department's waterproof pouches. He found one, stuffed the manila envelope in it, donned his trench coat and fedora, and headed out.

It was only when he stepped into the soft, warm rain that it came to him. He paused a moment, turned around, headed back to the bullpen, and studied his own handwriting. Yes, the pen taken from Trouville's body was filled with Parker's own blue-black ink.

He stared at the signature. Then he dug out the suicide note, the letter and its torn envelope, and examined them closely. Black ink. He took the letter and note and his own signature to the grimy window, and let the gray light tell tales. Black ink. Blue-black ink.

Silva was staring.

Sonntag returned to his desk, pulled Armand de Trouville's pen out, uncapped it, and tried again. Blue-black.

He handed the pen to Silva. "Write something," he said.

Silva scribbled his name.

Sonntag handed him the letter to Merchant. Silva looked puzzled. Then Sonntag handed him Trouville's suicide note, which had been in Trouville's breast pocket.

Now Silva got it. "It's evidence after all," he said.

Sonntag called Stan Bartles.

"I hate to trouble you again, sir. Do you have a file with some letters from Armand de Trouville?"

"Why yes, but they would be confidential."

"I don't need to read the letters, sir. We'd just like to see how Mr. Touville signed his name. We could do that under your supervision, if you wish."

"Oh, just come along. I'm sure it'll be fine."

He and Silva headed into the rain, with Trouville's papers secure in the waterproof pouch, and hiked over to the east side.

"This thing, I thought it was over, and it keeps coming back," Silva said.

When they reached Bartles's office, they were escorted to the conference room, where the file, labeled Trouville, lay on the waxed walnut surface of the conference table.

There were only a few letters. Trouville and his lawyer hadn't corresponded much, and mostly for the record. There was one handwritten note. The rest of the letters had been typed by Agnes Winsocket, and had been signed, in ink, by Trouville. They had all been written or signed with blue-black ink.

CHAPTER THIRTY-THREE

The lieutenant and Frank Silva hastened toward the Marquette district, ignoring the rain. They had one thing in mind, though it hadn't been expressed between them.

Potter was in the midst of moving. A trucking firm was at hand, with two teamsters loading crates of stuff.

Potter looked puzzled. Two cops weren't what he expected.

"Hey, we wanted to say goodbye, and get your address," Frank said.

"I don't know for sure . . ."

"We want to get ahold of you in case more stuff turns up," he said.

"It'll have to be a care-of address with a cousin."

"Yeah, okay. Hey, I forgot my pencil."

"I'll do it," Potter said. He headed into the bedroom, emerged with a fine gray Parker 51, along with a pad, and scrawled his name and an address in Denver.

"It's a shirt-tail relative," he said.

The ink was black.

"Thanks, Harley. We've enjoyed working with you," Sonntag said. "You gonna go into the document business on your own?"

"I think so, if I can't get a slot with the FBI."

The teamsters were loading crates onto their dollies and wheeling them out.

"You got enough experience here? From Trouville?"

"Three years."

"Yeah, that would be time for all that technical stuff, like typewriter fonts. But what about forgeries? You gonna be okay with that?"

"Listen, I could spot a forgery better than Trouville," Potter said. "I was born with the knack. You know how? Forgers take too long to write a name. They want to be accurate, so they go slow and careful and sometimes there's a tiny tremor that shows up. If you want to forge a name, master how it looks and do it fast."

"Learn something new every day," Frank said.

"Some day, come to Denver, and we'll look at a few forged names," Potter said.

"Too busy now?"

"Oh, this just isn't the right time. Thanks for stopping by, gents."

"When are you leaving?" Sonntag asked.

"The truck pulls out this afternoon. I'll camp on a cot in here tonight, and get off in the morning."

"That's a long drive."

"And an old car, too. Bald tires, almost. I'll just have to take it slow."

The detectives beat a retreat, and Silva tucked the address deep inside his suit, to protect it from rain.

"That sure as hell was black ink," Sonntag said. "But it doesn't prove anything."

"We'll see," Silva said. "There's a lot we don't know. Like whether the suicide note's a forgery. Ditto the letter. Who else might have a pen with black ink? Whether Trouville borrowed a pen with black ink. Whether Potter had the skill to forge not only the signature, but also Trouville's writing? I mean, the forger had to master Trouville's entire alphabet. And why. Always why."

"This ain't done yet," Sonntag said.

They were a long way from a chain of evidence that would connect Potter to a death a doctor was certain was a heart attack. If it had been Potter, he thought, they might never nail him. Blue-black ink. What the hell kind of evidence was that?

Back at his desk, Sonntag headed straight for the phone and got Bartles on the line. "Hey, I'm really sorry to bother you again. I'm really eating your time. But Mr. Bartles, this case is wide open again. We think the suicide note and letter were forged, and that suggests something very bad happened to Armand de Trouville."

"My God," Bartles said. "What can I do?"

"Dig every note that he wrote to you out of your files. We need them."

"For comparison?"

"Right. Comparison. Do you have some?"

"Oh, sure. There's notes scattered through the files. I used him as an expert witness several times, and he often wrote notes. Tell you what. Give me an hour and I'll come over there with what I got."

"We can pick them up, sir."

"No, I want to come. I have a reason. In all the years I've worked with him I learned a few things. We talked for hours about things, preparing our cases. I'm not the expert witness; I'm a lawyer, but I just want to help out. Give me time to shift some meetings, and time for my clerks to dig up stuff. Say an hour or so."

"We're grateful, sir."

Sonntag sat at his desk, absorbing the wild swing of fate. Outside, spring rain splattered on the windows, stripping city grime off of them.

He collected the suicide note and letter to Merchant, Trouville's pen, and also Potter's scribbled address, and headed for Ackerman's office.

The big cheese was on the phone, but waved him in, glowering. The captain was in a bad mood. He got that way sometimes, especially when an investigation went sour.

"Yes? Don't waste my time," Ackerman said after he hammered the earpiece down.

Sonntag steered around, behind the desk, until he was beside the captain. Then he spread the note, the letter, and Potter's address before the captain.

"This is Trouville's pen, taken off his body by the hospital." He uncapped the pen and slid the cap over the back of the smooth surface. "Here. Write."

"What the hell?"

"Your name will do."

Ackerman scribbled his name. "So?"

"Look harder," Sonntag said.

"Don't play Chinese checkers with me, Sonntag."

"What color is the ink in Trouville's pen?"

"Jaysas," the captain muttered.

"That address. We just had Potter write it down a few minutes ago. Black as the ace of spades."

"Well, arrest the sonofabitch." Ackerman was grinning again. That's how he was.

Bartles showed up even before the hour had passed, armed with a briefcase and dripping rain off his hat.

"Let's get at this," he said.

Sonntag steered them toward an interrogation room with an empty table. Bartles swiftly spread his cache, which amounted to seven memos and notes from Trouville. Two of them had been written in light blue ink; the rest in his typical blue-black. The ones with darker ink were more recent.

Sonntag laid out the suicide note and letter, along with its envelope, and Potter's scribbled address. By then, Silva and Ackerman had hastened in.

The cops simply waited while Bartles studied the material.

"I'm not a document examiner. This is not an expert opinion," he began. "But I learned a few things along the way. Armand de Trouville loved to share what he'd mastered. I can see a couple of things straight off. First, as Armand aged, he acquired a tremor. These lighter blue memos are from the war years, and there's no sign of a tremor. But look at the tremor in these more recent ones."

He pointed at the lines that seemed to proceed uncertainly, letters that were the work of an unruly hand. It was subtle, but there. Trouville's own hand had deteriorated as he lived through his sixties.

"Now, on these black-ink ones, the suicide note and letter, I don't see a tremor. They seem more confident. Does that seem right to you gentlemen?"

"Yeah, but I'd hate to arrest someone on that alone," Silva said.

That seemed a good enough response.

"Okay, here's another," Bartles said. "One thing Trouville was always saying was that people's signatures vary a great deal. They're affected by mood, tiredness, haste, and lots of things. That's why a document examiner collects every authentic signature he can. But a forger usually works from only one signature, and tries to duplicate it exactly. He does it over and over, until he can write a signature just like the one he's copying. Now look here. The signature on the suicide note and the letter to Merchant are identical."

He pulled the two sheets together until the signatures were as close as possible.

"Here's another," Bartles said. "These black signatures are larger than Armand's. Size is always a clue."

Sure enough, the black signatures were a bit bigger than the blue ones.

"He told me that forgers somehow make that mistake over and over. Maybe they're just so proud of their work that they don't notice it."

The black signatures were clearly more opulent than the blue.

"Now there's going to be different treatments of the individual letters, in spite of the forger's intent. That's where you'll need to get a document examiner. I don't have that skill. I just have a little knowledge on the cuff."

"There's still one in town," Sonntag said.

"Mr. Bartles, what do you make of all this?" Ackerman asked.

"I can't really answer. I can't give you an expert opinion."

"Well, just a wild guess, then."

"It wasn't a heart attack," he said. "And if I'd had the slightest inkling of any of this, you would still have Armand's remains to autopsy. I'm sorry."

"Yeah, well, we can't undo that," Ackerman said.

"So how do we go from blue and black ink to proving a homicide?" Sonntag asked.

"That's your province, not mine, gentlemen."

"If we've got the right suspect, maybe we can trip him up," Silva said.

"That's going to take some doing," Bartles said. "There's a valid death certificate citing cardiac arrest, and some ash in a small metal box."

"Does anything show up in ash? Like a poison, or arsenic?"

"You gents will have to talk to your expert."

"We'll need to keep this stuff for a while. That all right, sir?"

"As long as you want it. I hope it leads somewhere. Armand was my friend. And also the best expert witness I've ever met."

"You think Gilbert Merchant had anything to do with this?" Sonntag asked.

"Certainly. The last time or two I met with Armand, he was restless, agitated, not himself. I wondered what was wrong. He never said a word, and I didn't know what he was facing until I read Merchant's book, which was in the effects. Then I had a pretty good idea."

"Say, could you get that book to us?" Sonntag asked. "I'd like to look at it. Things that might be marked, folded corners, things like that. I'm wondering who read that copy. Trouville did, obviously. But who else?"

"I read the entire book," Bartles said. "But I rarely mark a book, especially one that belonged to the estate." He thought a moment. "I know where it is. I'll send it over."

They saw him off, and stood around.

"Now what do we do?" Silva asked.

"Get the expert, if we can," Sonntag said.

"Likely his phone's disconnected," Silva said.

"I'll find out." Sonntag headed for his desk.

The phone rang. Wisconsin Bell hadn't disconnected it yet.

"Yes?" Potter said.

"Sonntag here. I know you're busy, sir. This is a bad time for me to call. But something's come up. We need a document examiner. Do you think you could drop over here for a few minutes?"

"What about?"

"The trustee for the Trouville estate, Mr. Bartles, thinks that the suicide note and letter found in Trouville's breast pocket aren't authentic. He brought them over. He's worked with Trouville for years, and these items bother him. We told him we'd get some expert help if we could, and you were still around. Think you can make it?"

"Really? He's worried about that?"

"Yeah, he feels something's not right, and it's really bothering him. I told him we'd look into it."

"This isn't a good time, Lieutenant. I'm trying to shut down here. I'm waiting for Wisconsin Power and Light."

"It'd just take half an hour. We'd have to send these things off somewhere for an analysis. Look, I'll see about paying you. You're the man to help us."

Potter didn't respond for a bit. "Ten minutes. I'll eyeball it. A real examination would take hours. It'd just be a first impression. If you like my analysis, maybe you could give me a letter of recommendation. I'd sure like to hand something like that to J. Edgar Hoover."

"I'll ask Captain Ackerman about it," Sonntag said.

"Give me a half an hour. I've got to wash up."

"That's fine," Sonntag said.

He headed for the interrogation room and plucked up Potter's address. Then there was nothing on the table but Trouville's memos and notes, and the black-ink suicide note and letter to Merchant.

"What're we gonna ask him?" Silva said.

"Don't push. Maybe we can just let him wander into the woods without a shove."

"Joe? Maybe the dentist did it. Maybe Agnes Winsocket. Maybe Harry Truman did it. Maybe Cardinal Spellman did it."

"Maybe we'll end up with a suspect, some human ash in a box, a valid death certificate, and a case that will never close," Sonntag said.

"Yeah, there's one thing I want to know," Silva said. "Did Potter read Merchant's book about counterfeiting? I want to know that real bad."

CHAPTER THIRTY-FOUR

It took an hour, but Harley Potter finally showed up. He had donned a tennis outfit—white slacks, tennis shoes, and a white polo shirt—and looked like he was ready for some match games at the local club.

"Sorry," he said. "I needed to clean up. Moving's a grimy business."

"Yeah, well, glad you're here," Sonntag said.

He and Silva led Potter to the interrogation room, switched on the light, and waved at the display on the table.

"What we want to know is, the note and the letter. Are they for real?" Sonntag said. "Stan Bartles dug into his files and brought us a few memos from Trouville. That should give you some comparison, if I understand how this works."

"I think you do," Potter said. "Is there more light?"

"No, but I can bring you a flashlight."

"Please do. This isn't enough light. I wish we were in the lab."

"Well, have at it," Sonntag said.

"You must know how this works," he said. "I'd need some bright lights and a magnifying glass to say anything I'd stand behind."

"Just a rough idea, that's all we need. It probably won't come to anything, but Mr. Bartles was disturbed by this, to put it mildly."

"So much the worse for me," Potter said. "I'd hoped to

continue the firm."

Silva returned with a flashlight, and Potter began studying the various materials one by one.

"Is there a magnifying glass anywhere?" Potter asked.

"Gorilla Meyers has one in the darkroom," Sonntag said. "Would you get it, Frank?"

Potter stopped his survey until he could continue with a glass.

"The implications of this are awful," Potter said.

"How so?"

"There were people who suffered loss, disrepute, even prison time because of Armand's testimony," Potter said. "People who might want to hurt him. Does that say it clearly enough?"

"I guess it does."

"I just can't imagine anyone doing that. Not Armand, the kindest soul on the planet."

Silva returned with a magnifying glass, and Potter set to work, somehow vigorous and contained as he studied the documents. At last he stood straight.

"There is very preliminary bad news," he said. "These two suicide documents are forged. I have no doubt of it." He pointed to the note and letter. "There's plenty wrong, even with a cursory look. Let's take the obvious, which is that Armand never used black ink. These are black. That simply was not what he did. And these two signatures are identical. A sure sign of someone practicing a forgery. Forgers practice a signature until they can duplicate it. And that trips them up. And these are both larger than the authentic ones. But here's the main point, and why I needed the glass. Armand had a slight tremor. You can see it here, and here, and here," he said, pointing at the memos. "In fact, by following the dates of the memos, you can see it intensify. Here, these lighter blue ones, from the late thirties, there's none that I can detect. But here, the most recent ones, it's quite obvious." He pointed at various hesitations in the lines. "But there's another thing that's plain if you know what to look for. The person who drafted these signatures is left-handed."

"Left-handed?" Sonntag asked.

"Definitely. He had to control several things commonly done by lefties. He had to control the slant of the letters, make them look right-handed, and he didn't entirely succeed. Notice how the slant varies in the letter to Merchant and in the suicide note. Here and here and here. Now notice how the slant of the letters in Trouville's real hand is uniform. Here and here. You could say that the hand of the forger was rebelling against the task."

That seemed obvious now that Potter had pointed it out—with the index finger of his right hand.

"I just am sickened by this," Potter said. "I don't know what to think."

Ackerman, who had slipped in during all this, tried to sum it up. "So someone left-handed definitely forged everything in Trouville's breast pocket?"

"Yes, left-handed. This might be the work of an ambidextrous person. But it's definitely a fraud. I'll vouch for that."

Sonntag thought he could take it a step further. "Mr. Potter," he said, "could you put your conclusions in writing for us?"

"Sure. Then I've got to get back to the flat. My landlord's going to inspect it."

Silva eyed Sonntag and smiled. Ackerman's eyebrow arched. Bartles turned studious. Silva found a paper and pen, and Potter set to work, using his right hand to set down the conclusions, which he numbered.

The rest of them stood there, watching Potter's right hand as if it could tell tales, and indeed it could.

"I hope it helps," he said, and handed the sheet to Sonntag. "It's a point-by-point summary of my conclusions. I could type up a report later if you'd like."

Sonntag nodded. No one there really cared about what was being written. Potter's easy right-handed penmanship is what absorbed them. Silva eyed Sonntag and gently shook his head. Sonntag got the message: Potter wasn't their man.

"Did you read Merchant's book on counterfeiting?" Silva asked.

"Only the bookmarked chapter," Potter said. "The one about the most famous and successful ones. Armand told me to read it, so I did."

"Why did he ask you to do that?"

"He said that things might change, and if they did, he wanted me to carry on."

"And what did you conclude from that chapter?"

"That I'd taken a bullet through my heart."

"Could you explain that?" Silva asked.

"All those stories, Trouville's romantic nonsense—sir, they weren't nonsense, and he wanted me to know that. I put it together. We never spoke of it again. But it was there. Something terrible might happen to Trouville and his reputation and his practice. I didn't know what or when or what he wanted of me, only for me to carry on. I was the person he had given his knowledge to, and there was no other on earth. Oh, of course, there are other document examiners, but Armand was, well, unique. So I've been on a sort of watch for weeks, a watch that turned into a death watch."

"You expected him to kill himself?"

"I didn't expect anything."

"You've spoken of your unhappiness with him, shall we say . . ." Sonntag said.

"That puts it mildly, sir. I had moments of deep bitterness, moments when I thought he'd simply confiscated my own work, my own conclusions, and used them to glorify himself. But you have to understand something. I was in the presence of a genius. And Armand had chosen me as his successor, the one to carry on his work. That, well, in the end, it humbled me. He was never a father; not even a father figure. More like, oh, I was an apostle."

It was odd, the stretching silence.

Ackerman broke it. "How do you think your mentor died?"

Potter looked about, helplessly. "I'm not a detective, sir."

"Take a guess. Was it suicide? Heart attack?"

"I just can't say, sir. But those items in his pocket were forged. Now, are we done here? I really need to get back."

There was an odd pause. It seemed a decision that Captain Ackerman should make.

"Done, Mr. Potter. But write down your address for me," the captain said.

They studied Potter's writing once again. Then Potter capped his Parker pen and handed the forwarding address to the captain—with his right hand.

They watched the young man hurry out. Sonntag felt pretty sure Potter was clear. So did the rest, he thought, after glancing into their faces.

"We don't have a suspect," Silva said.

"I think we do," Sonntag said. "Kessler. The left-handed dentist."

"Next door?"

"It occurred to me when I saw these notes. Kessler's a man with disciplined hands. He can make them do anything he wants. They've been in Armand's mouth. He is a brilliant dentist. But he's also a man I would not wish for a friend."

"Why?"

"He's the most sour man I've ever encountered. He loves pain, and loves applying it, and loves his contempt for those who writhe under it. But that's not the part of him that I'm thinking of now. He's probably the finest dental surgeon in the country. He can repair jaws and restore teeth better than anyone alive. He can even move teeth in a gum, and do it all in his office. And yet he's won no great recognition for it. No one writes him up. He has no altar boys or pilgrims. No one crosses the oceans to sit at his feet. He hated Trouville, whose genius is obvious to everyone familiar with forensics."

"And he's a lefty," Silva said.

Sonntag smiled. "A lefty is right."

"Do you know anything about Kessler's claim against the estate?" Bartles asked. "Ten grand. For usurping the receptionist."

Ackerman shook his head and smiled wolfishly. The captain scented downed prey.

"Is he ever in his office evenings?" Sonntag asked.

"Who knows?" Silva said.

"Is he a record-keeper? Would he record a visit to his office, say, the night of the 17th?" Sonntag asked.

"He sure kept Agnes busy."

"Would he record the use of anesthesia?"

"I think he would account for every pill, every drop," Silva said. "That's one thing that kept his receptionist so busy."

"Even if his intent was . . . not dentistry?"

"It's his nature, Joe. If he does something, it'll be there."

Silva had a way of reading people.

"We've got a box of ash, a death certificate that says heart failure, a forged suicide note, a left-handed forger, and a bitter lefty dentist. You gents want to go connect the dots?" Ackerman asked.

"There's something I don't get," Silva said. "How would Kessler know enough to forge that letter to the writer? Merchant? How would he know enough even to forge a suicide note?"

"Good question. Agnes maybe?"

"Or Merchant," Sonntag said.

"Go kill the Easter bunny," Ackerman said, and began to peel cellophane.

"We gonna need search warrants?" Silva asked.

"Let's see what we find just moseying first," Sonntag said.

He clapped his battered fedora over his gray-shot hair and Silva followed along, hatless. Funny thing. Young men weren't bothering with hats.

He'd been over this route so many times he could almost count the steps to the First Mariner Building. The Milwaukee River flowed swiftly between walls of offices, bearing away the wetness of spring.

"What do ya think?" Silva said.

"I think we'll encounter one cool dentist."

"How should we do this?"

"Torture," Sonntag said.

"Ha ha."

"I think I'll torture him."

They exchanged the bright day for the gloomy confines of the First Mariner Building and made their way up mottled gray steps and down the long dark corridor, metered out by pebbled glass doors emitting melancholy light, with black names on them. Trouville's suite was dark, but light shown next door, from Dr. Kessler's offices.

Agnes was at her desk, looking pale and overworked.

"Why, it's the policemen," she said, mustering a smile.

"Yeah, we'd like to talk with Dr. Kessler. It's about your neighbor, Trouville," Sonntag said.

"He's, um, with a patient just now."

"How about after that?"

She peered over her half glasses at an appointment ledger. "Um, not a good time today, sirs. May I ask what it's about?"

"Yes, there's some questions about Trouville's last hours."

"Well—I suppose I could ask him. He's working on his wife's upper molar."

"We'd like a few minutes with him. Confidential, of course."

She slipped past three patient rooms. Sonntag could glimpse a patient in one, sitting there in the black and chromium-plated chair with a white bib on, awaiting his fate.

There was a lab in there somewhere, with a dental technician who manufactured ceramic teeth and plates and various other stuff. And a woman named Dandelion who acted as his assistant, spraying water over bloody holes and urging patients to spit.

Agnes reappeared. "He'll see you while he works. He says his wife won't mind."

Sonntag and Silva eyed each other and followed. Sonntag thought he'd never interviewed a dentist or patient in the torture chamber itself.

Agnes ushered them in. There wasn't much room. Kessler, in his white dental coat, was drilling away on a gray-haired woman whose head was thrown back until she was staring at the gray ceiling. The little pulleys whirled, and the belts delivered power to the chrome-plated drill that Kessler was deftly using in his left hand.

"We have company, Mabel," he said. "So don't whine."

CHAPTER THIRTY-FIVE

Mabel's sweaty white hands gripped the dental chair as the drill cut away enamel.

"Mabel's neglected this cavity for years, and now it's time to pay the piper," Kessler said.

Mabel's mouth was propped open and all she could do was arch an eyebrow in agreement.

Kessler relented a moment, sprayed water into her mouth, and let her spit it out. It was mixed with blood.

"I'm pleased to meet you," she said, and settled back fearfully.

"Ah, the last time you saw Trouville, was he fine?" Sonntag asked.

Kessler started drilling again, the whine making Sonntag's teeth chatter.

Mabel was squirming.

"Depressed, I'd say. Like a man about to meet his Maker."

He bore down cruelly on Mabel, who writhed a little.

"Did he say why, sir?"

"I don't think the world was giving him his due," Kessler said. "He was obsessed with publicity. If he felt slighted, even a bit, he went into a blue funk."

"I've never heard that about him," Silva said. "I remember a real cheerful little guy."

"All a facade, a fraud," Kessler said, boring in on Mabel, his elbows plastering her to the chair. "He was afraid of being found out."

"Found out?"

"Are you fellows not quite on top of things?" Kessler asked. "Found out is exactly what I mean. The man had a record a yard long, and was hiding it."

"How do you know that?"

"I can read as well as the next man."

Mabel wailed, her knuckles went white, and her hands clapped the arms of the dental chair.

Kessler drilled hard, peered into her mouth, which was dripping saliva, and then sprayed her mouth with water. She coughed and spat out the bloody residue.

When she returned to her head-facing-the-ceiling position, there were tears on her cheeks.

"You mean Merchant's book?" Silva asked.

"Certainly. An excellent researcher and writer. Too bad the local police don't have anyone of his caliber."

"How'd you come across that?" Sonntag asked.

"Anything in Trouville's office interested me. I bought the book."

He started drilling again. The drill chattered and whined, and the smell of heated enamel began to permeate the little room as the drill bit into the molar. Mabel groaned, but otherwise endured it.

"You want some pain numbing?" he asked. "I suppose you would. Can't get through some minor discomfort without a shot. I hope you didn't pass that along to the children."

She nodded. He set the drill on its hook and vanished, while Sonntag and Silva stared at the tear-streaked woman, not quite knowing what to say.

"It's a nice day," she said.

"Sure is, ma'am."

"He's a genius," she said. "I'm a lucky woman."

"No doubt about it," Silva said.

Kessler returned with a small glass syringe, half filled with a clear fluid.

He pulled her lip back, stabbed her rear gum, which made her wince, and injected the Novocain. "You always take some babying," he said, withdrawing the needle and handing the empty syringe to Dandelion, who was dressed in starchy white with a nurse cap. She carried it reverently away.

"We have to wait a little," he said. "I knew something was wrong with Trouville from the moment he moved in, back in thirty-six. He proved to be as much a phony as those graphologists that look at your handwriting and predict your future. Just more clever, that's all. But all went well with him for years. He played his game in court, and made a lot of money, and got a lot of attention, and it looked like he'd become the Barnum and Bailey of Milwaukee. But then it all caught up with him. That inflated reputation's going to collapse now. Merchant, solid journalist and a good digger, got to the bottom of it."

He eyed his wife, who had gradually slumped in the chair. Dandelion waited politely, a tray loaded with instruments of torture in her hand.

"We think Mr. Trouville opened up a whole new world of crime detection," Sonntag said. "He deserved his reputation."

Kessler glared at him. "If you think that, then the Milwaukee police are in far worse shape than I ever imagined."

"He helped us with some robberies," Silva added. "Where the stickup man shoved a note at the cashier. We really appreciated it. He actually figured out the nationality of the robber based on the way the letters were written. And that led us to the man. He was a gem, as far as we're concerned."

"Likely he bluffed his way through, and the wrong man's in

jail," Kessler said. He poked at Mabel's gum and she didn't wince.

"Trouville's reputation has grown. Even the Federal Bureau of Investigation's been adapting some of his techniques," Sonntag said.

"Too bad for the FBI," Kessler said, jabbing at the gum again. Mabel's head lolled. She looked a little glassy-eyed.

Kessler changed his drill bit and began grinding away again. Once in a while Mabel winced, but mostly she just flopped.

"She needs to be half-looped," Kessler said. "Can't stand anything at all."

He'd pried her mouth open and was industriously shaping the hole in her molar for the filling.

"The thing about Trouville, he pioneered the whole field. There were a few freelancers before he began to apply some science, but, you know, he became one of the most important men in crime detection," Sonntag said.

Kessler ignored him. He was hunched over Mabel, drilling away, a whine emerging from his left hand.

"Were you around the night of April 17, when Trouville suffered heart trouble?"

"He couldn't stand the pain, and asked me for help. You know what dentists are, to some people? Pain relievers. He wanted something."

"What did he say?"

"He said he was worried, and did I have anything to relax him. I thought, 'You bet you're worried, you crook about to get caught.' So I gave him a few drops of chloral hydrate in water. He quieted right down."

"You were working late that evening?"

"I was waiting for him to finish up over there. He'd been robbing me of my secretary's time, and I wanted to stop it."

"Did you succeed?"

Mabel winced, so Kessler sprayed her mouth with water. She coughed. Dandelion held a white enameled receptacle under her mouth, and she spit out water and gore.

"Succeed? How could I succeed with a man who'd flopped over his desk? He weighed fifty pounds less than most men."

He lifted some latex from the tray, and some clamps, and began building a sort of cofferdam around the molar, which would contain the cast of the filling. Mabel wallowed and said nothing.

Dandelion helped hold Mabel's jaws open while Kessler prepared to make the cast, which would be used to pour the gold filling.

"It must have annoyed you to be cheated by a man so successful," Sonntag said. "After all, you've done your own pioneering work, and get no credit for it."

"Of course I don't get credit. I build on the work of others. I studied dentistry with the best men in the country. My work is simply an addition to what they taught me. There's no fraud in it, and no credit in it."

"But you would have enjoyed some recognition, I think," Silva said.

"If it came to me, I'd shrug it off," Kessler said. "I don't invent quack science."

He was busy with clamps and other instruments, while Dandelion was mixing some sort of casting material. Sonntag had no idea what material was used for a dental cast.

"You keep good records, I hear," Silva said.

"There is nothing that happens in this office that is not noted," Kessler said. "Including the hours Agnes worked for Trouville."

"Yeah, that's what I'm getting at. Did you bill him for the sedative that night?"

"It's on the books. I included it in my claim against the estate."

"It's easier to get paid by the estate than by a live welsher, right?" Sonntag said.

"Mabel, hold still," Kessler said. His hand was holding the cast in place until it set.

Her hands were flopping.

Dandelion touched Kessler's hand, and he let up the pressure. Her hands stopped flopping.

"Yeah, after the dose, what happened?" Sonntag said.

"A sublingual injection did it," Kessler said. "It's a rare art. You wouldn't know about that."

"That took care of Trouville?"

"Absolutely painlessly," Kessler said. "I haven't spent years doing dental surgery for nothing. He left the way he wanted to go."

"What were you going to charge him?"

"The estate? For an infusion of chloral hydrate, and then some Novocain, plus an injection fee. It's all on paper. The trustee, Bartles, should have it by now."

"Bill the estate?"

"Certainly. My services are worth something."

"Are these services something Trouville asked for?"

"I supplied professional services. He was hoping to dodge the bullet. Merchant was in his waters, like a U-boat, you know." He pulled the cast from Mabel's mouth and examined it closely. "I suppose this will do, Mabel. The way you were squirming, I might have done another."

Dandelion pulled chrome-plated instruments from Mabel's mouth, and then Dr. Kessler pressed a temporary filling paste into the cavity and held a finger on it until it hardened.

"Now you can go home and feel sorry for yourself," he said.

Dandelion swung the tray aside, and Mabel staggered out of the chair.

"Isn't he a marvel?" she said to Sonntag.

Dandelion escorted her out of the room.

"When I'm done with her, that gold filling will be in so tight that it'll last forty or fifty years," Kessler said. "That's something I know something about. Not like Trouville."

"So you helped Trouville that night?"

"He got exactly what he asked for."

"What did he ask for, sir?" Sonntag asked.

"Quietness. He was agitated. It's a pity he chose that way out. A lack of character. I realized early on, maybe about nineteen thirty-seven, that he would come to no good. A dapper little fellow like that, putting on airs."

"You didn't supply more than Trouville asked for?"

"Why should I?"

"It's in your ledgers, I suppose."

"Certainly." Kessler led the detectives to an alcove where ledgers lined the shelves, and pulled the newest one off. He flipped pages to April 17.

There were several entries:

8 P.M. *Treated Armand de Trouville in his office. Complaint, agitation. Gave him infusion of chloral hydrate, followed by sublingual injection of—*

The remainder of the line had been heavily blacked out.

Time estimate: Fifteen minutes $15.00
Infusion $5.00
Sublingual injection $12.00
On account: $32.00

"I guess we'd better take these with us," Sonntag said.

"Why? They're mine. Where are you going?"

"You're coming with us, doctor."

"For what?"

"We'll get that spelled out at the station, sir."

"Oh, about Trouville's suicide, then. He certainly got himself into a corner."

"No, not about that. Not about heart trouble. You'll get the drill, sir."

"Would you mind if we look around your office, doctor?" Silva asked.

"Certainly I mind. Do you need something?"

"Have you some ink? For a pen?"

"I have some right in that drawer."

Silva opened the desk drawer and extracted a bottle of black ink.

"Do you have a writing pad, sir?"

"What would you want that for?"

"I'd like to look at it."

Kessler pointed. Silva pulled out a thick legal pad, and took it into an examination room where there was a bright light on an arm above the examination chair. Silva turned it on. This time the light wasn't probing what lay in an open mouth, but a lot of subtle indentations in yellow paper. He and Sonntag examined the sheet carefully. There were regular indentations on the blank page, left by pen writing something on the sheet above, which now was gone.

"Thank you, that is helpful," Silva said. "We'll be taking these to the station."

"What for?"

"To see whether this ink matches what was on the forged suicide note. Trouville always used blue or blue-black ink. People do have habits. He sure did. And to see whether the pen that made these almost invisible indentations was practicing a signature. You know, one of the problems with signatures is that they are rarely identical. People's signatures change with mood, tiredness, stuff like that. If signatures are all alike, doctor, that's not a good deal. That points to a little hanky panky."

"What's that got to do with anything? I require answers."

"We have a very good photographer at the station, sir. He'll take this sheet from the pad and light it in such a way that the indentations will show up, and then photograph them and enlarge the photos. We think there might be many copies of a name, practiced over and over."

Kessler seemed to lose height. In the space of a few moments he shrank half a foot, or so Sonntag thought.

"But Mabel needs a filling," he said.

"We can walk out of here any way you wish, Dr. Kessler. With cuffs, or voluntarily."

There were patients stacked in the waiting room. Kessler straightened his shoulders.

Sonntag nodded to Silva, who found a phone and called for a patrol car. This time, they all would ride.

Silva found Agnes trying to soothe the waiting, nervous crowd.

"Tell them that Dr. Kessler won't be seeing them today," he said.

Chapter Thirty-Six

Sonntag stared at a teletype report from the FBI about some fingerprints lifted from a Hudson hubcap. None of the prints matched anything in the FBI data files. Too bad.

Eddie Walsh loomed over his desk, a manila envelope in hand. "One thing about these deals, they never end," he said.

He dropped the envelope on Sonntag's desk. This one had been mailed from Forest Hills, New York, and was addressed in a feminine hand to Mr. Edward Walsh, Milwaukee PD.

"When you flirt a little, you never know," Eddie said.

Sonntag extracted several papers and photos from the envelope. The top one was a letter, in the same hand as the writing on the envelope. It was from a woman named Lydia Raphael.

Dear Mr. Walsh,

When you called us several weeks ago, you started something unexpected. What happened was that my mother began reminiscing about things that had been closed chapters in her life, and things that finally answered many questions I've had about my own life.

Eddie was poised over Sonntag's desk, looking pleased with himself.

You see, I never knew who my father was. I spent my early

years in Paris, with my mother, but I have little recollection of a father, and my mother would just turn my questions aside and say he was no good and I didn't need to know. But now, suddenly, she has been telling me things. She married a certain man named Bolivar Newman after the first war, and I am their daughter. They were both artists, and both worked in the same medium, and lived among the American expatriates there. From what she says, it was a stormy marriage, and also they were rivals, trying to outdo each other's work. But it lasted for several years, until she somehow discovered that he had a criminal record. Someone at the École, the art school, remembered him from before the war. There was a divorce, and he vanished.

So all these years, I've never known who I am. She found my birth record. And found the French registry of marriage. I had them photocopied and enclose them. She also dug out of an old shoebox a lot of photos of them together. My papa, Bolivar, and her. These were taken in the twenties, and into the thirties. I was born in 1928, and have some vague memories of him, but he vanished too soon. As you can see from the French records, I was named Lydia Newman, but I've always been known as Lydia Raphael.

I am simply curious about him. He became someone else, and I'd like to know who he was, and what he did, and if there is anything I could have as a small memento of my father, I'd cherish it. Just knowing about him would fill a void in my life. So if you can be of any help, I would be most grateful, and my mother would be, too.

Sincerely,
Lydia Raphael

There were photocopied records, and half a dozen photos. Trouville, with a young wife and child. A marriage photo of Trouville and his bride. Trouville with Edna and a pram. Trouville, standing on the front steps of their apartment, wearing a beret.

"I guess we should phone Stanley Bartles," Sonntag said. "There's an heir after all. He'll be pleased."

ABOUT THE AUTHOR

Axel Brand is the foremost practitioner of eye-level fiction. He is the pseudonym of a novelist whose surname comes near the end of the alphabet, and whose books are displayed where almost no one sees or buys them, at toe level. So Axel Brand was born to meet the eye and be first in line at the upper left in any bookstore or library shelf. He's happy there and does not plan to relinquish his catbird seat to anyone.